CW00431642

WOLF

TONY LINDSELL

Cover Image: 'Genesis' by Orly Shalem
www.orlyshalem.com

Cover Design: Molly Vincent
Image - IT Ltd

CONTENTS

TONY LINDSELL

PROLOGUE

WOLF is a reconstruction of the life of Wolf Albert between the months of September 1939 and April 1944.

The core story and timeline are true and are based on the transcripts of interviews undertaken with Wolf by the Imperial War Museum. However, the transcripts are sometimes matter of fact and lack colour – they do not offer a complete picture. Therefore, to bring the story alive, the journey and events have been fictionalised.

Some characters are real – Wolf himself, Hela and Chaim Sieradski in particular – but some of their dialogue and actions are fictional. Other characters are mentioned by Wolf but without detailed description and these have been further developed; others again are entirely fictional, or real but from someone else's account – in either case created to provide depth and continuity to the story.

Some scenes are built from the framework of a brief sentence in Wolf's account, others are fictional but are written to be true either to a specific account from another source or to the collective account – the very similar story recounted by many different people. In other words, they are a possible outcome at the time and in the circumstances.

Many sources have been used for the story over and above the IWM transcripts and a list is given at the back of the book under Sources *(page 323)*.

WOLF is intended to be historically accurate in terms of the wider picture of these war years. The first and last dates are true; many in the middle are 'best-guesses' based on Wolf's comments, other historical data anad cross-referencing. Geographically, again, the story is intended to be as accurate as possible based on place names provided by Wolf and other sources, the location of railway lines and logic. It has not been possible, as yet, to identify where, exactly, the labour camp in Siberia was. It is safe to say that it was somewhere in the huge area that runs North-East from Kotlas to Vorkuta, with Ukhta (formerly Chibyu) in the middle.

1 FLIGHT

People wondered, at the time of his birth, why his mother named him Wolf. They would have understood, years later - if any of them had survived.

******

Tuesday 5 September 1939

THE STUDENTS who had hung about for the last few months, harrying people to boycott the Jewish shops, had gone back to their own towns. No one wanted to buy anything from any shop now, Jewish or Catholic.

The explosions that, earlier in the week, had rumbled distantly from the direction of Warsaw, sixty kilometres to the North, thundered louder. News came through, sporadically, on the wireless and spread across Bledow, feeding new rumours. People passed on the street, their eyes cast down, looking nervously left and right or above them. The air was blistered with apprehension.

Every hour or more, a squadron of Messerschmitts roared low across the sky, tearing the heavy silence that hung over the town. Those who had dared to venture out ducked involuntarily and ran for whatever cover they could find. The fighters strafed the ground randomly, bullets ricocheting off the dirt and pockmarking the walls.

As the evening set in and the attacks stopped, Wolf Albert joined a group gathered in the town square. An engine roared from the direction of Grojecki.

"If they get any closer, we will have to leave," said Chaim Rindler, a schoolteacher, addressing the Jews amongst them.

Heads nodded.

His voice faltered. "There will be no future for us here. We will be safer in Russia than anywhere near the Wehrmacht."

Wednesday 6 September 1939

It was a little before 9 p.m. when they met again near the fountain that stood close to the synagogue. Flashes of light burst across the late summer sky. Wolf wished that it was lightning, but he knew that it wasn't. He turned. Hooves pounded up the narrow street that led to the square. The rider dismounted, breathless, beads of sweat tracking through the dust that lined his face.

"There are troop carriers this side of Biala Rawska," he said. "They're only fifteen kilometres away. They're coming."

"That is it, then," said Chaim solemnly, but firmly. "We go. We will be safer together. Get what you can, say what goodbyes you can, meet here in thirty minutes. We will leave at 10.30."

Wolf ran back to his home. His father was out, his sisters were out — only his mother was there. Her face carried a heavy burden.

"I'm leaving, Mother. They're close. A group of us are going; Mr Rindler is leading us. We'll be back before long, when this is over."

She nodded sadly.

"Wait," she said and disappeared into the darkness of the other room. She came back with a parcel wrapped in brown paper and string, his raincoat on top of it, and handed it to him.

"You'll need these."

She pulled him to her breast and hugged him.

"You are only nineteen," she said. "You should not have to suffer this, Welwul. May God protect you."

He searched for her eyes in the light of the lamp and held them. She had not used his baby-name for years.

"I have to go, Mother," he said, releasing her, and, clutching the package, he turned and ran back through the darkness to the square.

Hela Malakowska, his sister Naomi's friend, was already there.

"You don't need to come," he said. "You're Catholic. They won't hurt you."

"I'm coming," she said. "They have no right."

There must have been forty or more in the group when the clock on the town hall struck 10.30. Some who they expected to be there, were not there, but Chaim did not wait. Already, they could hear the clank and throb of heavy vehicles away to the West.

They took the road out of town Eastwards, running first, until Chaim said, "No, we cannot run all the way, we need to conserve our energy."

The weather, at least, was on their side – it was a warm evening and a pale half-moon lit their way. The main road, when they joined it, already seethed with people heading in the same direction — some on foot, some with horses and carts, some laden with bags, others with nothing.

"Stay together," Chaim shouted as they entered the jostling river of people. "Hold hands with the person in front of you."

Wolf coughed as dust swirled around them in the night air. He held out his hand to Hela and felt the warmth of her palm. With his other hand he held onto a man in front that he did not know. People were pushing through in the darkness, carts veering left and right in rutted tracks, dogs scampering underfoot and horses snorting.

In front of him, a woman tripped. He saw her go down. He reached his arm out to lift her but, before he could grasp her, the urgent tide pressed him forwards. He heard a scream and glanced back. He caught a glimpse of her head jerked sideways, but people did not stop or help.

He had lost contact with Hela in the melee, the man in front too. He shouted Hela's name.

"I'm here."

She was twenty yards behind him. He stepped off the road to wait for her.

"You go ahead," said Wolf, "Then I can see you."

Hela was small and she weaved her way quickly through and between people, somehow dragging Wolf's wiry six-foot frame with her.

"Chaim!" he shouted.

They strained their ears for a reply, then moved quickly on.

"Chaim!" he called. "Chaim Rindler!" He called again and again.

They squeezed past a family that clung to a wide creaking cart, loaded with furniture and pots and pans. The cart blocked the road, a grey draught horse panting at its front.

"We're here!" he heard finally and was relieved to see the schoolteacher's face in the pale light. For a little longer, he could cede responsibility for his existence to this man.

There was little talk; just a mutter, a curse, an occasional shout as people tried to find each other, the slap of leather on hide as someone willed their horse to take another step. They walked on, moving, moving, moving — the trance figures of a nightmare, hounded forward by the incessant thud of distant explosions to the West and North of them that momentarily lit the sky.

Wolf knew the roads of the area well, but, beyond the track they were on, he had no idea what route they were taking. They could not take the main route, which would lead them too far North, to Grojecki; they had to cross that road and take the side roads, anything that would take them East. He had to trust that Chaim, and those at the head of this fleeing cavalcade, understood where they were going.

Suddenly above the sound of footsteps, a bird started to sing in the darkness.

"It's a canary," said Hela. Wolf strained his eyes into the night. Ahead of them, a woman was carrying a tall wire cage in her right hand, a sack of belongings clutched under her left arm.

'A bird more loved,' he thought.

"We have to rest," said Chaim eventually. They had been walking for nearly four hours. An apple orchard spread out on either side of them and they moved into it. Already they were fewer, some of the Bledow people separated, lost in front or behind. Wolf walked with Hela deep into the orchard and lay down on one side of a tree, she on the other. It was quieter on the ground, but still he could hear the occasional crack of a branch breaking, overladen with fruit, and, in the distance, the unbroken drumbeat of footsteps marching, plodding, shuffling forwards on the road.

He was so tired.

He thought of the neighbours' apple orchards in Bledow. How he would play there as a boy on Shabbat, skipping the Shul service. He knew he was not supposed to play on Shabbat but he did not like rules. He thought of his father, a religious man and the lay leader of the Jewish community, who would know he was out but would not stop him; and how he would sometimes ask him to deliver potatoes to the poor people of Bledow, even though they had little themselves. He thought of his mother. Her eyes, just that evening, that had shone for him. Shone and wept. He thought of his brothers and sisters. Naomi – he wanted her here. Somehow he had to take care of Hela – for Naomi.

He thought of the comfort of their house. The two rooms. The kitchen. The front room where, somehow, they all lay down at night and slept. He pictured the feast on Friday evenings. Even if there was little food, it was always an evening of celebration, his brothers and all his sisters with his parents around the rough-hewn table, the gefilte fish and kugel. He remembered the suit he had been able to afford after working in the handbag factory in Warsaw and how proud he had been to go home to Bledow wearing it, to impress his parents.

He thought too of the Nazi-sympathising fifth columnists and shwabs.

How dare they? And why?

Thursday 7 September 1939

The dawn sun filtered into the orchard through a soft mist. For the four hours they had been there, his sleep had been only fitful. His feet ached and his right side was stiff.

Chaim walked past.

"We will leave again in fifteen minutes."

Wolf nodded. He looked across at Hela.

"Excuse me," he said.

He walked deeper into the field to relieve himself.

He found a tree with low branches laden with fruit, tall nettles beneath it. He went behind it and with his back to the road, undid his buttons. As his stream began, he heard a rustling to his left. A woman was squatting at the next tree, her thick skirts raised. She looked across at him and he covered himself, red with embarrassment.

"I am sorry," he said. "I did not see you."

She reached down for a clutch of dandelion leaves.

"This is what it is now," she said.

He picked four apples. They were red and plump, but he had to pull them from the branch. He knew that they would be bitter.

He returned to Hela and handed her two of the apples. He pulled a thick crust from the brown paper package that his mother had given him just a few hours before. He broke a section off for her and started to eat. Some of the other people from Bledow had nothing. They looked at him beseechingly – but he shrugged.

At the edge of the road, still upright, stood a bird cage. It was empty and the little wire door was wide open.

"I think I'd like to be a canary now," said Hela.

2 EARLY JOURNEY

THOSE with keen ears heard it first: the drone of aircraft bleeding from the sky behind them. Other people turned, following their gaze.

"Look out!"

An entire squadron came into view in arrowhead formation. They are high, thought Wolf, they might pass over. But two aircraft, different from the rest, peeled away. They flew fast and low through the scattered morning clouds, heading straight for the refugees like angry mosquitoes.

Wolf looked around left and right. A ditch had already filled with people.

"There!" he shouted to Hela. They ran across open ground towards a large beech tree and dived behind it. He leant his back against its broad trunk, and pulled her close to him, his arms around her waist.

The rat-tat-tat of cannon fire opened up, the guns raking the ground indiscriminately. A bullet spat into the front of the tree; others skittered across the earth just yards to their side and burst through the leaves above them.

In seconds it was over and the aircraft receded into the distance. There was a moment of shocked silence before the cries and screams started; a rough-haired dog howled pitifully, intestines spilling from its ruptured belly.

Hela was quivering, her face white. Chaim pulled himself upright nearby and surveyed the ground around him. Some bodies lay prone and still, others struggled to stand, bleeding.

"Bastards!" he swore, shaking his fist at the empty sky. "Bastards!"

"Help! Doctor!" a voice called.

It was Moshe, a man of about forty from Bledow, who often spoke to Wolf's father at the synagogue. He was kneeling beside another man, clasping his arm at the wrist. Wolf ran over.

"Press here," he said. In the mess of blood, Wolf could not at first see the site of the wound and blood gushed again from the shattered arm as they changed hands. Moshe tore off his shirt and pulled out a pocket knife. He slit the side of the shirt and ripped it in half. He tied the man's arm below the elbow and tightened the bandage, but still the blood flowed.

"Pass me that stick," he shouted, pointing.

Hela rushed over with it. He inserted it above the knot and tied again. He turned it and turned it like a corkscrew, until the flow of blood became a dribble, but already rivulets of deep red played across the dried earth.

The wounded man shivered uncontrollably and Moshe put his jacket over him.

"You're going to be all right," he said.

"Water," the man breathed. Moshe looked at Wolf, raising his eyebrows, but Wolf held his blood-drenched palms out, empty.

"We'll get you some soon."

A horse whinnied. It was the grey draught horse that had been hauling the family's furniture. A bone stuck out from its right foreleg, shattered by a bullet. It tried to move forwards, but, on three legs, toppled sideways. The cart tipped. A wardrobe and dressing table crashed to the ground, the glass of the mirror cascading, for a brief moment, like tiny singing raindrops in the midst of the devastation.

Potatoes rolled from a split sack and tumbled across the road. The horse whinnied again — more a scream than a whinny – and tried to lift its neck, but the cart pinned it. Another effort, but this time a shiver passed through its body and it settled, still, against the wooden shaft. The daughter ran to its head embracing it.

"Leave her," the father shouted. "It's too late. Get the potatoes!"

The family rushed about trying to collect them, but already some people who had rejoined the road were picking up potatoes as they passed.

Moshe looked at his friend.

"We're going to have to get going again. You hold the stick and we'll lift you up," he said.

Between them, they got the man upright and he shuffled forwards, leaning on Moshe, his face ashen. Wolf and Hela walked slowly behind, keeping an eye on the sky at their back.

They had gone barely a kilometre before the man crumpled to the earth. He muttered something to Moshe, waving his good arm away from him. Moshe bent down and hugged him. With tears in his eyes, he pulled him off the road and leant him against a wild hydrangea. Mops of mauve flowers enfolded the man's head and blood oozed again from his arm, but he had already lost too much. Moshe adjusted his jacket around him.

"Take it," said Chaim. "It is no use to him now."

But Moshe left it in place and kissed his friend's forehead. He stood up and put on the remains of his shirt, a shirt that had once been blue. It only covered his upper chest now, his stomach naked to the sky.

"On their way to Pulawy or Ljublin, I suppose," said Chaim, his face vacant.

"What do you mean?" said Wolf.

"To bomb them."

3 TWO BICYCLES

WOLF was impatient to move on. The Bledow group, originally forty or more, was splintered – some had been lost in the attack, others had gone on as Wolf, Hela and Chaim waited with Moshe.

Two black bicycles lay stranded beside the road — two bodies sprawled on the ground nearby. One of the bicycles had a wicker basket attached to the front of the handlebars. A rectangular bar of ivory-coloured soap, women's underwear and a bag of cherries had spilled out across the dry earth, but the bicycle appeared undamaged. Chaim nodded towards them.

"Let's take these," called Wolf, setting one upright. His bloodied hands were sticky on the handlebars.

Hela hesitated, concern etched on her face, but when she saw him pedalling forward, she took the other.

"They're not ours!" she called as she drew level with him.

"No, but they're no one else's either. You saw."

"Leich l'shalom," called Chaim behind them. "Go towards peace."

For miles and miles, they jigged and dived through the human wall. In places the road became wider and they could move onto the verge; elsewhere, they had to wait, like the rest, for the way to clear, their feet on the ground.

People cursed as they passed; some tried to grab the bicycles. Every now and then, when they saw a farm or homestead across the fields, they took the track down to it and begged for water. If no water was offered, they splashed their faces in any pond or water tub they could find.

It was early evening when the Vistula River opened out in front of them. There was only one road across: the road that led East. Wolf could see the town of Pulawy on the other side, a sea of people on the bridge, and instinctively he pulled off the road to the right onto a dirt track. From here he could see what appeared to be mud flats, small islands in the river, splashes of colour and movement on them, as if a flock of dappled geese had landed there.

"Where are you going?" called Hela.

"I just want to look down here," he said. Already they were riding against the flow of human traffic.

The drone of aircraft engines drowned her response. The sound grew louder and louder until it became a roar directly overhead, a skein of grey metal — black cross after black cross, a swastika on each tail.

A small wood lay a few hundred yards away towards the river.

"Pedal, pedal, pedal!" shouted Wolf, glancing across then glancing skywards, pedalling furiously himself.

Two, then four aircraft broke formation. And then the sound. Sirens. Trumpet sirens that wailed from the aircraft as they swooped down almost vertically.

Throwing the bicycles aside they dived onto the field beside them, searching for any cover, any ditch or hole, even the slightest depression in the land that could shelter them.

"Arms out wide, keep your mouth open," shouted a man to the side.

"Why?" called Wolf his voice muffled, his head hugging the ground.

"Protect the membranes in your ears," said the man. "Cover your head and the back of your neck …"

Through tips of grass, Wolf saw something fall from the belly of one of the aircraft. Everything became still. In slow motion, frame by frame, it dropped until it buried itself in a building across the river. In split seconds, the eruption - a cloud of smoke and dust and flame. A plume of water blistered the river and waves thrashed against the banks. Aircraft after aircraft, bowel after black-crossed bowel, dumped their cargo until the town was ablaze.

Wolf watched the aircraft intently until they became pinpricks in the distance.

"… with metal if you can, a spade, anything. Shrapnel," said the man eventually, breaking into the stunned silence between what had been and what was to be.

The aircraft disappeared from view. Wolf raised his head. On the bridge people pushed this way and that, a swarm of humanity moving like a kaleidoscope, but with no fixed pattern. At the far end the melee did not move, as if the swarm were paralysed, frozen. They're sitting targets, he thought.

Hela sat up and moved across to Wolf. He put his arm around her shoulders. She was shivering again.

"It's OK," he said. "I am frightened too. But you should not have to be. It is not you they are after."

"I think I might … Do you think I could?"

"Go back?" he filled in.

She nodded, looking down.

"Yes." he said. It was almost a command.

"Take the bicycle, you will be safer."

"I don't know," she said. "I just don't know."

"Go!" said Wolf. "Go now. Tell Naomi, tell my mother and my father, that I am fine. That I am going towards Russia. I will write letters."

Neither of them expected the explosion that shook the earth about them, spattering them with soil. A fragment of grey steel, the letter W visible in white on its warped side, sliced into the earth beyond Wolf. They dived to the ground again. For long seconds they could hear the anguish of the trees behind as one fell against another, the swish and brush and the long slow crash. He lifted his head – another tree was falling.

"Run!"

They raced to safety, but behind them a dull metallic thud told a different story of the bicycles. The wheels were twisted, the frames bent, a heavy branch splayed across them.

Wolf sighed. He nodded in the direction of the river. They walked down to the bank, numb. The mud flats looked inviting. Arms flailed in the water on either side. Some people stood in the middle, sodden clothes hanging limp, the colour drained. On the far side, a cluster of movement in the trees – some had made it across.

To his left, a man had found a boat. He beckoned urgently to his wife and son. Wolf understood – the man could not go back. It was the bridge or a boat. Perhaps the man was a boatman. Either way led to the inferno that had been Pulawy.

People crowded towards the boat.

"My child is sick!" cried a young woman, carrying a baby.

"My mother cannot swim!"

The man began to push the boat out. His wife climbed on board, but slowly. Their child, a boy of eleven or twelve, who appeared to believe in his strength beyond his years, pushed too, shouting to his father to get in. The father held his arm out for the woman with the baby but others raced towards them. Someone grabbed at an oar. In the seconds it took for the boy and the woman with the baby to clamber on board, the boat juddered against the shore, then caught the current. In the melee, the oar fell back on land. For a moment the father stood in the stern, his arms reaching for it, pleading.

Wolf ran down. He wanted to throw the oar out to him ahead of the boat, but he was too late. People were fighting over it and the boat had already been swept out, the man sitting now, paddling helplessly.

There was nothing Wolf could do. He picked up a stone from the shoreline. He did not know why but he liked its shape. It was grey and, though sharp and pointed at one end, was smooth and rounded at the other. It had a delicate white line pattern on the surface, as if some person from another time, who wrote in a different script, had left a message. He put it in his pocket.

Something caught his eye. A piece of flotsam, a branch wrapped in litter, he thought at first. But when his eyes focussed, he could see.

"Oh God," said Hela.

They walked back up to the woodland.

"Wolf Albert!" called a voice.

Chaim leant against a tree, his shoes off, rubbing his feet. His eyes were still bright behind his damaged spectacles. One lens was missing, the other cracked.

"How did you get here so quickly?" Wolf asked.

"A truck came by. Gave us a lift in the back until it ran out of fuel."

Moshe and another man, whose face and tall, lean figure Wolf recognised from somewhere in the back of his mind, nodded. It was Josef, he realised after a few seconds. He came from Mogielnica, a town not far from Bledow.

The flames had subsided now in Pulawy but a continuous crackling spread across the river and small explosions punched the air. Air that tasted of smoke and charred timbers and cordite.

"Did you see?" asked Chaim.

"What?"

"The bombs did not touch the bridge. Nowhere close."

"How do you mean?" said Hela.

"The bridge itself is safe. They need the bridge. They want to bring their army and their tanks over. It is safer to go across the bridge than to try to swim or find a boat. I say we rest here for a little while until it is completely dark, then cross in the night. What does everybody think?"

Wolf looked about the assembled group. Apart from Hela, all were now men and no one dissented.

"How do we know where to go on the other side?" asked Josef.

"Follow the main road, it will be obvious." said Chaim. "Even if we are separated, follow it. It's the way East, towards Ljublin."

.

4 A BARN

PEOPLE bumped and jostled against each other in the darkness. To right and left, the water glinted orange as small fires still burnt in the city. There was no moon, just the flickering flames that dimly lit the night – shadowy figures ahead of them moving this way and that. Wolf had watched the crowd earlier, from the relative safety of the western bank. Now they were part of the crowd. He kept looking up at the sky behind them.

Someone stumbled into him and his hand was jolted from Hela's. He strained to see her ahead of him. It was, in reality, barely a minute before he was across, but already he had lost her. He stopped on the other side, not knowing if she was ahead or behind. He called and called, but amid the crackling of the fires and the multitude of voices and footsteps he could not make out a reply.

Then he heard his name shouted, close, as if for the last time.

"Wolf!"

"I'm here, I'm here. I thought I'd lost you."

He embraced her. He felt her chest heaving against his own, both of them relieved yet fearful.

Chaim, Moshe and Josef joined them as they reached the far side. Chaim, almost blind in the darkness with his damaged spectacles, had clung tight to Moshe in front and Josef behind. In single file, refusing to be broken, they had advanced across the bridge.

******

They walked through Pulawy like figures in a dream. No one bothered them and no one attacked them. No aircraft came. Beyond the town, all they could hear was the steady footfall of hundreds of feet moving East. Then, like the song of one bird plucked from the cacophony of the dawn chorus, they heard the clip-clop of a horse. As the sound drew nearer, they could make out a hay cart through the darkness.

"Can you give us a ride?" called Chaim. The horseman slowed. He was seated at the front of the cart, long reins in either hand. Twenty or more people were already on the back. Wolf and Josef leapt up and, amidst the cries and shoves, held out their arms for the others. There was barely enough space to stand but, holding onto a waist-high wooden rail, they jolted and swayed down the road at a speed far faster than their own feet would have carried them.

It was still the depths of the night when the driver stopped the cart at a junction. He knew, it seemed, where he was headed and it was not East.

"Where are we?" called Chaim

"Ten kilometres from Ljublin," said the man. "Or thereabouts."

Dazed, they shook their rattled limbs on the road. The other passengers had walked on and behind them, for the moment, the road was empty.

"We don't want to get there in daylight," said Chaim. "Let's see if we can find somewhere to rest."

"There's some sort of track here," said Moshe.

They followed it along the side of a field, feet tripping sometimes in hidden ruts. In front of them loomed a tall shape, a roof rounded against the sky. Josef went forward to explore. Wolf cursed as his shin hit something metal.

"It's a hay barn," Josef called.

The sweet smell of the cut grass welcomed them. It was still warm after the day. Wolf relieved himself at the side of the building, then scrambled up until he found a lair where he could make himself comfortable. A chicken clucked distractedly somewhere in the depths of the building.

"Are you OK, Hela?" he whispered, and he heard her whisper back from the other side before his eyes closed and sleep took him.

8 September 1939

A cockerel woke him in the dawn light, its call so loud he looked for it beside him.

The barn had a semi-circular, corrugated-iron roof, but it was open to a height of five metres or so on all four sides. Chickens were clucking now on the dirt floor, pecking at anything they could find, oblivious of the human jetsam that had washed up there in the midst of the night. On the right side of the barn, on which he now lay, was the stack of hay. To the left, to his amazement, was an old bus. It was a dirty yellow and had once, perhaps, carried children from the country to school in Ljublin. Now it lay rusting in this barn, the chickens fouling its steps.

He could see Chaim's green trousers on the other side, apparently still fast asleep and, near him, Josef was stirring. Wolf was starving. The last apple had gone a long time ago and most of his mother's bread. He tore the remaining crust in two and tossed one half to Hela.

In his mind he knew that today was Friday. The Sabbath would start this evening. He did not consider himself a religious person, though his father was second only to the rabbi in Bledow, but he honoured the Jewish traditions. Tonight the family would have feasted – feasted, so far as their income allowed. They would have eaten challah – the plaited bread that his mother made and was so delicious. He had wondered, when he had eaten challah at other houses, why it was not as good as his mother's, what it was she secretly added to make it so tasty. He could have eaten a whole loaf now.

Trumpet sirens stole the remains of the morning quiet.

From his soft hay bed, Wolf could see the formations pass, one, then two, then three. Safe here, for the moment, he thought. No one spoke, though all now were awake. In the distance they could hear deep booms as the bombs landed on Ljublin. Josef yawned and sat upright, his tall body erect, his beard, somewhere between light brown and ginger, still proud and shapely on his carved face.

Occasionally, there was an explosion closer to them – a burst of soil in a field in the distance, an aircraft miscalculating or out of fuel; but mostly the thuds and flashes were far away.

One by one the squadrons returned, their bowels empty, finally harmless.

"I think we'll be better to go through Ljublin at night again," said Chaim.

Wolf looked out. He could hear the sound of an engine. A tractor was bumping across the fields towards the barn. There was no point in running and they did not hide. The man, when he arrived, was about sixty. He wore blue dungarees, scuffed with soil. He clambered down with difficulty and hobbled forwards.

"Forgive us, sir," said Chaim. "We sheltered here for the night."

The man looked at Hela and then around the barn.

He grunted, then spat onto the dirt where the chickens pecked.

"Didn't think the bastards would come this far," he said. "I'm going to see if I can get this old girl going. Then we can all get a long way from here." He patted the bus.

He hobbled round to the snub-nosed bonnet, unclipped a latch and folded the cover up and back. He peered into the petrol tank, then released the starter jack, fixing it into a slot at the front of the engine.

He opened the cab door, a cloud of hay, twigs and dust billowing out, and pulled a key from his pocket. He inserted the key and turned it to the right.

"Flat as a pancake," he said.

"Would you like me to turn the crank handle sir?" asked Josef, who clearly had some experience of these things.

The man nodded and Josef turned the handle, straining against the crankshaft. There was nothing.

"Try again," said the man, making some adjustments.

With two hands this time, Josef turned, and this time the engine coughed. Frantically the man pumped the accelerator. Briefly the engine roared, then settled to a noisy thudding beat, not unlike the tractor's. He put it into reverse and it shuddered back, screeching as brakes that had been unused for months or years released from their rusted pads.

"Are the planes coming?"

Wolf scanned the sky West and East, North and South.

"It's clear at the moment."

He put the bus into first gear and turned the wheel, edging out of the barn. For twenty yards it moved forward until, with a metallic thud, it lurched to a standstill.

Josef spun the handle again but this time there was no response. The bus slumped like a snub-nosed pig in the field, its days done. Their hopes of a speedy journey past Ljublin and further East evaporated .

"Those German bastards can have it," said the man. "But they can't have the petrol. "

He picked up a crow bar that lay in a corner of the barn beside a hay fork and shovel. He hacked at the bottom of the petrol tank. Flakes of rusted metal fell from the sides and it did not take many blows to puncture it, leaving the fuel to spill out into the ground.

He limped back towards the tractor, then turned.

"Have a chicken if you're hungry," he grunted.

"What does he mean?"

"I think he means we can kill a chicken and cook it," said Chaim.

"Does anyone have matches?"

From a webbed bag that had hung around his neck through everything, Chaim pulled a box. Now they spread out and searched for wood until the drone of engines from the North-West forced them back to the barn. Wolf dived behind the thick stack of hay, Hela close behind, as another wave of aircraft came into view.

"Close," he said.

They could hear the rat-tat-tat as bullets strafed the road.

******

Eventually they had enough wood. They cleared an area for the fire in the dirt of the floor where the bus had stood. The slicked edges of what had once been a puddle of oil told a story.

It was Moshe who grabbed the chicken. He pulled a penknife from his pocket and, as Hela looked away, slit its throat. For a few minutes he held it upside down, allowing the blood to drain, then plucked and gutted it, separating the liver and kidneys from the innards.

Inside the bus, they found an old biscuit tin and this they used as a baking tray. They rigged up the pitchfork and shovel to hold the chicken above the fire and turned it as it began to release its own fats and juices. Between them, they worked to keep the fire stoked and to watch for aircraft.

The smell of the cooking bird filled the barn, driving Wolf to distraction. He wanted to sink his teeth into its half-cooked flesh.

Eventually, with the penknife, Hela tested the meat.

"It's cooked," she said.

"You divide it up, Hela," said Chaim.

It would have been easier, thought Wolf, if there had been four of them. But no one complained. Those who had wings rather than legs received more breast. Chaim, who had neither leg nor wing, had the largest portion of breast.

Wolf gnawed at his leg long after every speck of flesh was eaten. When the juices dribbled down his chin, he caught them with the back of his hand and drank them too. It was, he thought, one of the best meals he had ever had though his hunger was not satisfied.

What he wanted now was water.

5 LJUBLIN

IT WAS nearly eight and dark again when they set off.

In tacit agreement, they spoke only rarely, reserving their energy. Figures moved in front of them when they rejoined the road. They could hear what they could not see – the footfall of more people, like them, heading to the East, the occasional muttering.

There was not, in reality, any choice in the route. Behind lay the German armies, to the North lay the Pripyat marshes; Lvov, to the South, was bound to be another Nazi target.

Wolf's ears were attuned to the sky. He listened for the staccato beat of aircraft engines above the repetitive sound of footsteps. He tripped, sometimes, on bodies that lay in the road – the victims of the day's strafing. The sickly smell of cloying blood lingered through the air.

The barn seemed a distant memory already — the sweet warmth of the hay, the clucking of the chickens and the taste of the roasted meat, a vestige of home.

"I'm so thirsty," whispered Hela, and Wolf nodded in the darkness.

"Me too. We'll find some water in the town perhaps."

Their easy night-time passage through Pulawy, once they were over the bridge, gave them confidence; sheltered them from any thought that Ljublin might be different. Surely they had out-thought the Luftwaffe? And so they were caught unawares when they heard the engines behind them as they entered the outskirts of the town. The pilots had not even bothered to turn off the aircraft lights. Fear coursed through Wolf – they were vulnerable here.

Two aircraft led the formation. He could hear the power boost in their engines. He waited for the sirens, but they did not dive. They flew low overhead, engines screaming. A carpet of explosions burst across the town, the outlines of buildings and ancient church spires suddenly drawn in yellow light as if the curtains of the night had been opened. To the right, other aircraft dropped their load until the whole city was alight in a miasma of magnesium and flames.

They raced for the nearest shelter.

"Stay together, incendiary bombs!" called Chaim, but already he and Moshe had dived behind a wall.

Wolf grabbed Hela's hand and raced towards a taller stone building he could see across a square. It was a synagogue, he realised at the last second.

"No!" he shouted to Hela, but he was too late.

Another device landed just metres away. The explosion threw him to the ground and in seconds he was blinded by the flames and smoke. He pulled himself upright and ran from the searing heat. He looked around for Hela. He called her name again and again, but in the roar of the flames he could barely hear his own voice. He raced back in the direction he thought they were going, but nothing now was the same. He spun, trying to get his bearings. A rafter, red with heat, fell from a roof above him — it seemed the very bricks were on fire. He leapt sideways, shielding his eyes, trying to pick out Hela in the people scuttling this way and that.

He thought he could see her. A small body crouched in a doorway.

Holding his hands above his head he began to run over. He was half-way across when he saw the lights. Another aircraft was coming in. He dived to the ground, edging behind a pile of rubble. Shots stuttered from somewhere behind him. Perhaps, he thought, someone was trying to shoot down the aircraft with a hunting rifle; perhaps the town's citizens were trying to fight off the refugees.

Strangely, in the noise and unnatural chemical light, the aircraft gave him his bearings. Its line of bombs fell further to the right. He had to go in the same direction as the aircraft but to his left, away from the flames.

He looked to where the body had crouched in the doorway, but now there was no one there. He had no choice. Masonry tumbled from burning buildings. Sparks and small explosions burst all around him. He sprinted down a narrow street. People were running from their homes in pyjamas and nightgowns, smoke engulfing them as flames licked at the fabric of their wooden houses.

Out of breath he came to a small square. In the centre was a fountain, water still running from the mouth of a fish. He bathed his face in it, held his mouth to the trickle, swallowing and swallowing until his thirst was sated. He wanted to pick some up, to take to Hela when he found her, but he had nothing to hold it.

The light of the flames seemed to flash on and off, illuminating momentarily the dark streets and alleyways he found himself in, then darkening them again. Ahead, he caught sight of movement in the darkness, someone running – a familiar shape, the angle of the body, the tall, lean figure.

"Josef!" he called, and the figure stopped and waited for him.

"Have you seen Hela? She was with me. We were by the synagogue …"

Something exploded in a building nearby and they sprinted away. For minutes they ran, until Wolf stopped, unable to run further. He held his hands on his knees, breathing heavily.

"We have to find Hela."

"And Chaim and Moshe."

They were in the outskirts now, emerging on the other side of the city. They looked behind them. Buildings were silhouetted against the fires, strange shapes appearing, then disappearing —a house lit up as if by a spotlight, one moment the colour of the woodwork plain to see, the next flames leaping from upper storey windows.

"Shall we go back?"

"Where to?" said Josef. "We have no idea where they are."

There were few people about in the area they found themselves in.

"How about we try to find the main road again, this side. That's where Chaim said to stick to. Perhaps they are waiting for us there if they are OK."

"You're right," said Wolf and they criss-crossed streets, trying to follow the direction the aircraft had flown, keeping the flames on their right until they receded behind them. They came to a cobbled street. People were jostling this way and that, racing in and out of houses, bundling up belongings, children crying. At the far end, the street joined a larger road where a stream of people were walking. It had to be the main road.

They looked up and down. They could not make out faces in the darkness, just the flickering light of movement.

"Hela, Chaim Rindler!" they called out, but they could barely hear themselves above the roar of the destruction behind them, the rushing footsteps and the shouts of others searching for their loved ones.

"Let's move to somewhere quieter further on," said Wolf.

The last buildings gave way to open countryside. A clump of oaks stood beside the road and they squatted against them.

"Chaim Rindler, Moshe!" Josef called again and again.

"Hela!"

For an hour they repeated their calls.

"They must be ahead of us somewhere," said Josef finally and they got to their feet and walked on through the darkness.

.

6 AMMUNITION TRAIN

WOLF thought about Hela's house in Bledow, her parents. The potatoes they grew, the straw that they gave the Albert family at Easter for their palliasses. All this now seemed like a dream, but as he clung to it, he wanted to tell Mr and Mrs Malachowski how he'd tried to look after her; how the Nazi incendiary bombs had so exploded their world that they had been, literally, blown apart; how, the last time he had seen her, she was crouching in the shelter of a doorway, uninjured. He wanted to tell them this though they had no idea, perhaps, where their wilful Hela was; they had no idea that Wolf, the younger brother of her Jewish friend Naomi, had been with her, trying to protect her on the journey; that he had shared his mother's bread with her and picked two apples for her, though they were not yet ripe.

His thoughts turned now to his own father. 'I tried to look after her, father. They were bigger than me, the bombs, the aeroplanes. Are you OK? I will come back when it is safe. I will come back and restore our home when these people have gone.'

They reached a fork in the road and stopped, uncertain. At the point between this future and that future, on a patch of worn grass, they watched the other travellers. Some went left, some went right. When they called out, some said Russia this way, some said Russia that way. A woman pointed to the left – Chelm, she said. She pointed to the right — Lvov.

"I am holding a twig in one of my hands," said Josef. "If you choose the hand with the twig, we go right, if you choose the empty hand, we go left."

Wolf studied Josef's form, facing him in the darkness, trying to glean any message as to the twig hand, though the twig hand held no more certainty than the other. For no logical reason, he preferred the right-hand fork and touched Josef on his right side. Josef shook his head, holding out his empty palm and they walked, without discussion, to the left.

In the dim dawn light, they could pick out a shape in the distance, long and low, like a factory. To the left of it, something glowed red. From a distance, above the footsteps of the people, they could hear a rhythmic sound. Closer and louder the sound came until they could make out a funnel that moved Eastwards against the skyline, smoke trailing behind it.

"It's a train," said Josef as an urgent whistle scattered the crows across the flat lands. "Let's get over there. See if we can get on the next one that comes past."

"Or at least we can walk down the line until we come to some sort of station," said Wolf.

They crossed the dirt-dry fields that separated the road from the railway. The sun was up now, and, even this early, had begun to warm the air. The glow, as they got closer, had turned into a raging fire. An engine was slewed across the track. The flames had spread to the wagons behind. Some were slumped on their sides, others burnt-out shells, still smoking. On either side, the earth was pockmarked with bomb craters but the track on the far side was clear.

They moved closer. Food, water, anything that might help them was foremost in their minds. The explosion that suddenly erupted from the wagon closest to the fire flung them to the ground. Dazed, they scrambled between burnt out bushes and dived into the nearest crater, metal, wood and burnt-out debris falling all around them. The wagon grumbled like an angry wasp, threatening to burst again. They braced themselves.

It was not another explosion that came. It was a storm of bullets, ricocheting off the ground, bursting in the air up and down and around them like a firework display. They scrambled deeper into the bomb crater, hugging the side closest to the train, scrabbling for cover.

"Ammunition train," said Josef.

They waited. The sun grew hotter and the crater gave them no shelter. Still the bullets blew, as if fired by a hidden sniper, ripping through the air above them at random angles. They'd stop for a few seconds, as if offering the men a chance to escape, then blow again. Wolf was thirsty, hungry and desperate to move on; to one side was open land, but they were trapped.

When eventually the shots stopped for over a minute, he began to scramble up the steep side of the crater. It was not far to the top, but his feet slipped; he could find no grip on the bomb-loosened soil.

Josef tried to help him from below, holding his feet, giving him support, as if legging him up onto a horse. But no sooner had Wolf got his head above the rim than another series of small explosions began. In the split second before he threw himself backwards, he could see, through a hole torn in the side of the next wagon, smoke curling around olive green boxes. Once they might have been stacked neatly, but now they were slewed across the floor; some had burst, releasing the hand grenades inside.

"Cover!" shouted Wolf as he fell backwards.

For what seemed like hours, they did not dare to move. The grenades exploded in waves. Sometimes a whole box would explode at once, shards of metal flying through the air above them in a deafening din. At other times, there would be just the pop and crackle of one or two. Pieces of twisted metal landed all around them. Josef picked up a larger piece and, once it had cooled, laid it over the back of his head and neck as he burrowed as deep as he could into the earth.

They could hear a train go by in the other direction, going East. Something splintered as it passed, but it did not stop. It was late afternoon before the explosions finally petered out. Wolf climbed out first. He lay on his stomach, reaching down to help Josef. All the wagons now were burnt-out shells and the engine blistered with fire and bullet holes. Everything was scorching hot to the touch. Already they knew that there would be nothing they could retrieve from this waste land.

They started walking along the track, the setting sun behind them, their legs barely able to support them. Somehow, through everything, Wolf still clung to the brown paper parcel that his mother had given him as he left Bledow, his arm threaded through the string and held over his shoulder. It was his link with home; he might have lost Hela, but a piece of his mother was still with him. He looked down at himself. His clothes were covered in earth, stained with the green of the grass and the coal black charcoal. He wondered what was inside the parcel. The raincoat that he had carried, tied around his waist, had gone. He wondered if it lay at the bottom of the crater by the train or on a street in Ljublin.

Either way, he took another step away from his past.

Ahead of them, they could see a village. The railway line ran through it and they could see that the road intersected here. Figures, some upright, some bent over, some singly, others in groups, moved along the road. Some had stopped at the railway station. Wolf walked up quickly to see if Hela was there, but there was no sign of her. Nor of Chaim or Moshe.

A small rough shelter stood on the outskirts of the village, close to the track.

"Let's sleep here," said Josef. "Then, if a train comes in the night, we can get onto it."

A family of four were already inside. The man of the family nodded as they entered. He pulled a loaf of bread from a bag and tore off a small section.

"It's all I can spare," he said.

"Please," said Wolf. "You have a family to feed." But the man pressed it on him and he did not refuse a second time.

Thirst, however, still haunted him and there was no water.

7 EMBANKMENT

IT WAS early morning when the rumble of a train from the West woke them. Quickly they pulled themselves upright. Wolf felt for his mother's parcel and looked down the line.

"They're goods wagons," said Josef. "It may not stop."

They stood poised beside the track, ready to leap onto a coupling if necessary, but the train slowed and they followed, running for the station. There were two passenger carriages at the back. No one got out, and the people on the platform hurried to get in, stumbling over each other and tripping over bags to find a seat. The guard was shouting and waving his arms as Wolf and Josef climbed onto the end of the platform, helping the family up. The driver, clearly impatient to get further East, did not wait long. With a whistle and a belch of smoke, the train lurched slowly forward as they clambered into the second carriage, Josef's long arms sweeping up the last of the family's children.

The benches of their compartment were upholstered in a lined pattern of red and brown. The material was worn and torn and greasy in places where thousands of hands had been wiped against it. Above the benches were metal racks with netting between the spars. Wolf helped the father lift his heavy bag and place it up there, then leant back in his seat and smiled at Josef opposite him.

"The train to freedom," he said, and Josef smiled back.

The train chuntered through the countryside. Its rhythmic clacker lulled Wolf into a reverie. He lowered the window, releasing it with a webbed sash. The smell of cinders entered the compartment as the carriage caught up with the smoke from the engine. Outside, hills, valleys, rivers and orchards sped past in fractured images like the single frames of a film, with no time to learn the end of each story or to understand its beginning or its fullness. For mile after mile he watched, until the farmland gave way to forest.

One of the children, the boy, suddenly burst into sobs.

"I'm hungry," he cried clinging to his mother.

"We will have lunch soon," she said, a sad look in her eyes as she gazed out, as if pleading with the gods that this were true.

That was when Wolf heard it. The sound that haunted him, haunted all of them. Everyone froze. His fingers, he saw, as he clutched at the seat frame, were white, as if clutching harder would protect him.

A huge explosion rocked the train and shards of wood peppered the left-hand side. They could hear the engines whine as the aircraft turned. Now he could see them, three of them, heading back, following the track through the pine.

They lined up. Wolf lost sight of all bar the right-hand aircraft as they dived. The whine drew closer and closer until, with the too familiar rat-tat-tat, the machine guns opened fire. Bullets spat into the back of the carriage and thudded into the horse hair of the upholstery. Glass shattered in the windows. Wolf dived to the floor - blood, mixed with broken glass, already trickled across it. He turned his head to see who had been hit. In the pandemonium that had spread forward through the train like a flood tide it was impossible to tell who was hurt and who was merely terrified.

Then the screaming started. It was the woman of the family, a bloodied stain spreading across her chest, her children climbing on top of her, desperate. Wolf lay still. For a few moments he could hear only the cries of the wounded and the rush of air through the broken windows and punctured sides. Then the engines again. This time the bullets came from the front, rattling against the roof of the carriage and bursting into the compartment.

"Take cover!" shouted Josef, but there was no cover to take.

Another bomb rocked the train ahead of them. Wolf caught a glimpse of trees crashing to the ground as they passed. For a while, the bullets stopped. Glancing out, he could see the aircraft turning again.

"We have to get out!" said Josef and pulled himself upright, brushing shattered glass from his red pullover. As the train entered a sweeping bend, it slowed. Ahead was a steady incline up a high embankment. Josef yanked at the door handle. The door slammed open against the outside of the carriage. A cold wind whistled in.

"Now! Jump!" he shouted.

Wolf looked behind. In the sky above, the planes were lining up for yet another attack. He looked down. The grass-strewn embankment was steep and the train, though slowing, was still moving fast. But there was no time.

"Go!" shouted Josef as he jumped himself.

Wolf caught the briefest glimpse of arms and legs flailing, a red ball tumbling and bouncing against the hard earth. Instinctively wrapping his arms around his head, he leapt. He hit the ground rolling, head over heels, side over side, the air knocked from his lungs. His mother's brown paper parcel burst against brambles, scattering pieces of underwear. Still he was rolling. He thumped into a bush, slowing his chaotic descent, but his momentum took him on. He caught a glimpse of the back of the train in the distance, the planes still chasing it, the machine guns sputtering.

Finally, at the bottom of the slope, a lifetime from the top, he stopped. To his right were the thick pines. To his left the embankment, a narrow path at the bottom. He lay for some minutes dazed, panting for breath. Something trickled down his cheek and, when he swiped it away, he saw that it was blood. Blood spilled too from lacerations on his arms and legs and chest. He raised his right leg - it was not broken. Then he raised his left and cried out in pain, but it, too, was unbroken. He tested each arm and found that he was whole.

He pulled himself up on his knees and looked down the path for Josef. There was no sign of him.

"Josef," he called.

There was no reply. He stretched upright. His left hip ached and he could step only gingerly on that side. In the distance he could hear the drone of the aircraft and he retreated into the pines, shaking his fist at the sky

"Josef," he called again.

The only sound was the cry of the crows in the woods and the sigh of the trees and the wind. He looked up at the railway track and the steep bank he had fallen down. Further back the bank turned into rocks half way down. A wave of fear grabbed him.

He scrambled amongst the rocks where Josef must have fallen. He was searching for the colour red. Had anyone else jumped, he wondered. But there was no one, nothing. No one answered his call. He was on his own.

Bruised and limping, his mind too tired to feel, he walked forward. He followed the bottom of the embankment, desperately thirsty, stumbling sometimes, listening for the sound of water. He saw a blue flower, a cornflower, and, as if in a dream, he grabbed it and ate it.

It was hours, it seemed, before the embankment ended and the track finally levelled out, but still there was no water.

8 A JEWISH CEMETERY

A SMALL town lay ahead of Wolf across a plain. A dusty road led towards it, parallel to the railway track. A group of four men walked in front of him - he thought he could make out Chaim and Moshe.

"Chaim, Moshe!" he called out and tried to pick up a jog. But as the men turned and he joined them, he saw that they were not amongst them. Three of them were around Wolf's own age and the fourth was an older man, his hair greying at the temples.

"I am Eliasz," said the older man. "There is no Chaim or Moshe here. But what happened to you?"

"What?" said Wolf.

"You are covered in blood and bruises."

Wolf looked down at himself. The leap from the train had left its marks all over him but he was barely aware of them. He told his story briefly, but they did not linger on it – each of them had their own story to tell.

The small town was deserted. Curtains moved sometimes in the windows as the small group passed, but no one appeared. They walked on. Wolf's shoes, too big for him from the start, slid backwards and forwards on his feet and blisters were forming. He wanted to take them off but the sharp stones on the road deterred him.

A farm cart stood outside one of the houses and in the field beyond a skewbald horse, chestnut and white, its shoulders and haunches jutting from its skin.

"Let's see if we can use that horse and cart. That will get us to the next town a lot more quickly," said Eliasz.

They knocked on the door. A woman in a stained ankle-length apron that once might have been green opened it, scowling.

"What do you want?"

"Could we have a jug of water please, Ma'am? And … we wondered if we could hire your horse and cart?"

"Hire them?" she said, ignoring the request for water. She called into the back room. "They want to hire the horse and cart!"

A sarcastic laugh came from inside.

"They can buy them if they want."

"What do you want for them?"

"Thirty zloty for both."

The men looked at each other. Some of them fished notes and coins from their pockets and began to count. They had about twenty zloty between them. Wolf held his hands out empty.

"I have no money," he said.

He fingered a chain around his neck. It held the pocket watch that his father had given him at his Bar Mitzvah. It had belonged to his grandfather and was of a grey metal, the roman numerals etched in a fine line round the face. It was dented on one side, the glass cracked now from the leap from the train. He honoured this watch as if it was part of his family. Reluctantly, he pulled the chain over his neck and handed it to the woman. She inspected it.

"Ten," she said.

"Fifteen," said Wolf, instinctively.

But the woman shook her head. The promise of food and water in the next town overcame his shame at letting it go so cheaply and, with the other men looking on, willing him to agree, Wolf nodded. He wondered what his father would have done.

Eliasz walked out into the field and led the horse towards the cart. It dragged its every step, its legs riddled with arthritis. He backed it between the shafts, then looked around.

"Do you have leathers please?" he shouted towards the door that now had closed.

It half-opened again and the woman held out the tack. She spat on the ground outside before finally closing it.

Eliasz sat at the front of the cart, while the rest of them clambered onto the back. A signpost pointed to Kovel and they set off, the wheels creaking and bumping down the uneven road, throwing up a small dust cloud behind them.

From time to time, Eliasz would cajole the horse into a trot, slapping its neck with the loose end of the reins. The horse would snort and whinny weakly in protest and no sooner had it picked up speed for a few paces than it would slow again, like a clock unwinding. Wolf wondered if they were actually moving faster than they could walk, but he was glad of the relief from the blisters.

Three hours or more passed, the sun beating on their faces, before they made out a large town in the distance. It sprawled across the landscape in front of them and, as they drew closer, they could pick out a walled area on the Western edge, standing out from the dry fields around them.

"Matzevot," said one of the men.

Some of the headstones in the cemetery were painted in red or blue or ochre — those who had recently died and had been spared the theft of their country. Many more were plain stone or showed faded versions of the same colours — colours that had once been bright but had faced the wind, rain and frosts of decades and were weathered now to a replica, just a hint, of what had been.

In one section, headstones, some rounded, some ornate, some with long Hebrew inscriptions, lay at a slant, or on the ground, cracked and broken. Wolf sighed.

They saw a man in the fields.

"Can you tell us which is a Jewish household please."

The man pointed to a house; its plaster walls were faded to a dull brown. Wolf knocked on the door. It did not occur to him that a group of five men in tattered clothes, blood-stained and bruised, would appear threatening. There was no answer and now Eliasz stepped forward and knocked.

"We just want to sleep," he called in Yiddish. "We have walked for miles; we are exhausted." Still there was no answer and this time he hammered on the door.

"OK, we will break the door down," he shouted. "We mean you no harm."

One of the other men kicked at the door near the handle. Another took a run and kicked again. They could hear the sound of wood splitting. With a final kick at the bottom where a bolt must have been, the door toppled inwards. A frail old man appeared in the hallway, leaning on a polished stick, his hands shaking.

"I … I saw the planes. I heard the bombs. I am sorry …" He paused. "Food, I will give you food," he said, beseeching them. "And water."

"Thank you, no," said Wolf. "We will just sleep here on your floor and leave in the morning."

The other men looked at Wolf and began to demur, but he held up his hand.

"We cannot accept hospitality from a fellow Jew that is not freely given," he said, surprised at the strength of his own conviction.

"But water for our horse, and oats or hay if you have any."

The man shuffled past the broken door and pointed to a yard behind the house. Loosely baled hay was stacked in the corner of an open stable.

"Please help yourself," he said, plunging a bucket into a water-tub. The water was brown and brackish, dead flies floating on the surface. Wolf pictured his mother when, as a child, he had started to drink from a stagnant pool that collected some of the waste of Bledow.

'No, don't drink it. It will kill you,' she had cried.

He cupped the water in his hands and sluiced it over his face and head, but he did not drink.

******

They had hardly left, soon after dawn, when the planes came back, high above. For a few seconds, nothing happened; then two of the aircraft separated, the whine of their engines intensifying in waves, and dived, the air filling again with the sound of the sirens. As one, they leapt off the cart, sprinting for whatever cover they could find.

Wolf watched helplessly as the horse, the cart still attached, the reins dangling across the ground, panicked. It raised its head and, with a terrified whinny, broke into a canter, the cart careering behind it, crashing off houses and denting walls, until it disappeared behind a church.

Bullets spat into the ground randomly – there seemed no target here. Wolf could see some of the other men sheltering behind buildings nearby; a few people were running from street to street, shouting and lifting the wounded. As the Messerschmitts pulled away, two bombers began their run.

Wolf could judge now where a bomb would land as he saw it released. He dived into an old crater, covering his head as dirt and shattered brick and stone clattered about him. He moved from one crater to the next, trying to get away from the town. He shouted for the others to follow, but he could not wait and in the melee of people and dust, he lost sight of them. He found himself on his own again.

He was desperately hungry and thirsty. He cursed himself for being so proud as not to accept the old man's food and water the previous evening. He was not thinking clearly. Almost delirious, not knowing where he was, he took a track that led off the road through a forest.

9 A STRANGER

THE SHOES which had clackered back and forth across his feet, he finally threw off. Blisters had formed around his heels and on the right foot on the outside of his little toe. He tied the laces together and hung them around his neck and walked now, barefoot, along the track.

Images tumbled through his mind as he stumbled from tree to tree: Chaim, arms flailing desperately for his wire-rimmed spectacles, one lens splintered on the broken ground, the other cracked and glazed; the headlong dive from the moving train and the shuddering somersaults down the embankment, the Luftwaffe screaming above him.

He could smell wood smoke, he could see open fields. A small white-washed farmhouse stood in front of him, a cherry tree either side of it. A few of the red cherries still clung to the higher branches. In front of the house a boy of perhaps ten was whispering to a copper-coloured chicken that he held in his arms. More chickens fussed about the dry earth.

For a few moments the boy stared with wide, unfrightened eyes at the wild-haired, barefoot figure that came out of the woods, as he might stare at an exotic animal that he had not yet come across. Then, excitedly, he dropped the chicken and ran inside, calling for his mother.

She appeared at the door, her dark hair tied in a knot, her face kind. She beckoned Wolf forwards. He willed his legs to move but they took him barely half way before he collapsed amongst the chickens, overwhelmed, finally, by the distance he had walked and the time that had passed without food or water.

He was naked in a large metal bathtub when he came to. The water was hot and welcoming and around him now were not just the mother and the boy but also a daughter, younger, who carefully carried, in both hands, another jugful of water. She poured it into the tub.

"Thank you," he said in Yiddish, but they looked at him blankly.

"Dziękuję," he tried in Polish, and the mother nodded.

Through the doorway to the kitchen, Wolf could see his clothes hanging above the fire; he could smell onions cooking. The daughter passed a bar of soap and the mother, without any embarrassment, began to wash him. She washed him from head to toe, all of him, asking the children at times to support his shoulders or hold his legs. Very tenderly, she washed the blisters and lacerations on his feet and heels. Finally, she passed him a large towel, torn and frayed at the edges.

"When you are dry, come into the kitchen," she said.

She pointed to a chair with a spindle back and arms. He looked around him. Against the wall was a wooden dresser with a few plates displayed of different sizes. There was no chanukiah that he could see or mezuzah on the door; nor was there a crucifix. The woman beckoned him to the table and set a bowl of broth in front of him. She called to her son, and he brought a thick slice of rye bread. The daughter, again with two hands, carefully poured water into an earthenware pot and stood back to watch him, her brown eyes wide.

He ate and he drank as a dog does, as if there is no tomorrow and this is the last meal, and when he was done, his eyes were leaden.

"Come," the woman said. She led him to an alcove where a straw palliasse lay on a wooden frame. He looked at her as if to say, 'Where is your man? This is your bed, you and your man's,' but she pulled a thick grey blanket over him and touched her hand to his chest.

Another slice of bread waited for him in the morning.

"Dziękuję, dziękuję,"he said again, bowing his head to her.

She gave him an egg, hard-boiled, when he left, and pointed. She seemed to understand which direction he should go and he did not doubt her.

.

10 AN ORCHARD

18 September 1939

WOLF studied the signpost. Something about one of the names on it rang a bell in his mind – Velykyi Omelyanyk. Then he remembered.

His brother, Shmil, had married in June. It was only three months previously, but it seemed to Wolf like another lifetime, a different existence altogether. It had been a very happy time. Erika, his new sister-in-law and her parents came to Bledow. Erika and Shmil were married under a chuppah outside the synagogue; it was decorated with wild flowers from the nearby fields. Afterwards there was a great party, so much as the meagre finances of the two families would allow, with food and dancing; it had seemed like hours that they had danced the hora, singing Hava Nagila over and over.

Wolf had worn the suit that he had purchased when he worked in Warsaw. He had felt proud of his brother and he had talked to Erika's parents, Natan and Lutka. He had liked them. They spoke to him as an adult.

"We are renting an orchard in a place called Velykyi Omelyanyk, near Lutsk. It is not very far from the Russian border," Erika's father had told him.

Wolf folded his hand around the grey stone that he had picked up at the Vistula river, his talisman, and walked the four miles to the village.

"Do you know of a family by the name of Fajnsztein?"

The second person he asked directed him.

"There is a pear and apple orchard behind a tall rusting gate between two stone pillars. The house is a little further along the road."

Wolf hastened forwards. He could not believe the good fortune that had brought him here. He knocked at the door. The dark hair of a young girl fell in a cascade of curls around her face and her feet were bare. She looked at him, uncertain.

Wolf had not met Erika's sisters before, only seen them at the wedding and he stood for a moment, unable to speak.

"I... I am Wolf Albert. Is your mother or father here? I met them at the wedding."

"Who is it?" came a call from inside the house.

The girl had scuttled away and was quickly replaced by the man that Wolf remembered, though now in dungarees and not a suit.

He looked him over quickly.

"Wolf, my dear boy." His wife came out too and they both embraced him. She was weeping.

They stood back.

"You are so thin and bruised, look at you. Did you come on your own? What news of Erika and Shmil? Are they all right? They have not written or sent any message."

"I wish I could tell you," said Wolf, "but I do not know. I did not see them. I left in the night when the Germans were close. I did not see any of the family, only my mother."

Erika's mother urged him to sit. She gave him water and made tea.

"The German planes came here," said the father. "They came twice. Just a few days ago. We heard them, saw them overhead, waves of bombers and then the noise. Like a wailing siren."

Wolf shuddered. "I know the sound only too well," he said.

"They did not touch us here but we were like rabbits caught in the chill of a buzzard's cry. We could hear the boom as the bombs dropped. We could feel the ground thud. Again and again. Someone said the government came here from Warsaw. We saw helicopters the day before and many military vehicles on the main road. Now we are hearing that Russia is invading us from the East. That is the news that came from Lutsk yesterday."

"What do you mean?" asked Wolf.

"Germany from the West, Russia from the East. People do not want our country."

"But…" He looked behind him as if, in looking there, he could find an escape route. He could not accept the truth that was being shown to him — that the country towards which he had been fleeing, where he thought he would find a safe haven, should now have turned on him.

"With bombs and planes and bullets?"

"No, not that yet. Occupation is the word they use."

"You must stay here with us, until this is all over and you can go back to Bledow," said Lutka. "You are part of our family now. You can sleep in the stable. Karola – this is Shmil's brother. He will stay with us and work with us. Please show him to the stable and the water pump."

"Rest and wash and the girls will call you when it is time to eat."

Another girl appeared, this one the spitting image of the first but older and fuller. She was perhaps seventeen or eighteen. She was shy and inclined her head.

"Rywka, are you coming too?" said the younger girl.

Wolf followed them. They walked without speaking through lines of fruit trees on either side. Wolf had to duck under the laden boughs of russet apples.

"Pears here," said Rywka eventually, as they reached a different section. The tang of the fruit, freshly picked, but some of it accidentally trodden, filled the air. Wasps were busy boring holes into pears that had dropped, gorging themselves. In places the trees were already stripped of fruit. Wicker baskets sat under others, waiting to be filled. More baskets, these ones already filled, stood by a small building, thatched and whitewashed, with a stable door. A palliasse and a worn grey blanket, stained in one corner, lay on the earthen floor. Outside the building was a pump and a bucket.

Rywka opened the door.

"This is for you," she said and stood back to let him in. He brushed past her breasts as he did so.

"I'm sorry," he said, and she blushed.

"We will call you when food is ready."

Wolf tore off his clothes. He pumped vigorously, filling the bucket again and again, hurling the water over his face and his chest and his genitals and his feet, as if to wash away all traces of the last ten days. At last, he shook himself, like a dog after its bath, and lay down on the palliasse. He did not know how long he slept but when he woke, aromas of frying latkes filled the air. He put on his clothes again, such as they were.

"Wolf," came a little voice out of the trees. "Dinner time." He followed Karola back to the house.

He fell upon the food and, when he looked up, he saw the girls staring at him.

"I am sorry," he said. "Do I look like an animal? I was so hungry and your mother is such a good cook." They all laughed.

Slowly, over the next hours and days, Wolf told his story. Natan listened, nodding sometimes and sighing, while Lutka busied herself with the food and the dishes, trying to distract Karola from all she might hear.

"For the moment," Natan said eventually, "we are safe here. We have begun to harvest the pears. When they are picked, we will pick the apples. The strong arms of another man will be very useful."

"Of course," said Wolf.

"What do you mean?" cried Rywka. "I can lift up the baskets!"

"You can, my loved one, you can. But twenty, thirty of them. My old back is not what it was; we do not know where Shmil is. Wolf is a young man. When he has got his strength back after all his journey – he will be able to do the work of two of us without thinking."

Rywka looked across at Wolf and her eyes caught his before they slipped to the side.

******

It was after 6 a.m. when the clank of ladders heralded the new day. Natan showed Wolf how to pick the fruit – a gentle twist, not a tear. If the fruit does not come off easily, then leave it for the second picking. Be gentle with the fruit. Unripe fruit cannot be sold, nor bruised and damaged fruit. Put your arm through the bucket and load it with fruit and then, when it is nearly full, not so full that pears are tumbling out, go down the ladder and carefully unload into the baskets. At the end of the day, the baskets are lifted onto the cart at the gate where the market man comes to grade them and pay.

Bees hummed through the ankle high grass that grew beneath the trees and the late summer sun quickly wore away a thin mist. Blackbirds called between the trees and Wolf marvelled at the spiders' webs that hung between the branches.

"Wolfie, Wolfie, Wolfie, Wolfie," Karola would sing out, skipping between the baskets. It seemed to Wolf as if he had stepped into some other world — a world entirely different to the one he had faced on his way here.

From time to time, after loading up the basket from his bucket, he would look up to see Rywka staring at him before her head turned. At other times, at the top of the ladder, he would see her black curls preceding her as she reached the top of the next tree. Invariably, she would chuck her head, tossing the hair from her olive brown eyes. Their eyes would meet for a moment across the trees and it would be his turn to glance away, as if interested in something else.

As time passed, at the top there together above the world, she would take an apple and sink her teeth deep into it, and he would take one too and they would eat together.

"Let me," he would say, when they both reached the ground at the same time,

but she would shrug. "I can do it."

She would laugh, if he dropped an apple: "Careful, Wolf. Bruised fruit is worth nothing."

At midday, Lutka and Karola would bring bread and cheese and tomatoes and a pitcher of water and they would all sit in the shade of the trees.

Friday 22 September 1939

As the Sabbath approached, they started on the last row of trees.

In the evening, Lutka lit the candles. Wolf had done his best to wash himself and had put on an old shirt that Natan had given him. Rywka's hair was still a little damp when she came into the room and Wolf had to look away. Natan included him in the blessings as if he was their own son, before they each broke a piece from the two loaves of challah.

"In the morning we will go to the synagogue," said Natan.

Saturday 23 September 1939

Wolf heard a soft footfall and a rustle through the low branches. The midday sun caught the green leaves, making them almost translucent. Their shadows played on the floor in the light breeze like a troupe of dancers.

The top of the stable door hung open. The leaves framed Rywka's dark curls as she looked over at him. Both of them knew the significance of the moment and both were silent. The only sound was the bees buzzing amongst the fruit trees and the thick grass beneath them.

"May I come in?"

He motioned with his hand, paralysed . She sat on the end of the palliasse.

"I said I was going to feed the chickens. Karola is with her friends."

Wolf didn't know what to do. He had never been with a girl. In his body he wanted to draw her to him and gorge her all over; but in his mind he was frozen.

She edged a little closer, moving her hand towards his knees.

"I am glad you are here with us," she said. Her voice caressed him like honey.

She leaned towards him.

"I suppose …" he said.

He touched her hand, working his finger nervously around the top of it.

"Shmil and Erika. It makes sense. Me and …"

He never finished the sentence.

A shout from nearby. It was her father. She broke off quickly and ran out. It was a few seconds before he heard her reply.

"I'm here. A chicken escaped."

At tea that evening Wolf could not bring himself to look at Rywka, his desire was so strong. But something had changed. He felt a coolness from her parents, a hint of disapproval. The mood was sombre. Wolf did not know if it was her father's suspicions or what he was about to say that changed things.

"This week," he said, "We will have finished the harvest. We cannot stay here when it is done; our tenancy of the orchard comes to an end. Tomorrow I will go into Lutsk and find somewhere where we can live. It will not be easy."

11 LUTSK

Monday 2 October 1939

THE LATE summer sun that seemed to have escorted their days in the orchard — days that would have been magical had the cloud of war, the lack of information about Erika and Shmil and the uncertainty of what the winter would bring, not hung over them – turned to cloud and rain. A chill descended as they all clambered onto the cart that had stood near the stable. All the family's belongings and a few baskets of apples were perched precariously between them.

Wolf tried hard not to bounce and jolt into Rywka, but at one point, as the cart lurched over a deeper rut than most, she grabbed his arm for support. An electric shock passed through him as their eyes met, but quickly she took her hand away.

The apartment that Natan had found was cramped and bare. A small cooker stood in one corner of the kitchen where one of the window panes was cracked. There was just enough space for Wolf to sleep under the table. All the family shared the only bedroom. They had not been able to sell all the fruit from the orchard — there was little money for food, let alone any kind of heating.

With only a shirt and another on top of it that Natan had given him, the cold penetrated every inch of Wolf. From an old worn saddle that they had found in the stable, they had sewn together shoes for him with twine, but the leather on the soles was quickly wearing through.

******

The bombing had stopped before the Russians marched in. The Luftwaffe had succeeded in destroying only some administrative buildings and Lutsk remained the wealthy capital of the Volyn province. Natan told Wolf how the Nazis and Russia had signed a non-aggression pact just before the war. Now that the Russians were here, the Germans would not come back, he said.

Russian soldiers strolled through the streets of Lutsk in their grey serge coats. Their families came and the women found items to buy here that they could not buy in the Soviet Union – watches and dresses and the like. For them life was easy and comfortable. For the Fajnsztein family, however, and most of the large Jewish population, swelled by refugees from the West, life was harsh.

Work was in Wolf's nature and it was the only thing he could do. Work to bring in some money in order to buy food for his adopted family and to keep warm as the temperature plummeted. At least, thought Wolf, the Russians do not treat us as the Nazis had.

He fought his way through the winter months, doing anything he could. Sometimes he would stand in a bread queue all night to earn a few szlotys; sometimes he would pump a wheel all day, drawing water at a bath centre for the Russian incomers; sometimes he would help make crude hessian underwear, pack it into large bales and load it onto trains. Eventually, as the year turned to 1940, he got a more regular job hand-making ice cream in a factory and serving it from a little shop at the front called 'Lucky's Ice Cream.'

He barely saw Rywka. She and her mother and sister would go out cleaning and cooking for the Russian women for many hours a day and, even when they were both in the tiny apartment, there was no chance to be together and little desire, anyway, to do anything but eat or sleep.

15 March 1940

Wolf stood in the queue as the instruction had said. *'A census of new arrivals in Lutsk'* it was headed.

"What's this about?" he asked the man next to him.

"I think they want us to become Russian citizens. They have taken over the country, now they want us to be an official part of it. Not bloody likely I say. Did you hear about Stalin's show trials? And all the people who died in the countryside? These Russians here seem OK, a lot better than the Germans we used to see in Krakow – even before the bastards overran the place. Of course, the Russian women go around flaunting their pretty dresses but … well, we can look. At least no one is making us wear armbands or smashing our windows."

A Russian soldier beckoned Wolf forward into a small office. From the window he could see the long queue winding round the city library. A young officer sat behind a wide desk. On his arm was the insignia of the NKVD — a downward-plunging sword overlain with the hammer and sickle, on a background of red flames. To the side, a pile of beige files threatened a landslide.

"Please, sit down," he said waving his arm in the direction of a chair with a green leather back.

Wolf sat and waited expectantly.

The officer adjusted his wire rim spectacles and pulled forward a sheet of paper.

"Albert, Wolf?"

"Yes, sir."

He picked up an ink stamp and thumped it onto the sheet.

"So, you are, let me see, 19 years of age, nearly 20. You have been in Lutsk for how long?"

"I am not sure, sir. I do not have a calendar. I think about five months."

"I see."

"Any family here?"

"No, sir."

"Why not? You have family somewhere I presume."

"Yes, sir. I had to leave Bledow to escape the Germans."

"Good. I don't blame you. You got here and now we, the Soviet Union, are looking after you."

"Yes, sir."

"Your country, Poland, is finished. Germany has taken a bite out of it from the West. We have re-taken what is rightfully ours on the East side. And now you have a wonderful opportunity. Today I am authorised to offer you full Soviet Union citizenship and a Soviet passport."

Wolf paused. It all sounded very plausible, very simple, but he remembered what the man in the queue had said.

"Sir, as you say, I am only 19. These are big questions and I am not qualified to answer them. When I can see my father again, I will discuss them with him and then, with his blessing, give you my decision."

The officer stood up. He tore off the spectacles. The voice that had been mild and conciliatory rose now to a scream.

"Get out of here!" he shouted, raising his arm and pointing to the door. "You will not speak to your father. You have had your chance. You can get on your knees and pray to me; you can kiss my bare arse, but you will never get a passport or anything else from Mother Russia."

Wolf walked out of the library building in a daze. The Russian soldiers that stood by the door were stone-faced. One of them he recognised – he had come into the ice cream shop and joked with him about a large-bosomed girl who had been standing outside. Wolf had not said anything about Rywka – he held an image of her as his secret, not to be sullied by boyish chat.

There was an air of apprehension on people's faces as he walked away. He made his way back to Lucky's Ice Cream, surprised that he was not arrested.

.

12 RUSSIAN PRISON

6 April 1940

IT WAS to the same Lucky's Ice Cream that they came, early in the morning, when Wolf had just opened up the shop. He was preparing to serve them a scoop in a cone.

"Wolf, Albert!"

"That is me."

"Come with us. We are conducting a survey. There's no need to bring anything. You'll be back soon."

Wolf did not resist – these Russian soldiers were his friends. He served them ice cream. They directed him to the same library building where he had been interviewed.

"In there," said one of them.

It was a large room, cleared of shelves and books, and filled with faces he knew: the man from the bakery, a friend of Natan's, the woman who had delivered some dresses for Lutka to repair, a man called David Solomon, leader of the Bund in the city and the owner of a shoe-making business. There was a set look on all the faces – as if fate had finally caught up with them – no one complaining, no one crying or weeping, no one raging. Wolf looked around for Rywka and for Natan, Lutka and Karola but there was no sign of them.

"What's happening?" he whispered to the man next to him, but his voice sounded eerily loud in the silent room.

"Silence," shouted a soldier.

More people arrived and as the day warmed, the room began to stink. A large woman fainted and the man beside her moved to open a window.

"They said I'd be home soon," Wolf whispered again. They were now squeezed up against each other, sweat dripping from their bodies. "That was first thing this morning."

"Same here. I think they're up to something. Perhaps they're sending us back to where we came from."

It was late evening when they heard the belch of engines outside and were counted out of the room.

"Twenty-eight, twenty-nine, thirty." The soldier lifted a stick to stop the next person. Wolf was keen to get out, even if just to breathe fresh air for a few moments. He was herded into the second lorry, jammed so tight on the narrow wooden bench that the surplus rolls of flesh of a corpulent woman next to him came to rest on his thighs. It was not a long journey. After fifteen minutes, the lorry stopped. He could hear gates opening and, through the gap in the back, he could see lights and a sentry post and fences.

"This isn't a railway station," someone muttered. "This is the prison."

Guards searched them as they climbed down from the lorry.

"Strip!"

Wolf released his belt and stepped out of his trousers.

"All of it!"

He removed his underwear and the guard felt in his anus.

"Open your mouth. Hold it open, look down and shake your head."

Wolf followed the instructions.

To his side, a young woman stood naked. The guard seemed to take glee in sticking his fingers first up her backside and then her vagina. Her breasts drooped. Wolf had seen only glimpses of womanhood and now to see it all at once, being so treated – he could not entirely process it.

"What is this?" asked the guard rifling through Wolf's pockets.

"It's a stone — my lucky stone."

"You'll need that," said the guard and, inexplicably, returned it to him.

Dark, cold stone lined the narrow corridor they were led down, guards in front and behind. A fetid stench filled the place. The corridor went on and on. Wolf looked around. The front guard stopped and, with a large key, released a wide metal door with a peephole to the left. They filed in. It was a large room, high ceilinged. In the centre was a single bare bulb which threw a dim light across the concrete floor. There was one window, high up and oblong, bars across it, the pane smashed, and beside the door was a tarred barrel. Nothing else.

The room filled. Wolf counted. There must have been at least ninety people in there, he thought, as he was crammed up against a wall, his space to exist reduced to an area just big enough to lie down and sleep in a foetal position. Where it had been hot and airless in the library building in Lutsk, here it was bitterly cold, the chill air seeping into the room through the broken windowpane.

The door eventually clanged shut and for a while there was just the rustling and jostling of bodies shifting and anxious. From time to time there would be a shout as someone tried to reach the barrel, and then the farting or the furious release of urine falling on urine. It was inevitable that before long, someone would not make it.

"Fuck, you've pissed on my trousers," came a shout from the other side. Quickly, the room began to stink.

There was a clanging outside and the door was opened again. One guard stood at the door while another wheeled in a metal pot, lightly steaming. Liquid spilled over the sides as he released it. There were two bowls.

David Solomon was a tall man. His beard was greying at the fringes but his voice was loud and commanding. He was closest to the cauldron.

"There are only two bowls," he said. "I do not know how many of us there are but there are a lot. If we divide the room down this line," he held his arm out, cleaving the crowd in two, "I will pass this bowl to this side and this to this side. Let us say two mouthfuls each until we see how far it goes. Is that all right with everyone?"

For the Jewish amongst them, and there were many, this was entirely in the spirit of tzedakah; others muttered and mumbled until someone said loudly, "It's good enough."

David now filled the bowls and passed them to those nearest to him. Minutes passed as the progress of the bowls, their journey back to David for a refill and then their return, hand by hand without spilling, to the next person, was followed in a kind of fascination. The further each bowl progressed, the longer it took to come back, be refilled and make it out again to the corners of the room.

"I only had one mouthful," called someone as the full bowl came back past him, but there was no arguing.

"I think there is enough for another mouthful each," said David when the first ration was complete and the whole ritual began again.

******

It was still dark outside when the cell door crashed open again. This time, four soldiers came in. Two of them carried wooden chairs.

"Your ID and photograph will be taken here," the sergeant called, pointing to one of the chairs.

"For your health and cleanliness, your heads will be shaved here." He pointed to the other chair.

"Form two queues."

Without further ado, the person closest to the left-hand chair, was told to sit down.

"Name! Where from? Family?"

They have all this information, thought Wolf. That is what they took down in the library building a month ago. But it did not seem to have occurred to them.

The first man was told to press his index finger onto an ink pad, then onto a document that carried his number. Finally, he was told to sit upright and look straight at the camera, then turn for his profile.

"Next."

When it came to his turn, Wolf looked down at the document that was handed to him. B167. That was his number. He was, he said to himself, Wolf Albert. He was not B167, but he would play that game, do what was required of B167, for so long as that protected him.

The barber was a ruthless man. He might, in other times, have been a butcher. His extravagant arm movements were better suited to cutting up a joint of lamb than to shearing a person's head with blunt scissors. First he cut off the long hair, virtually dragging it from its roots; then he worked furiously across the head from front to back and back to front with clippers, like a farmer ploughing a field.

Wolf's head was sore and blood seeped from the scratched skin when he was told to stand up. A pile of hair, black and brown and blonde and grey, had built up on the floor.

"Here, B167" said the barber, holding out a sack to Wolf. "Clear it up."

There was no brush. With his bare hands, he gathered up the hair. On it, he could smell the personalities of its former owners. The scent of hair oil and perfume, the odour of the farmyard, the tang of urine that some hair had fallen into on the floor, the smell of onions that had been frying when the soldiers came. All of this jumbled mess of hair he pushed into the hessian sack and glanced up. All he could see was a sea of shaven heads, the individuality of those heads now subsumed into this bag.

At a signal, the soldiers left the room. Wolf returned to his space – already an unwritten rule had been established that, where you started in this room, that is where you stayed, that was your home for the moment. Two different soldiers entered. One wheeled in another cauldron of tea, another carried a sack which he dumped on the floor. David Solomon looked inside.

"It is bread," he said. He held up a slice. It was black and sticky.

People stirred and moved, but he held out his hand.

"Wait, we will pass it round. No one will lose out. Remember, we are Jewish. We respect others and take only what we need."

People mumbled their agreement and the bread moved quickly through the mass of them. Whatever else the Russians had done, they had calculated the quantity needed exactly. Everyone had a slice and none was left.

Now the tea ritual followed, eager eyes chasing the bowls across the room. This time there was a small sugar lump for each of them.

13 A TOILET

WOLF was desperate to empty his bowels but it was only on the second morning that a guard came in and shouted:

"Toilet."

He counted out twenty-five men and they were marched out. After only ten minutes, they were back.

"Next."

Wolf was in the second tranche. The air outside the big cell was different. Not full of sweat and urine, but dank and oppressive, yet still he scooped up great lungfuls of it. Guards escorted them in single file. In front, he could see that the corridor reached a junction. He could hear other footsteps, then a whistle.

"Halt," shouted the guard. "Stand facing the wall."

Wolf did as he was instructed, but a guard came up behind him.

"Against the wall, I said." He jammed his face right into the uneven stone, scraping his nose. Behind him, Wolf could hear the other group walking, returning the way he had come.

"No looking," shouted the guard, then "Walk forwards," as the footsteps receded into the distance.

They turned to the left and, shortly, stopped. Beside Wolf were a set of five steps, the smell of excrement spreading down in a nauseous wave. The guard blew his whistle and pointed.

"Quickly!" he shouted.

Wolf climbed the steps. They led into a large bare room. In the centre, like a volcano's crater, was a huge concrete funnel, perhaps four metres across, sloping down to a stinking hole. Urine and faeces and blood lined the concrete.

Wolf moved to the far side; there was no time to consider the niceties. He turned his back on the hole and positioned his feet. He lowered his trousers, his bottom hanging over the very edge. All around him, faeces and urine splattered. The stench was unbearable. One man, older and infirm, toppled sideways, scrabbling to hold onto the rough concrete and save himself from falling into the hole. The person next to him pulled him back but already he was smeared in excrement.

Wolf had barely finished when the whistle blew again. There was no water, nothing to clean himself with. He could feel the dampness of the faecal remnants as he pulled up his underpants and trousers.

******

In the cell, the stench of sweat and unwashed bodies became overwhelming. David Solomon designed a system for people to rotate their position so that they could spend some time near the door where fresher air leaked in, or beneath the broken window.

"Sir," he said one day to the guard who brought in the morning urn of tea. "It is too cramped in here. There is barely room for us to lie down and sleep. The air is thick with the stench. It is not healthy. People are getting very sick."

"I will tell an officer," said the guard, pleasantly enough.

"Perhaps they will listen to us," said David. "He seemed quite reasonable."

A senior officer came in.

"I hear you have a problem," he said. "You think ninety-nine people is too many in here."

"Yes sir," said David. "Many people are getting sick in this fetid atmosphere and there is not enough space to lie down properly."

"Well, if you have a problem with ninety-nine people," said the officer, "I have a solution. I'll give you another person. Then you'll have a nice round one hundred. How's that?"

Without waiting for an answer, he turned on his heel and a little while later a single man was pushed into the cell.

******

"Who is on A?"

Two NKVD men stood in the doorway. The crashing of the door and grating of the lock had already woken Wolf. All the inmates had become used to the nightly disturbance – people being called away from the cell for interrogation. Whether it was 10 p.m. or 3 a.m. Wolf had no idea.

"Sir," Wolf answered.

"Second name, first name and name of your father?"

"Albert, Wolf - Jankel."

The warden checked his list.

"Prison number?"

"B167."

The guard checked the paper he held in his hand.

"Follow."

He followed the guard to a small office.

"I am your Citizen Judge," said the man inside. "We have information that you were in Lutsk to spy for the Germans."

"Sir, I am Jewish. I was in Lutsk to escape the Germans. They bombed my village and I ran from them."

"That is not true you Polish son of a whore. You sold out to the Germans, and you know it."

The man held a pistol to his head.

"Here, sign this." He thrust a piece of paper and a pen in front of Wolf.

Before he had time to lift the pen, the office door opened and a Russian officer, his face familiar to Wolf, walked in. The interrogator stood to attention.

"What are you doing here?" asked the newcomer, looking at Wolf. He was a regular of Lucky's Ice Cream. Wolf would fill his bucket generously – he imagined that there was a family of ice-cream loving Russians to keep happy.

"I don't know, sir. Ask him."

The officer spoke sternly in Russian to the interrogator, then rapped out a command.

"Take him back," he said to the guard.

******

4 May 1940

The heavy door rattled and grated again. This time the warden came in. He had a large sheet of paper in his hand.

"Step forward if your name is called."

He began to read out from a long list.

"Wolf Albert."

People shuffled and cursed as Wolf pushed forward in the confined space, breaching what had become their property.

"You have been convicted under Section 58, Paragraph 8 of the Statia as a person unknown to the State threatening to weaken or subvert Soviet power. You are sentenced to three years in a labour camp."

"But I…"

The man raised his arm for silence and read out the next name. To a rising chorus of angry shouts, others were sentenced to five or ten years.

"What do you mean? How can I be sentenced? I have not had a trial."

"I cannot leave Lutsk – my wife is sick."

"I am no threat to the Soviet state. I have been helping it. You know that. I gave you all the information in my interrogation."

But the warden remained firm.

"These are the sentences we have received from Moscow. Follow the guards."

They followed and this time a whole platoon of guards, all armed, were ready to escort them outside. Wolf blinked in the new daylight, his eyes unaccustomed to the brightness. In the yard, many more prisoners were lined up. They were ordered into two lines.

People were silent at the roadside, staring, cowering out of the way of the Russian soldiers, as the ragged troop marched through the dusty streets. Wolf searched for Rywka, for Natan and Lutka and Karola in the crowd but they were nowhere to be seen and the eyes that he looked into looked down as he passed.

.

14 TRAIN TO SIBERIA

STRAINED faces greeted them at the railway station, all sentenced. People were five deep in a line that snaked back towards the town. Many were Jews, some of them families with small children, but native Poles were dotted amongst them too. Some carried small cases, others held a knot of possessions in a sheet or blanket. Children pawed at their parents' legs as the guards marshalled the crowd.

Wolf saw a woman twenty yards ahead of him in the throng. The back of her head, the colour of her hair, the way it hung, the worn green coat she wore - his mother! He did not stop to wonder how she could possibly be here at Lutsk Railway Station, how she could possibly have taken the same journey he had – something visceral took over.

"Mother!" he shouted, trying to push his way forwards. People near him shook their heads and blocked his path. They wanted to retain their place, to get out of this place and on to the next place, to be on the train that would, perhaps, take them home.

"Mother!" he shouted again, but in the din of the crowd, guards shouting and a train clanking on the far side of the station, the woman did not hear.

Eventually she turned her head. It was a careworn face, a face that carried sadness in its veins, but it was not the face of his mother. She looked around her, taking in, it seemed, the faces beside her and behind her. Across the void of the crowd her eyes met Wolf's and he smiled and waved anyway; but it was an empty smile and something inside of him died as she turned forward again.

The guards' rifles were not slung loosely round their shoulders but held at the ready. Every now and then, Wolf heard a shot. He looked about him. Was there an escape route? The land was flat to the railway buildings. Behind and on either side were more guards. The trees of a spinney beyond promised some cover, but it was four hundred metres away.

In a siding, a line of cattle wagons lay silently. He wondered how long it would be before their carriages arrived.

"Where do you think we're going?" he said to a man next to him.

"Don't think there is much doubt about that. Somewhere way up North, I imagine."

He turned to the others around him and pointed to the spinney.

"What do you think?" he said.

They looked in the direction he was pointing.

"No chance." Heads shook as one, seemingly resigned to whatever fate had in store for them.

At that moment, anyway, one of the guards shouted something to the other soldiers and approached the closest cattle truck. It was made from reddish brown wood with crude diagonal struts. Tiny windows were set high in the sides with thick metal bars across them. The domed roof was of corrugated metal. The soldier released the bolts and hauled the heavy side door open. It slid and creaked along its rusting track.

"Board," he ordered, beckoning the first prisoners forward with his gun.

More and more prisoners he ushered in until, to a volley of curses, he hauled the door shut again. Wolf manoeuvred himself to be one of the first into the third wagon; more and more people shoved in behind him.

Planks sat on crude brackets one and a half metres up to provide an extra 'floor'. Opposite the door, a hole, roughly square, had been cut in the wall at waist height. A plank was nailed to the lower and side faces, sloping out and downwards, creating a chute. Remnants of dried faeces clung to the rough-hewn timber, as if someone had made a half-hearted attempt at cleaning it, but the stench of urine and excrement seemed to live in the very fabric of the wagon.

Wolf chose a position on one of the upper planks close to a little window.

"Move up, move up," shouted the guard.

The light of the day and the station platform diminished and disappeared as he hauled the sliding door shut again and slid the bolts home.

In the semi-light there was a restless stillness as people took stock of where they were. The wagon lurched suddenly forward and some of those standing in the middle, unable to find a handhold, fell back. A little girl cried as the wagons clanked against each other. Outside, Wolf could hear, slowly at first, the start of the engine – da da da di-da, da da da di-da – until the train shunted forwards. Instinctively, he felt that they were moving East. It was not so much a conscious conclusion as an innate knowledge.

Back in Bledow, in the warm days of summer when he was a child, the Polish boys would come to his door.

"Hey, Jew Boy, want to come out and play?"

It wasn't a judgement. It was his name as far as they were concerned; it might have been Pieter or Matheus. That had been when they were fourteen or fifteen, before the virus of thought that came out of Berlin had filtered through the cities of Poland, and then the towns and the villages, until those same boys that he had played football with, that he had explored the fields with, seeking out the mice and the hedgehogs, hiding behind thick bushes or camouflaging themselves in plain sight in the thick grass, had begun to sneer at him, to stand guard outside his father's shop, warning people that the owner was Jewish.

But, in those earlier years, which were to Wolf now, in his mind, years of unalloyed happiness filled with blue skies and a freedom of spirit and body that now he could only wish for, he always knew what time he should return home.

His mother had said, "We will eat tea together. Whatever you are doing Wolf, Naomi, Rosa, Shmil, Moshe, you will come home at tea-time. Sometimes, there may not be much food, but always I will have something for you."

There were times when, after a whole afternoon with the village boys, roaming in the fields, play-fighting, exploring, Wolf was starving hungry, dying for the food that his mother promised would be there. Some of the other boys, he knew, would have two or even three-course meals waiting for them at home with fish and green vegetables and honeyed cake from their well-to-do parents. Once, Pieter had said to all of them, "Come on – let's all eat at my house."

Wolf ran back home and told his mother, begged her to be allowed to go.

"Of course, darling," she said.

Pieter's mother had raised her eyebrows, unwilling to let Wolf into the house when he arrived after the others but unwilling, too, to let her son down. And so she had said, "Boys, sit out in the yard, and we will bring the food out there."

True to their word, Pieter's mother and father had brought the food out and served the boys. Wolf had felt like a king. Never had he had such a meal.

"Thank you very much," he had said to Pieter's mother and father when they left to play again, and Pieter's mother smiled but the father looked down.

He knew that he could never repay that invitation because sometimes, on those heady days,
he would find at home just a potato. Cooked, lightly salted, but barely enough to assuage the first pangs of his hunger.

But, behind the food, there was something else that Wolf had learnt. It was not something learnt consciously. Early in his life, his father had pointed to the sun in the morning.

"Do you see where the sun is this morning, Wolf?" he had said.

It was mingling with the branches of the tall trees that stood behind their house. At the end of the same day, when his father finally finished his work and set down the sewing machine, he took Wolf's hand and led him outside.

"Do you see where the sun is now, Wolf?"

It was on the other side of the village square, low to the right of the synagogue.

"Why does it move?" Wolf had asked.

"This is the way it is, the way that God made it. We, the earth, move around the sun and sometimes it is daylight and sometimes it is night. The sun rises in the East and it goes down in the West. It is different at different times of year, but if you look at the sun, look at the sky, anytime, anywhere, you will know what time of day it is. And you can work out where you are."

He pictured his father now, wished he was with him, wondered what was happening in Bledow. From that lesson he had learnt the angle of tea-time. If there was no clear sky, no sun, he had learnt from the light what was tea-time.

And from the light in the sky before the wagon door was hauled shut, he knew now, as the train stuttered and strained into motion, that they were heading East. He craned his neck towards the window, craned for one last glance of the platform that was all that remained of Lutsk, craned, in hope, of one last glance of the girl from the orchard. But there was nothing. Instead, Wolf tried to count the shifting heads. Forty or more, he thought. A baby that had been stunned into silence until now began to wail at the other end.

"Does anyone have water?" came a woman's voice.

"There's a barrel down here, love. I think it's water, as long as no one's pissed in it."

An older man climbed up to the bunk opposite Wolf, the top of his bald head preceding him.

"I am Nikolay," he said with a wide smile.

"Wolf."

Their embryonic conversation was disturbed by a tall Ukrainian whose face resembled a broken cliff-face. He pushed his way towards Nikolay who was not a big man.

"Off," he said, with the authority of one who knows that his appearance will ensure that he will get his way.

Nikolay did not move.

"I was here first," he said.

The Ukrainian grabbed his shirt in ploughshare fists and lifted him off the plank, pushing him away. He beckoned to a woman in the scrum of the wagon, then turned his attention to Wolf. Wolf did not bother to resist. He had, anyway, no desire to sleep, if there was to be sleep, anywhere close to this man.

He settled on the floor close to Nikolay. Although the man could have been his father, he felt an affinity to him.

"Tell me about Wolf," said Nikolay. "Where does he come from? How did he get to Lutsk?"

Wolf painted the picture for him.

"And you?"

Nikolay told his own story. He was a piano teacher. He was not a man that Wolf would, in the ordinary run of things, have come across or befriended. His hands were elegant. Wolf imagined the long fingers dancing over black and white keys, the fingernails clean and manicured, a child beside him looking up intently at the sheets of music on the stand.

Already people jostled past to get to the toilet hole. The train rattled and swayed over the lines for hours and hours, the heat and stench and stale air dulling its inmates into silence. A man relieved himself, then came over to talk to them. He wore a dark, crumpled suit that had clearly suffered the privations of days and nights of incarceration.

"I understand you are of the Jewish persuasion," he said. "My name is Father Lenkovski. I do not know where these people are taking us, but I am praying that God will protect us all. I am just letting everyone in this wagon know that I am here and if I can help in any way with prayer, I will."

"Thank you father," said Nikolay. "But how come you are on this train?"

"Well, of course, it is a misunderstanding. I held a normal service, but the Russian women who had come into Lutsk said it was not a Russian Church service. I said this was all I could offer, but the authorities came. They said I was subverting Soviet doctrine. I am sure it will all be sorted out when I can speak to someone who understands."

It was hours later that Wolf felt the train slow and heard the grinding of brakes as it came to a halt. For a while, nothing happened; then there was shouting and the clanking of bolts as the door slowly opened.

"Out," said a guard. "Sit on the ground, do not move."

The guard counted the inmates of the carriage out.

"Thirty-nine," he said, then nodded to two other soldiers. They carried buckets of water into the wagon and sloshed it into the barrel. Then they filled the buckets with pieces of black bread. Thirty-nine pieces.

"Back," they shouted, and Wolf resumed his seat on the floor next to Nikolay.

7 May 1940

"It would not be that hard to escape if we all just ran for it," said a voice after they had got back in the wagon after another bread stop. "What do you say? We outnumber the guards by a long way. Most of us could get away."

"The problem is," said Father Lenkovski, "that we are not in Poland now. We don't exactly look respectable in these clothes after we've been locked up, and all we have in the way of documents are the sheets of paper they gave us when they locked us up. From everything I have heard, if you do not have the correct documents in the Soviet Union, the NKVD lock you away without any more questions."

"And I can't run, not with my baby here. I'd be one of the ones to get shot."

The wagon fell silent, people ruminating. Hopes had for a second been raised, only to be dashed by the realities of their situation. At the next bread stop no one moved.

11 May 1940

Monotony and hunger and a creeping tiredness ruled the hours. And worse, dysentery had caught a hold of the inmates of the wagon. Wolf did not notice the stench now, the urine and congealed faeces that pooled around the floor beneath the toilet chute. The visits to the chute were continuous. It was not a surprise now to see a woman lift her skirts, nor to see the shape and size of the men's penises. It was not that Wolf was deliberately looking – simply that, in this cramped space, if you opened your eyes that is what you saw.

Through all of the night, the baby had screamed, but now it was silent. In place of the wailing was a sobbing. The little girl, whose name, Wolf had discovered, was Lena, was with the mother, stroking the baby's blue and lifeless head. Lenkovski went over. He knelt and prayed with them, but there was nothing they could do with the body.

"That is very sad," said Nikolay. "But perhaps it has escaped a painful life."

Wolf had seen more dead bodies over the preceding year than he wished to remember, but those were the result of bombs and bullets. This baby had not died from a bomb or a bullet. His father had talked to him once of the sword of Damocles. Up until now, and despite his hunger, he had felt his life to be invulnerable, but suddenly that sword had become very real.

He turned to Nikolay.

"Why did you get arrested anyway? A good citizen of Lutsk."

"I was teaching the son of one of the Russian families that came into Lutsk. He was a colonel, high-up in the military anyway. The house was very plush – deep carpets and thick curtains – and looked out over a park. The wife seemed to wear a new dress every time I went. Anyway, one day when I went, she asked me:

'Nikolay, have you seen the figurine that sat on this mantelpiece?'

'I am afraid not,' I said. 'What sort of figurine was it?'

'It was of a ballet dancer.'

"I did not think anything more about it, but the next time I went, in the middle of the lesson, the wife called the boy out of the room. Two soldiers came in and began searching the leather briefcase where I carried my music. One of them held his arm up triumphantly, holding a different figurine – a sailor. I had never seen it in my life before.

'That confirms it,' said one of the soldiers. 'He is a thief.'

And they led me away."

"That is ridiculous," said Wolf.

He sensed the slowing of the train as if it was straining up a gradient. He angled his head to the side. Through one of the little windows at the top of the wagon he could see a pine-covered hillside.

"I think it's the Ural Mountains," said a voice from one of the upper bunks.

It was not many hours later that they entered a large station. The sign board said 'SVERDLOVSK' when the door was dragged open. They were ordered out onto the platform. This time, the women and little Lena were separated out. Lena clung to her father's trousers but the guard dragged her away as the men were ordered back inside.

Over the heads of others, Wolf saw again, in the crowd of women and children that they were leaving behind, the woman he had mistaken for his mother, her hair hanging lank and greasy now, like a moulting bird. Her eyes crossed his and, though they were empty, he waved anyway, as if, in waving, he could communicate with his mother, tell her that he was all right.

******

There was more room in the wagon now; it almost seemed like luxury and Wolf and Nikolay took their chance to lay claim to two bunk beds at the opposite end to the Ukrainian. As the train moved out of Sverdlovsk station, Wolf felt it cross some points and head North.

It was only minutes before it stopped again. It shunted slowly backwards, a shudder ricocheting down the line of wagons as contact was made. A loud metallic clang signalled completion of the new coupling, but now the bolts were drawn and the door re-opened. Five men climbed on board.

"Where is this train going?" asked one of them.

"We have no idea. We came from Lutsk. You?"

"We were imprisoned in Starobelsk. They said it was near Lugansk."

None of these places meant anything to Wolf and he looked out of the tiny window. It was a relief to feel the breeze come through and to see the country going by. Sometimes there would be a few wooden buildings, people cutting trees in shabby dress. A few would wave towards the train and call out.

"Good luck," Wolf thought he heard from one woman.

A vista of mountains and forest opened out to the left of the train. They were heading North-West. Wolf called Nikolay over.

"Look, I think we're going back over those mountains again. What were they called – the Urals?"

******

Sometimes the train seemed to change direction, to take a branch line, like a pigeon correcting its flight path on sighting danger. At other times it would stop for hours, sometimes days, on the track. The air in the carriage, without the movement of the train, became yet more fetid and stale.

At night, guards would bang on the sides and roof with hammers, checking if the prisoners had broken through. People screamed at them to stop, clamping their ears, as the din thundered down the length of the train.

Dysentery and monotony took their toll. From the top bunks liquid excrement dripped onto the bunk below, men too weak to get to the toilet chute. Every day, it seemed, another person succumbed. Every time, Father Lenkovski, though sick himself, would stumble across to the body and recite the prayers for the dead:

Eternal rest grant unto them, O Lord, and let perpetual light shine upon them. May their souls and the souls of all the faithful departed, through the mercy of God, rest in peace. Amen.

A desultory 'Amen' would follow from around the wagon. Religion, of whatever faith, did not seem to Wolf to have much meaning in this hellhole. Quite apart from the dysentery, they were starving, drained of all energy.

They had quickly learnt that, if they told the guards that someone had died, their bread ration would be reduced by one portion. Now, they piled the bodies close to the door and waited until the bread had been put in the wagon. Then, as the guards began to haul the door shut, they would tip them out.

******

"Tell me a story, Nikolay." said Wolf.

Other men gathered closer or leaned towards them – anything to escape the empty walls of the wagon. A man in one of the upper bunks on the other side, said:

"Tell me a story, tell me a story," in the voice of a parrot.

"Shut up," called the Ukrainian, but the dysentery had drained him and it came out as a croak.

"Every summer I would go to stay with my grandparents for three weeks. They lived in a village near the River Varta. Their house was up in the hills, the wild flowers would be out – it was beautiful. My grandfather played the piano – it was from him that I got the love of the piano. Sometimes, after swimming in the river, I would come back and hear him playing. He would play with the garden doors open and the sound would carry across the hills.

"One year, when I was about seventeen, I arrived there to find that a new family had rented the house next door. They had a daughter of sixteen, called Lola. She had long blonde hair – she was blonde everywhere else too…"

Some of the men chuckled lustily from their corners.

"blonde everywhere else, blonde everywhere else," recited the parrot man.

"… and then they had adopted another girl, Dora. She was nineteen. She was completely different, a bookworm and very serious. But when she took off her glasses and threw back her dark hair…"

Wolf was transported back to the orchard and to Rywka at the top of the ladder on the next tree, munching an apple. He could imagine the rest of Nikolay's story anyway.

"Talking of women," said another man, "I am a hunter. I come from Augustow in the North-East of our country – it is a good area for wild animals. I trap and shoot deer and hare and wild boar and sell them to shops and restaurants. I tried getting married once, but the problem is, in this job you are away from home a lot of the time. I discovered my wife was having an affair. I showed up unexpectedly one day – the guy was there, completely naked, on my bed. He was white as a ghost. I aimed my twelve bore right at his three-piece suite.

'Please, please,' he said. 'Give me a sporting chance.'

'All right,' I said. 'Swing them.'"

For a few seconds there was laughter in the wagon.

The parrot man climbed down from his bunk. He stood unsteadily then flapped his elbows, squawking, this time like a chicken. He crumpled to the floor, and sat with his head in his hands.

"Does anyone have a knife so that I can end it here?" he said in his own voice. "I know I am going — it would be easier to go quickly."

"It is an unforgiveable sin to take one's own life." Father Lenkovski's voice was frail. "Our Lord suffered unimaginable agony for us to live and to never give in."

"Shut up father. Our Lord was not locked up in a cattle wagon by these bloody Russians."

"The father is right, we should listen to him," said Nikolay.

"Who asked your opinion, you scabby Jew?"

"Come on then father," came another voice. "If your Lord is looking after us so well, why not ask him to turn that man into a real chicken. Then we can have some nice chicken soup for supper."

There was no response from Father Lenkovski. Wolf went over to his bunk.

"Are you all right, father?"

Struggling to speak, the priest whispered: "Fight, hold on, trust, Wolf. Fight, hold on, trust."

A deep sigh ran through his body and his eyes closed.

.

15 ON A BARGE

25 May 1940

AT THE end of the line, where the train finally stopped, a large sign proclaimed the place to be Kotlas. Plane trees stood at either end of the stone, single-storey station building. Nearby, Wolf could see a large stockade surrounding what he thought was must be their camp. At intervals, watchtowers were built around the perimeter. Outside people were moving about, cutting wood or digging.

There must have been around one thousand men who finally disembarked from the train, but the soldiers that met them did not lead them to the camp.

"Follow", they shouted "March."

Some tried, at the start, to swing their arms, but as the journey progressed and the guards themselves toiled, it became a matter, simply, of putting one step in front of another, just one more step. They marched for mile after mile. People pleaded with the guards for water, but it was useless. The guards had none and there was none around.

Starving and thirsty, Wolf could feel his remaining strength draining from him. Ahead of them up the dusty track was a small field camp. It was a place where two tracks intersected and canvas tents stood in the land around. Soldiers languished on the ground smoking, shouting at the group of prisoners as they shuffled past. At one end, there was a field bakery. The tantalising smell of fresh bread spread through the air and Wolf watched with envy as the officer leading their group walked in.

He came out with a large piece, its crust crisp, rounded and tanned and, Wolf imagined, still warm to the touch. It looked to him like the most delicious meal that anyone, anywhere might eat.

"Sir, please," he said. "I'm starving. Can we not go in too and get some bread?"

The officer leered at him, taking a great mouthful and chewing it deliberately.

"If I can fuck a woman, you can get some bread," he said, sweeping his arms across the empty landscape, no women in sight.

"Shut up and march on."

It was two hours later when they reached another tented encampment.

"We will sleep here," said the officer. "Line up for food."

Expecting only a meagre piece of black bread, Wolf was surprised to see great barrels of fish. There was no rationing. He took as much as he could carry, and secured more between his shirt and his skin.

He sat on the ground beside Nikolay and began to eat ravenously. It was salted herring. To begin with, its taste was nectar to his starved body, but soon a fire began to burn in the back of his throat, small at first, just glowing embers, but then, as he ate more, unable to stop, it turned into a raging conflagration. He was desperate for water.

If his earlier thirst had been that of a parched man, this thirst now clawed at him, torturing him. It raged through the night and was not assuaged by the morning water ration.

They marched again with the morning light. They marched for five hours, he judged, from the journey of the sun. Some men collapsed, clutching their throats, their legs giving way, but the guards goaded them on.

As the fish next to his skin mixed with sweat and grime, a crowd of flies formed around Wolf.

"You stink," said Nikolay.

Suddenly, In front of them as they rounded a bend in the track, were trees and a green hillside, a wide river below. Water. Wolf wanted to run forwards, to drink great shafts of it, to drown himself in it.

As they drew closer, he could see that they were heading towards a makeshift port. A pier ran out from the river bank and two huge river barges were tied up beside it. Over the centre section of each barge a sheet of canvas had been slung between poles that were lashed along the sides. At the back was a small wheelhouse for the barge master, otherwise just the flat cargo bed.

They marched straight down to the pier. The officer pointed.

"Board!"

The water was low and the bottom of the barge was some way down. Wolf turned, on reaching it himself, to help anyone else. A Pole, grey-haired and exhausted, was about to jump. Wolf held out his hand but the man turned his head.

"I don't need help from a Jew," he said. He landed in a heap and fell. Wolf held his hand out again and this time the man took it, his eyes downcast, still unable to utter his thanks. More and more men piled onto the barge. Some tried to hold onto a position beneath the shelter, but the guards ordered them further and further back until the full five hundred men were crammed in.

The metronomic thud of an engine broke into the vast silence of the water and round a bend in the river came a tug boat. It moved slowly towards the barges. The bargemaster shouted something, pointing. He went to the front and, with the tug alongside, hurled across a coil of rope, as thick as a python, then released the mooring ropes.

Slowly the tug pulled away. Wolf watched as the rope stretched and creaked in protest at the load, until slowly it took the strain. The barge was now free on the water, the bank receding. Soon, they were in the centre of the river. Water was all around them and there was still no way of drinking it.

Lying discarded in the bottom of the barge was a rusty tin can. Wolf tried to lean over the side to fill it with the river water, but it was too far down. Nikolay pointed to the length of orange twine that served as a belt around Wolf's waist. Expertly, he tied the twine around the can and tested it. The knot was strong. Wolf dangled the can over the side of the barge like a fishing line and hauled it up. Nikolay took the first mugful in one long draught, then sighed deeply. He handed the mug back to Wolf with a burp. The next mugful Wolf drank himself. The water had a green tinge and tasted brackish, as if the oil of the tugboat's engine had spread through it. Wolf had heard his mother talk of disease from unclean water, but it was all they had.

The can and its string attachment were a prized possession. The knot of people around Wolf and Nikolay gathered closer and it was not long before they too were satisfied and they could go into a second round. By the third round, some people were not drinking the water but holding their heads back and tipping it onto their faces.

Wolf's thirst was, for the moment, sated, and he felt able to nibble at the fish again. Its taste was rancid now, the salt mixed with the sweat and dirt of the journey, but, as his tastebuds grew accustomed to it, he ate faster, surreptitiously. He handed a piece to Nikolay.

******

For hour after hour, day and night, the barge ploughed through the water, the steady chug of the tug ahead of them. They were heading North-East, Wolf calculated. Sometimes steep tree-lined banks bordered the river, at others flat taiga dotted with larches and spruces.

Life was suspended. Sleep was a matter of leaning against the hard metal of the sides. Sometimes someone would stand up and stumble between the outstretched legs to reach the back to relieve themselves. Shouts and curses would follow their progress and the guard stationed there would give them no assistance.

From the angle of their backs and the position of their arms silhouetted against the dull river, Wolf could tell when someone was urinating. To defecate required a more agile stance that meant climbing onto the back platform, holding precariously onto the pole that held the canvas roof. Twice, Wolf heard a scream as someone lost their balance and toppled backwards into the water.

"Don't touch me!" a Jewish voice shouted now from the back. Two guards were changing shifts.

One of them laughed.

"We don't want to touch you, I can assure you, filthy Jew."

The man said something that Wolf did not catch. He was squatting at the back, his trousers around his ankles, one arm clinging to the pole.

"Better clean yourself up then," said the guard, and slammed his rifle butt against the man's knuckles.

"Help!"

Desperately, the man clawed at the side of the boat with his other hand, but he could get no purchase and, in slow motion, toppled sideways into the river.

"You can't do that, that's murder," came another Jewish voice, but the guards cackled, enjoying the spectacle as if they were watching some town square fairground fun.

"You need to stop the boat and get a lifebelt out to him."

But the tugboat pulled interminably on and the arm that flailed in the water, the head that bobbed, diminished into the distance.

"Anyone else for a swim?" the guard sneered.

******

28 May 1940

The sun dipped behind the steep sides of the river and a chill descended on the boat. Wolf shivered. Nearing a bend, the tug cut closer to the bank. A narrow stream tumbled down through the trees, creating, for a few metres, a flatter strip of land at the bottom. Visible on there, though they were still some hundreds of metres away, was a rough dwelling, a small boat hauled up beside it. A thin column of smoke rose from the hut. Wolf looked about. Could this be an escape route? To right and left of the hut were steep stone banks, trees jutting from the rocks. Behind it, there was a hint of a track, fit more for goats than humans.

"I'm going to swim for it," he whispered to Nikolay.

Nikolay put his hand on his arm.

"It's too dangerous, Wolf, you'll never make it."

Wolf pushed his hands against the bulwark, summoning the energy to get up, but another man stood first. He climbed quickly onto the side, balanced there for a second like an Olympic diver, his torn white shirt billowing behind him. A guard shouted and raised his gun, but the man stuck two fingers up at him and dived expertly into the current.

Wolf watched fascinated. The man did not re-appear for nearly a minute and when he did, his head was some distance away from the boat. It was only brief seconds before he dived again, the water around where his head had been peppered with the splashes of the guards' bullets. When he emerged again, he was a tiny speck, but he was making headway to the hut.

Involuntarily, Wolf clapped.

"Zol zein mit mazel! Good luck on your journey!" he said and sat back down.

He wondered who the man might find there, what he would eat. Would he learn to fish? Would he take the path up the steep bank?

"Perhaps you were right, Nikolay," he said.

******

29 May 1940

An eagle owl flew overhead, casting a dark shadow over the boat as the water passed interminably.

"How much further?"' someone shouted to a guard.

"Far enough."

And so it was a surprise when, from his semi-conscious doze, Wolf heard Nikolay call out. Ahead of them, the steep cliffs had given way to a land that was flat and swampy. Trees lined the horizon and the air was warm and loud with the whine of insects. A wooden pontoon stretched along the far bank.

.

16 MOSQUITOES

TWO HORSES, their shoulders gaunt through dull coats, nibbled at the sparse grass that grew amongst the sedge where they landed. Two carts stood to the side, the metal rims of the spoked wheels worn and pitted. Each cart was laden with great folds of canvas and wooden cases.

They had moved from the barge in a straggling mass, unsteady at first on their feet, their bodies used to the silent swell of the river beneath them. Wolf was glad to be on dry land if only to feel that they were making headway to some destination.

It was when they reached the swamps that the mosquitoes attacked. Attracted perhaps by the stench of herring that arose from Wolf's body, they quickly found a way between the folds of his filthy shirt. He slapped at his chest as they bit, and gasped when he saw the bodies fall out. These were no ordinary mosquitoes. They were huge. A centimetre or more long in the body, their black legs dangling behind, their evil proboscis protruding in front. Tundra mosquitoes. Light-coloured shirts turned to black as they swarmed over the men. They came in great waves. Wolf shivered. Their whine was like the merciless dive of the Luftwaffe. He rubbed his inflamed chest helplessly. All around him, other men cursed and slapped at themselves.

Every step that they took, feet dragging through the cloying swamp-mud, released another cloud of mosquitoes into the air. Wolf looked across at Nikolay. His face was set, his eyes slits in a swollen orb, his bald head pitted with red bites. The left side of his lip had blown up like a balloon and when he spoke it was barely audible.

"Save your breath," said Wolf, unable to offer more than words for support as he thrashed his arms in the air to beat the insects away. The guards were in barely any better shape. Though they had been provided with a rudimentary gauze net around their faces, the mosquitoes were getting in around the edges and down their collars. They waved their guns around as if a gun might help.

It was only, in the end, when they climbed out of the swamp onto slightly higher ground that relief came for a while. Ahead of them lay a huge forest landscape. A narrow track was marked by posts, the tops painted crimson as way marks. This, said a guard, is where the railway would go. For hours they followed through the forest, the light darkening as the trees closed around them. The carts trundled behind, the horses snorting and wheezing with the effort as the wheels alternately buried themselves where there was mud or lurched left or right as they negotiated a tree stump.

Every six kilometres they skirted an encampment. They could see the rudimentary huts and the fires and the scrawny backs of men, dirty and emaciated, working in the trees. They could hear the curses and shouts of guards, but they did not stop.

The smell of woodsmoke brought back memories of Bledow. The mosquitoes, Wolf noticed, already fewer in the forest, did not come into the smoke and so he tried to fill his shirt with it, to engulf himself in it as he walked.

They passed camp after camp, until suddenly, without warning, the officer cried 'Halt.' Wolf looked around.

There was no camp here. On a tree was painted the number 96 in large red letters. Above the 96 was a white arrow pointing to the North-East and beyond it more white arrows until they disappeared in the tangle of the forest.

To one side, in a small clearing, a tent had been set up. Two men sat at a wooden table, their faces lean and grim-set. A cardboard box containing a pile of index cards sat on the table. The officer addressed the crowd of men.

"This will be your camp," he said. "Line up and give your ID to the clerks. Then we will start building."

The line of men stretched to the edge of the clearing and then, as the entanglement grew too thick, snaked back on itself. Slowly, the line moved forwards. Wolf felt for the paper he had been given in Lutsk. It had somehow survived the journey in his pocket, curled at the edges now, soiled with sweat and stinking of fish.

The man in front of Wolf had no papers. He was turned over to the second clerk.

"We will call you Mister Nobody 23," Wolf heard.

He handed his own document over to the first clerk. The man curled his nose at the smell of it.

"You are Albert, Wolf?" asked the man.

Wolf nodded.

"Age?"

"Nineteen, sir. Or twenty." He did not know whether the 15th June had yet come round.

"Twenty, near enough," grunted the man.

He smoothed out the ID and wrote a number on it, then handed Wolf a thin metal disc, the number 317 stamped on it. At the top was a small hole through which a leather cord was threaded. Wolf hung it round his neck like the other men.

'I am not No. 317, nor B167, I am Wolf Albert,' he said to himself. 'I am not No. 317 nor B167, I am Wolf Albert.' Whatever was thrown at him here, he was going to find a way to deal with it.

He moved away to the clearing where the processed men had gathered. Trees and shrubs encircled it in a strangling thicket on three sides. The two horse-drawn carts appeared through the trees and the attendants dismounted. They pulled from the back of one of the carts a metal trough and placed it on the ground in front of the horses' heads. From a churn, they poured water into it. Men rushed forward, but the attendants waved their guns. The horses drank in slurping, thirsty draughts.

Wolf turned to Nikolay.

"They're treating the horses better than us," he said.

"Get the tents up," the officer shouted.

The guards pushed men forward. It took as many men as could reach around the cart to lift the canvas. And, once out, no one was sure where to lay it.

"Here," said the officer eventually, indicating to the horsemen to move the carts out of the way. "Set it up here on this flat piece of land."

The tent was unfolded and laid out on the ground like the carcass of an elephant. There were no posts, but from the second cart a guard produced two axes. He handed them to the men nearest to him. The officer pointed to two trees with slender, straight, trunks.

"Cut them down, we need three of them," he ordered, sending a small group off with the axemen and the guard, then measuring carefully where the three main posts should go.

He pointed to the carts, shouting at other guards. Two of them clambered up and started turning the contents over. Thick metal tent pegs, milk churns that sloshed with water, and wooden cases that Wolf hoped contained some sort of food. Eventually, three shovels were uncovered. Another group of men were assigned to dig the post holes. The rest, exhausted, sank to the ground.

Wolf stretched out on the sedge next to Nikolay. The man's face resembled a raging boil. Wolf had an idea. They had already learnt that the mosquitoes did not like smoke.

He started to pile together brushwood and, though the cold of the evening air had not yet set in, built the fire in the way his father had taught him. Other men joined in. Some, he could see, knew what they were doing; while others, those with delicate hands that were more used to office work or giving orders to a servant, picked at the branches and fronds as if they were infected. They are going to have to get used to this quickly, Wolf thought to himself.

A guard handed him matches and, gradually, cupping his hands against the breeze, he cajoled the flame to take. Slowly at first, and then with a burst and a great crackle, the flames soared into the air momentarily before settling to a real heat, grabbing the solid wood and searing the branches. A circle around the fire was clear of mosquitoes and Wolf dragged Nikolay close, as more and more men leaned in trying to escape the insects.

In the clearing, the three cut trunks were laid against each other, then two of them sawn again to match the height of the shortest. The thick lower ends were positioned in the holes, their narrower top ends inserted in the canvas. Men lined up behind each trunk to raise them. Sweat poured from their faces as they leaned into the huge weight. Slowly, the posts moved to upright.

"Hold them," shouted the guards as the men strained to keep the swaying structure upright, whilst others worked furiously with the guy ropes, tightening them against each other on either side.

.

17 TOMCZYK

THE FIRE that Wolf had started was commandeered by a guard who said he was the cook. He set up a giant pot over it and heated water, throwing in some herbs and leaves.

"Kipiatok," he said.

Wolf did not know what kipiatok meant – all he knew was that anything liquid he would drink and anything edible he would eat. It was, he quickly discovered, a sort of tea and was handed out with a piece of dark, black bread. He took a portion for Nikolay. Around them was the huge silence of the forest, broken only by the cry of insects, unseen, murmuring in the thickets and the occasional call of an eagle owl.

The flattened scrub beneath the canvas was not uncomfortable to sleep on and the smell of the grasses and bare soil carried Wolf back to Bledow. He slept fitfully. From time to time, someone would make their way across the sleeping bodies and into the forest to relieve themselves.

30 May 1940

The morning light had barely penetrated the branches of the forest when Wolf was woken by the harsh cry of a guard. He shivered. The ground had become damp with the night dew and a breeze whistled through the bare sides of the tent carrying the smell of faeces. A sound of brushing and crashing and rolling came from behind. A team of horses approached, the contents of the carts that they pulled rattling and jostling and sliding from side to side.

The men were ordered into a line to unload them – axes, pickaxes, shovels, wheelbarrows and long double-ended saws, the jagged blades sharpened like sharks' teeth. A different officer had arrived with the horses. He ordered everyone into a circle around him.

"My name is Morozov," he shouted. "I have been appointed your commandant. Your first job is to build your camp. Cut down trees, make planks, build a fence and watchtowers, build huts for yourselves and your guards and myself." He paused.

"And build a kitchen where the cook can cook you delicious food," he added with a sneer.

"We will build it there," he said pointing to a thick entanglement of forest, out of the way of the line of white-arrowed trees. "When you have built the camp, then you can start work building the railway."

"Form into brigades of twenty-four men. Find a leader amongst yourselves. The leader is to report to the engineer here." He pointed to a weasel-faced man whose lank black hair draped across his eyes. Wolf took an instant dislike to the man, but knew he must not show it.

He whispered to Nikolay.

"You're older. You have experience of dealing with people. People will respect you. Why don't you be a leader?"

But Nikolay shook his head, his face still disfigured by the mosquito bites.

"I can lead." It was a Jewish man that Wolf did not know. There was no selection process. Amongst the thousand-odd men who had arrived here, there was a smattering of urki — ex-prisoners — whose only language was intimidation and violence.

"I'm not being led by one of your kind. I will lead," one of them snarled.

Several Poles seemed to like the idea of this arrangement and moved closer to the urki, fulfilling his twenty-four man quota.

Wolf dropped back with Nikolay and the Jew who had offered to lead. Nearby, a man in torn and faded orange trousers held up his hand. His tall frame and mop of curly black hair had survived the journey so far. Dark stubble formed on his mosquito-bitten face but it was not yet a beard.

"I am Tomczyk, Szymon," said the man. "I can see that some of you are Jewish. I do not have a problem with that. Our job is to cut down trees and build the camp. I have done some of this kind of work before."

They joined him and quickly a brigade was formed.

He called over to the weasel man.

"I have a brigade here, sir."

The engineer led him over to a section of the forest.

"Clear this area," he said, pointing out the section in question and allocating the tools for the brigade.

"You look strong," said Tomczyk, turning to Wolf. "You take one end of this saw."

Another younger man was assigned to the other end. They began to work on the nearest tree but soon the blade became stuck. Tomczyk came over. Leaning against the tree, they hauled the blade out. He showed them how to cut a V so that the blade would not become stuck and the tree would fall in the right direction. First study the tree – which way was it leaning, which way did they want it to fall? Then a horizontal cut one-quarter of the way into the tree on the side they wanted it to fall. Then a cut above that, at an angle, to create a wedge-shaped V. Then cut from the other side towards the apex of the V until the tree was ready to topple. Then run like hell. Already, trees were crashing to the ground in other sections and the air was filled with the sway and swish of branches falling through branches. There were loud curses too as men shouted warnings and leapt out of the way.

As one tree was felled, other men came with smaller saws and removed the branches, and yet more men lifted the felled trunks into a pile. Others, with just shovels and axes, dug out the roots and levelled the ground.

The sun passed over midday.

"I am dying of thirst," Wolf said to Tomczyk. They had taken down five trees in the morning and already, with the space created by others, the area looked bigger. Across the clearing, smoke rose from the fire. A different man was stirring the giant pot.

It was barley soup. Something green, perhaps cabbage, floated in it too. Somebody called it schi. The barley could be counted on the fingers of both hands and, having drunk it, Wolf felt more hungry than he had before doing so, but the day did not stop. The light here was virtually continuous and the commandant was in a hurry to get the camp built, so the work went on, the men's energy flagging, until late in the evening.

Nikolay's face was drawn. He had been pushing a wheelbarrow loaded with earth and severed roots all day. His eyes were covered in a dusting of dark soil.

"At least we will get a meal," said Wolf seeing smoke rising as they eventually stumbled back; but when they joined the queue, there was just a slice of the black bread and a mug of tepid kipiatok.

.

18 BUILDING CAMP

9 June 1940

IT WAS the people who were used to eating fresh white rolls for breakfast, with fresh linen napkins and steaming coffee that were the first to go. Their soft hands were not used to the work and their bodies had never known the hunger and grinding toil that they experienced now.

Already, in a dish in the clerks' tent, lay a small pile of identity discs. Wolf had seen some of the bodies. A man from a different brigade said that they had spent the morning digging a deep pit in the forest.

It was the first body that Wolf saw at the camp that was imprinted on his mind. It was not the deadness of the man – it was the behaviour of the other men. The clothes were torn from him, even his soiled underwear, his shoes a prized possession, his belt; and those that stole them from him then put them on over their own clothes – the only way to keep them safe.

Nikolay was gaunt and pale but he was still going. His eyes had sunk behind their sockets and he walked as if trying to hold his balance, as if his legs might break with the weight of his body. His long, piano-playing fingers were scratched and blistered, dirt ingrained behind the nails. Hunger and exhaustion had already arrested the growth of stubble on men's faces and even Tomczyk had developed a stoop, as if carrying some great sack upon his shoulders.

Wolf looked about him in the warm morning air.

It looked very different to the place where they had arrived just ten days previously. Where there had been a canopy of spruce and birch, now there was open sky. The cleared space stretched out for metres. At the far corner, a cabin was taking shape. This, word had it, was the commandant's house. Posts had been set up around the perimeter of the encampment, the beginnings of a fence. Pegs were laid out in a series of oblongs to mark where the prisoners' sleeping huts would be. There were four rows, each with a line of four huts.

To one side, latrines had been dug. Wide rough planks bestrode three large holes. The smell and a constant murmur already hung over them. The sound was of not just mosquitoes but of all manner of insects seething in the maelstrom of faeces. It became a race for the prisoners, how quickly they could evacuate their bowels and get their trousers up again before the insects bit their backsides and the undersides of their scrotum. Hands were the only things that they could use to clean themselves off and the grass and dirt around the latrine was smeared with the mess of a thousand men. Outside the perimeter, a rudimentary sawmill was taking shape. Piles of logs lay on trestles, waiting to be sawn into rough-hewn planks.

Wolf saw the weasel engineer in silhouette across the land, speaking to the commandant. He came across and spoke to the brigade leaders. Tomczyk spent some time talking to him. He looked frustrated. Eventually he threw his hands out in resignation.

Up to this point, a target system had been in place, food the reward. The brigade was given a task each day. If the task was completed effectively, then the men were given the watery barley soup for lunch and a larger slice of black bread with the kipiatok in the evening. If it was not, there was no lunch and there was less bread in the evening.

"It is completely irrational," said Nikolay. "How can men work harder to meet the target if they are given less food?"

Wolf nodded.

But now, Tomczyk told his men, the target and reward was going to apply by pairs of men, not by the brigade. There had been too many shirkers, the weasel man had told him.

"Just men exhausted and half-starved," muttered Nikolay.

Wolf knew that he and his own young partner could achieve their own target – six trees down – but felt helpless for Nikolay. The weasel engineer, who went by the name of Zielinski, seemed to have eyes in the back of his head, noting down the work of every brigade and every man in it. Sure enough, when the evening came, he pointed to Nikolay.

"You have not met your target," he said and allowed him only a small portion of bread.

Other men pleaded their own cause, some on their knees, weeping and begging for more bread. Nikolay was too proud for that.

"I am not going to paw at his feet," he said.

Wolf was glad of that. He could not abandon Nikolay. His only chance was to use his own youth, determination and remaining strength to carry the piano teacher to the target. He spoke to Tomczyk.

"Can you put me with Nikolay tomorrow?"

Tomczyk nodded. As they spoke, a small man stumbled out of the food queue. He peered about him short-sightedly. One lens of his spectacles was missing, the other a crazed pattern of cracks. An urki grabbed at the man's bread. He dived for a pickaxe that lay abandoned on the ground and swung blindly. The urki ducked, but tripped. The small man, his face contorted with anger, brought the pickaxe down again. It caught the urki in the temple, the bone splitting with a crunch.

"Deserved it," said one of the onlookers. "You can't take another man's bread."

An unwritten rule had been established. Bread was their only possession, their only fingerhold on life. To take that was verboten, and to kill someone who did so was permitted. The urki had broken this rule and suffered the just punishment.

.

19 JANKEL'S DEATH

Saturday 13 July 1940

THE SYNAGOGUE in Bledow was built of wood. It had been constructed in 1855 soon after the first Jews had come to the village.

It was to here that Wolf's father, Jankel Zglinowicz, was called one Saturday. No doubt the Nazis deliberately called the meeting on the Sabbath. The rabbi, other lay leaders of the Jewish community, members of the town council, were called too.

Hela had finally turned back in Ljublin after she lost Wolf and the others in the fires and bombing. She had been home nine months now. She was in the yard when she heard the Nazis next door. They sounded polite, not the usual harsh orders, and she felt that something was wrong.

"We would like you to come to a meeting in the synagogue, Mr Zglinowicz. We need to discuss accommodation in the village for the Jewish community and for our soldiers, how we can work it best for all the village. Please could you be there in half an hour."

From the back of the house, she heard Wolf's mother.

"Don't go. It's a trick. They're up to something."

"I must go," said Jankel. "The Jewish people in this village are suffering. Heaven knows — if there is something that I can do to make things better for them, then I will do it. And anyway, if I did not go, what will they do? They will come for me anyway."

"No," said Hana. "Run. Run like Wolf. Escape. Do not worry about me."

But Hela heard the door close shortly afterwards and saw Jankel's back heading in the direction of the synagogue. With a pounding heart, she left her house by the back door and moved through the small gardens and fields. On her way, she whispered to Krystian, a Catholic boy, and he joined her. They made their way, crouching low through the undergrowth, to the wood half a mile outside the village. They had been here before and it was not a memory that Hela cherished.

They climbed a huge oak whose branches spread like a fan over a clearing, the thick foliage and unusually large leaves camouflaging them from sight. Beneath them, a section of ground some fifteen metres long and three deep was disturbed, the soil broken. There was an acrid smell in the wood, not just of turned earth and rotting leaves.

Hela put her finger to her lips and they listened. In the distance, from the direction of the village, they could hear a spitting and crackling and shouts. A pall of smoke rode across the sky above the tops of the trees. They could taste the burning wood.

Presently, they heard footsteps approaching down the track. The Nazi officers who had been to Jankel's door spoke now in harsh tones. They held their pistols ready. Other soldiers escorted the prisoners, the rabbi, Jankel and the councillors amongst them. At the back, a Jewish man who Hela did not recognize pushed a cart that carried many shovels. The officer drew a line in the soil with his baton - an oblong, parallel to the earth already turned.

Each man was handed a shovel.

"Dig," said the officer.

It must have been obvious to them what was going to happen, said Hela. They knew that some of the villagers, those who had tried to remonstrate with the Nazis or oppose them, had disappeared.

The men started digging.

"Faster," said the officer as sweat and soil besmirched their clothes and faces.

"Please," said Jankel, "I have seven children and a wife. They need me. I will do whatever you ask, but please let me live."

The officer just laughed. He walked over to the side and lit a cigarette. He was directly beneath Hela and Krystian. She could smell the cigarette smoke and stifled a cough. She was gripping so tight that her foot slipped. A twig, a small length of dead wood, broke off. The officer looked up. He held his left hand to his eyes and scanned the tree. Hela froze. She thought the sound of her heart pumping must be audible to the German, but he turned his gaze back to the trench. The men were waist deep now and a large mound of soil had formed at the back.

"Deeper," he said.

There was desolation on their faces when they finally climbed out. Desolation, faith and fear mixed with sweat and tears.

"Spare us, sir, please," said the rabbi. "God will look after us, but you, you, if you shoot us, he will not spare."

This seemed to enrage the officer. He shouted now at the men, his face red.

"Stand there on the edge of the trench! Face that way!"

One man, younger than the rest, turned and ran towards the thickness of the woods. He had barely taken five strides before the first shot hit him. Blood spurted from his chest and he slumped to the ground.

"Please, I do not want to die," he screamed. But a soldier took his arm and dragged him towards the trench and dumped him in it.

The others, cowed into obedience, stood as instructed. The rabbi, Hela could see, had soiled himself, his bowels released. The officer and the soldiers now moved up behind the men. They must have felt the cold hard metal of the pistols at the base of their skulls before they died.

The spits from the guns were not simultaneous. They were staccato, as if one was waiting for the other, or one was thinking. The rabbi seemed to be in mid-prayer, words that Hela did not recognise, when the shot came. He toppled forward. The bodies that fell sideways, the soldiers kicked into the trench.

The man who had tried to run still screamed.

"Help, please get help!" Another body had slumped on top of him and he squirmed beneath it.

"Fill it up," ordered the officer, shrugging. The soldiers picked up the fallen shovels and began to fill the hole. Gradually the sounds of choking fell silent.

Hela and Krystian stayed in the tree for a long time after the Germans had gone.

.

20 NIKOLAY'S DEATH

3 September 1940

THOUGH Wolf made sure that he and Nikolay met their daily quota, the weasel Zielinski continually marked them down, reducing their ration.

Tomczyk tried to intervene:

"These are some of my best workers, sir. I need them strong. I know that they are meeting their quota — I check for myself."

But it was to no avail; Zielinski merely shrugged. And now the rains arrived. They arrived hard and they arrived with a vengeance and they continued for a month and more. The entire camp became a bog, a quagmire. The only thing that was fully built was the kitchen. The canvas tent that had been used at the start was replaced by a wooden shelter, open at the front. Just the foundations of the huts had been built, no more. The rains had beaten them to it.

At least there was wood. The fire outside the kitchen would burn and glow and crackle and fizz in the rain, but the cook kept it going. On it a huge cauldron, supported by a scorched chain that hung between two iron posts, heated the kipiatok day and night.

The men divided into their brigades and built more fires around the camp. In the evening, they gathered in front of these fires stoking them up, lying in front of them on sawn-off trunks, warming their fronts as their backs soaked in the rain, and then turning over to warm their backs, steam pouring off them.

The railway line was unbending – anything in its path had to go. It was not just the trees but little hills too. With pickaxe, shovel and wheelbarrow, the hills themselves had to be moved. At least, Wolf thought, in the trance-like state of these sodden, muddy days, it was better to be moving and working than to be lying in the rain being soaked. He barely slept.

Sometimes, bodies would fall in the mud. He would see a leg or an arm sticking up, a puddle forming around it. Sometimes he would recognize it as that of a friend, if friends they could be called. Friend or not, Jewish or not, he would offer to dig the grave. Any of them, so far as he was concerned, deserved the respect of a burial.

He would dig in the area at the side of the camp that had been designated as a burial ground. If they were Jewish, he would speak the words of the kaddish, those that he remembered; if they were not, he would bow his head in one last acknowledgement of a life. He wondered, these men, did they have wives, a family like him at some far-away home in Poland or Russia?

Payment for this work was an extra slice of bread – the engineer did not have the power to refuse it or reduce it. This was how Wolf had worked out that he could supplement his meagre ration. With it, he could sustain his own strength and give some to Nikolay. Even so, he wondered how Nikolay kept going. He coughed constantly, and a gash on his leg had turned a grey-ish green.

******

By late September, the rain, at night, turned to snow. It was strange, at first, to hear the soft touch of the snowflakes on the pines and not the steady beat of the rain. Morozov, the camp commandant, and the guards shouted at the men louder now, urging them to work harder. A sign went up at the entrance to the camp '*It Never Rains or Snows in the Workplace*'. They needed to get huts built to form some sort of shelter through the Siberian winter.

More groups were deployed to the sawmill, cutting more and more planks; others began to build huts. The walls were lined with the planks, the roof sloping off to one side and lined with soil. Inside, a system of bunks was built from the split planks of younger trees.

15 October 1940

The huts were mostly built. Wolf took a bunk next to Nikolay. The planks were coarse and rough and gave him splinters, but the hut felt like a palace after the grime of the canvas and the mud. Across the camp, a curl of smoke seeped from the commandant's hut. The commandant's mother had joined him in the camp. They called her Baboushka, for she was a cheerful soul though so bound up in thick coats and scarves that no one had any idea of her real appearance.

A fever was draining Nikolay now. Mucus poured from his nose like a baby and his breath came in a broken wheeze. Wolf pleaded with the lekarskaya-pomoc, the lek-pom as they called him, the man who served as the camp medic, to help, to take Nikolay into the newly-built sick-hut and treat him there, but he just shrugged. He was, Wolf suspected, qualified as a nurse at best.

Back in the hut, Wolf could feel the other inmates encircling Nikolay like vultures. They knew when a man was near the end. Wolf looked across at his fading body, his piano fingers swollen and torn. A man sentenced for a crime he did not commit.

In reality, there was no sentence – no sentence of three years or ten. The only sentence was that day, to get through the next second, the next swing of the pickaxe, to survive the rain and the chilling cold, to live on the tiniest portion of bread. The cards had been dealt, none of them had had any control over it; this was their fate. There was nowhere to run to. Each of them, it seemed, had drawn a two. Wolf was not to know what he learned afterwards, when he found out about the cards that others had drawn, that theirs was actually a three or a four.

Nikolay's bread lay untouched in the gap between his emaciated back and the wooden slats. Wolf broke off a piece and held it to his mouth. He tried to grasp it with his lips, but could not take it. Wolf tried again, but the bread crumbled without being eaten. Carefully, Wolf caught the crumbs, cupping them and placed them, with the rest of the bread, close to Nikolay's hand.

He tried to sleep, but to sleep like an animal, alive to movement around him, aware of the seeping life beside him. The shadow of a figure tip-toed silently across the dirt floor, any sounds muffled by the snores and broken breathing of the sleeping men. A man stood in the pale light above the bed. Wolf did not move. The intruder reached his hand out for the bread. Wolf unwound. He leapt up and butted him in the stomach. The man fell back, crashing his head against the wooden side of the hut. As he tried to recover, Wolf smashed his fist into his jaw.

"Don't you dare steal a dying man's bread!" he shouted, breathing heavily from the effort.

The man slunk off. Other men had woken in the outcry. Wolf had laid down a marker.

In the morning, he listened for Nikolay's breath but there was none. He took the crumbs and ate them. The rest of the bread, he kept for later. He took Nikolay's jacket that he had used as a pillow and put it on.

He remembered Father Lenkovski's last words in the cattle wagon.

'Fight, hold on, trust, Wolf. Fight, hold on, trust.'

Zielinski, the weasel engineer, he determined, would be the next subject of the fight.

******

The wind tore through Wolf's clothes and the rain soaked them. He smelt like an old sheep. He looked around him at other men who, at the beginning of their journey, had been powerhouses and now clung to life. His own strength, he knew, was ebbing.

He took out the last of Nikolay's bread. He resisted the temptation to eat it like a hungry dog. He chewed it, extracting every last ounce of goodness from it, drawing the juices until it tasted like nectar. He felt no guilt in drawing another piece of bread from the kitchen after burying his friend.

Tomczyk came over.

"I am sorry about Nikolay, Wolf. I am going to put you with Andrei now."

Wolf nodded. He respected Tomczyk.

"Andrei or no Andrei," said Wolf, "the problem I have is Zielinski. Even though I meet the quota, he drums up some reason to mark me down. I cannot keep up the work on so little food."

"I understand. I am not sure what I can do, but I will keep trying," said Tomczyk, but Wolf had already decided to take matters into his own hands.

******

Andrei was Russian. They took either end of the two-metre handsaw and fought their way through the day.

"We have to make the quota," Wolf said, using the few half-words of Russian he had picked up, when he saw the other man flagging.

"You didn't make today's quota, Jewish; only four trees," said Zielinski again in the evening.

"We did five, look," said Andrei.

"Don't worry, I will take care of him," Wolf muttered when they were out of earshot.

He stood by the cook's fire, his arms wrapped around himself. To others, he might have been warming and drying himself, but he was watching Zielinski closely.

The self-styled engineer went to what the prisoners called the office, carrying his notebook. After a little while, he came out and walked towards a small hut, set away from the main rows.

Wolf drank the thin kipiatok and went in the same direction. A candle was burning inside the hut and, through a gap in the slats, he could see Zielinski snoring. A large section of bread sat on a plank beside his bed.

The next day, Wolf talked to Andrei more. He liked him. They communicated in a pidgin language made up of the Russian half-words, hand signals and drawings traced on the ground. Andrei had been a mechanic in Kirov. He fixed wheels on carts and exhausts on motor cars such as there were. Wolf did not ask him why he had been imprisoned, but he told him that he would make sure that they got more food.

They worked through the quota. That evening, he watched Zielinski into the office and then walked warily across to his hut. He had perhaps a five-minute window. Checking behind and around him that no one was looking, he pushed at the door. It scraped across the earth inside but there, beside the bed, was a large chunk of bread. Quickly he thrust it into his pocket and walked deeper into the trees to eat it.

He kept some for Andrei.

"Here," he whispered, passing the bread beneath his palm when he got back to the hut.

He knew he would be watched the next night, but the one after he went back. This time he had to search for the bread but he unearthed it along with some sugar lumps beneath the thin paliasse that was the weasel's bed. Again, he shared the food with Andrei.

Zielinski glared at them the next morning.

"Someone has been stealing my bread," he said.

"What are you talking about?" said Wolf.

"Serves you right," came a voice from behind them.

21 BABOUSHKA

13 November 1940

THE GREAT White Bear bit hard that winter. Wolf clenched his teeth against the fierce relentless cold. It was a cold that penetrated every corner of him. It numbed the body and stultified the mind. One day turned blindly into the next. He neither fought it nor submitted to it.

Though Zielinski was now allowing his full quota of bread, it was still a minuscule ration. Hunger stalked Wolf like a tiger.

He could not now remember the hunger he had been used to back in Bledow when times were scarce and the potatoes had run out. He knew he could endure that. Often enough he'd been to school without breakfast, without dinner even, the evening before. Later, on his journey, he had still been able to pick an apple from a tree, even if it was unripe, or, at the ice cream factory in Lutsk, slip a spoonful into his mouth before the commissar saw him. But now... there were no apples, there was no ice cream. There was nothing. Nothing but him and the snow-clad pines and the snow itself. The lack of food in those earlier times was of no account against this gnawing cyclone of hunger.

This hunger taunted him, willing him to surrender. It stole any fat that was left on him and then it stole his flesh and his sinews. It held him in its jaws trying to diminish him, but he would not let it.

He did not think, if thinking it could be called, about his family. He did not think of health or wealth. He thought only of food. Not, even, of a square meal. Just one more piece of bread, of the dry, black bread that they were given at dawn to prepare them for sixteen hours of work. Just one more piece and how he could get it.

Every morning, they were awoken before dawn. They had sealed the hut from the biting wind with the snow itself, like eskimos, but, as the thin light came, Wolf would look around. How many this morning? Bodies lying rigid on the narrow slats. It was the first job of the day. They would lift the dead men outside. A grave could not be dug now in the frozen land, and so they carried them to a giant pit, their ID disks first removed.

Back in the autumn, a horse and cart had come, laden with packages of hessian-coloured material, pressed flat together and wrapped in string. They contained clothes – clothes that were supposed to last the winter and protect against the Siberian cold.

A pair of woollen trousers, a jacket of the same flock material, a shirt like sacking, rough and coarse and prickly on the skin, and a woollen hat. The guards had handed them out. There was no question of sizes, they were all the same size. Tall men had trousers that hung above their ankles, shorter men turned up the legs. There were no fat men — all were starved and angular. For some the trousers held around the hip bones, while for others, they would constantly slide down their backsides, until they could find a piece of string or a belt to hold them up. Shoes were of the same woollen material, wrapped around a piece of rubber cut from an old car tyre.

If a man had a chance to lay his hands on a second jacket or shirt or hat or pair of trousers, then he would grab it without hesitation, whatever the condition. Invariably, then, the bodies that they carried to the pit would be naked, the clothes torn from them. Anything to hold off the creeping cold.

******

30 November 1940
"Come over here. Look at this!"

The shout came from the direction of the latrine.

A thin film of ice had formed over the putrid mix of urine and faeces —the ice punctuated by small mounds of frozen excrement that men were still, somehow, able to produce despite their tiny intake. From the murky stinking depths protruded an arm. The entire arm was caked in filth, the torn shirt sleeve frozen rigid. The fingers of the hand were splayed out as if trying to grasp hold of something or to call out.

The lek-pom was called, though clearly it was far too late for medical treatment. The guard called the commandant.

"Prisoner 523," he said, consulting a note book. "Hershel Mendelevich. He was missing from roll-call this morning."

"I can get him out, sir," said Wolf, thinking only that he might earn another slice of bread.

The commandant looked at him.

"All right son, you get him out, if that's what you want to do. I will give the order for the usual burial when he is out."

Tomcyzk had now joined the group.

"You'll never get him out, Wolf. It is no way to die, but you'll end up in there yourself if you try. It's not worth the effort. I don't want to lose a good worker."

Wolf saw that he was right. Even for another piece of bread, it would have been an impossible task. He stood for some moments beside the latrine muttering the kaddish until a Pole pushed him away.

"For Christ's sake – I need a shit, not some Jew muttering over my bare arse."

As he walked away, Baboushka, the commandant's mother, passed. She was heavily wrapped in scarves and snow-shoes and the men around stopped and stared. She seemed to recognize them from the shape of their heads and the set of their eyes.

"How are you today, handsome?" she called to Wolf with a wink.

******

3 December 1940

"The commandant needs his firewood pile replenishing," said Tomczyk. "I'd like you to go over and do it, Wolf."

Wolf walked through the snow to Morozov's cabin, an area that was normally out of bounds to the prisoners. He could see Baboushka through the glass-less window. Her grey hair hung lank beneath a black headscarf. An orange smock, embroidered in fraying purple, peered above her battered coat, frost forming on its outer edges. Her face carried the contours of the swamps and hillocks of the ancient forest they were cutting through, but, when she saw him coming with an axe, her mouth widened into a gap-toothed smile that lit up the frozen taiga.

She pointed to the woodpile, then nodded towards the potatoes she was peeling. She peeled them roughly and threw the thick skins into the snow. Wolf fell on them, filling his mouth and collecting them in his pockets. But Baboushka was not finished. She heated oil over the fire and began to make pancakes. She picked one from the pan with her left hand and moved to slip it out to him, but at that moment her son appeared. Quickly she held it up.

"Dinner is nearly ready, Dmitri," she said. "What have you to go on these pancakes? Syrup, blueberries, honey?"

The commandant cursed her. No one in the camp, prisoner or guard, had seen any of these things for months and she knew it.

For long minutes, he watched, ready to punish the slightest lapse, as Wolf split and piled the wood. He worked ceaselessly, terrified that the potato peelings would fall from his pockets, until the commandant seemed to become bored and left. Without hesitation, Baboushka passed Wolf a pancake. She made some more and, with a furtive glance either side of the window, tossed him another.

Finally, for that day, his hunger was tamed.

22 THE KNIFE MAN

23 December 1940

WOLF lay back on his bunk, exhausted. He scratched at his skin. Lice again. He had hoped that the wash he had had a week before in the bathhouse that had finally been built would have got rid of them for longer, that they would not survive the cold. The bath was a ramshackle affair that leaked from every joint and the water was tepid, but he had, at least, been given a piece of soap, albeit the size of a sugar lump. He had had lice back at home in Bledow one summer. His mother had made him and his brother and sisters dip their hair in a tub of strong-smelling foamy water every night for a week. He took off his shirt and inspected it. Lice were crawling through the seams and over the grimy remnants of his collar.

He pulled the grey stone from the Vistula river from his pocket and laying the side of the shirt flat against the wooden slat of his bunk, he aimed the stone at them one by one. With each successful blow, he flicked the dead louse onto the dirt floor. Sharp staccato blow followed sharp staccato blow.

"For Christ's sake! I'm trying to sleep," came a cry from across the hut.

Wolf went outside.

From time to time new people would come into the camp. People said that the commandant was under constant pressure to get up to full strength, to get more work done, to replace the dead. On this day he noticed, as he collected his kipiatok outside the cook-house, a new man in there. Long curls hung over his neck and, though lean, he looked healthier than the rest of them.

From his mouth came a constant volley of invective that even the urki could not match. It was not just his language. With his kitchen knife, he seemed to be practising a circus act. He was hurling the knife — a knife which, between throws, he sharpened — at a target on one of the support posts ... and hitting the target. Suddenly, he spun. An urki was trying to sidle up the far side of the cook-house, his arm leaning over to grab more bread. The knife flew. It landed on the bench close to the urki's hand.

"Blyyyat," he screamed, and ran back.

"Don't you ever dare try to steal from the kitchen again!" the knife man shouted after him. Then he turned to Wolf.

"What are you looking at, you stupid fucking puppy?"

"Just watching," said Wolf.

"Want to watch some more, get a better view?"

"Stand there," he said, without waiting for an answer. He positioned Wolf beside a post. "Stand still. Don't move, just look me in the eyes."

Wolf did not have time to think or object. A crowd of men had gathered round. They stood on either side of him, at a respectful distance, but no one stood behind him.

"Don't worry if you hit him," came a cry from the back. "No one will miss another Jew."

Wolf was not frightened. There was not time to contemplate death at the hands of an inaccurately thrown knife – he was too cold and hungry and numb to think about it. Had he done so, he might anyway have reasoned that, if this was to be the end, it was a better way to go than to waste away from sickness, cold and hunger.

The man pulled three knives from a bench inside the cook-house and began to sharpen them.

"Are you ready, Pup?" he said. "What is your name?"

"Wolf," said Wolf weakly.

"Well, Wolf, do you think you're going to die? Are you chicken?"

His voice transformed into a loud squawk and then a raucous clucking. He flapped his arms and bent his neck and his clucks took on a note of surprise. He held his hand to his bottom and made as if to lay an egg, then slapped his thighs, clucking again. Some men clapped. He stood upright and turned to his audience.

"What do you think? Is he going to die?"

The commandant had joined the crowd now. He was about to say something, but the man shushed him. Fear finally gripped Wolf, paralysing him.

The first knife slammed into the post at chest level. The sound of it left Wolf with little doubt that, had it sliced into him rather than the wood, then it would have been the end. He did not have time to consider it further — the second knife entered the wood millimetres from his left eye.

Now the man passed Wolf a section of log, the size of a thick wooden plate.

"Hold that in front of your balls," he said.

Wolf's focus, that before had been on his life, now descended to his private parts.

"No children," cackled the man, "if you move."

The knife whistled through the air. The force of it slammed the plate against him. The topmost tip of the blade peered straight through the plate. Wolf was too dazed to speak. He handed the plate back.

The man, normal, civilized now, held out his hand.

"Shwili," he said. "I am Shwili the Armenian. I will look out for you Wolf."

******

Wolf was still shaking when Tomczyk came up to him.

"Are you OK, Wolf? You were very brave. I couldn't have stood there."

"It all happened so fast, I don't think I knew what was happening. The guy's mad."

"Yes, mad but brilliant."

They moved to the side and sat down, each clutching a mug of kipiatok.

"Tell me something," said Wolf. "You are different to a lot of the other Poles. You don't bad-mouth us Jews, you treat us the same as everyone else."

"I suppose it is the way I was brought up," said Tomczyk. "My father was a jolly man, very kind. He worked on the PKP, the railways. He always said, 'Jewish people have done a lot for Poland. They have never done me any harm.' My mother was a schoolteacher and some of her pupils were Jewish. 'Some of them are naughty, some of them are well-behaved, some are clever, some are not so clever,' she said. 'Same as everyone else.'"

"I think I'd have been one of the naughty ones," said Wolf. "I don't know about clever. I wasn't at school long enough to know. We had very little money. I went to Warsaw to work."

"I think you'd have been one of the clever ones," said Tomcyzk. "I wasn't clever myself, but my mother spent hours with me and I passed the exam into the gymnasium. I joined the cadets there and really enjoyed it. That's why I joined the Air Force."

"Ah, that explains it," said Wolf. "So what rank are you?"

"Flight-Lieutenant, if I ever get back in. But right now I'm a prisoner just like you."

"Lieutenant Tomczyk. That sounds good. But can I call you Szymon?"

"Of course."

"At least you weren't shot down."

"No, nothing like that. We were stationed in Dubno, way to the East, south of Lutsk. It was the Russians who took us. One minute the squadron-leader was giving us directions on which way to go, then he disappeared in his car and we were all taken prisoner — twenty-four of us."

"And how come you know how to chop down trees?"
"Oh, we did it first in the cadets, just the theory of it; then at the beginning of this year we did it for real, just a few trees near Dubno — a kind of squadron team-building and firewood-collecting exercise. I never thought …"

23 SHWILI THE ARMENIAN

25 December 1940

"SHNORHAVOR Amanor yev Surb Tznund. Happy Christmas, Wolfie!"

Wolf and Szymon looked across blankly. It was Shwili.

"Christmas?"

"Yes, so Baboushka told me. Today is Christmas day, whatever day that is. Christmas in a hellhole."

"Ah, so do you have some dumplings and carp for us?" said Szymon.

"You'd be fucking lucky. Who are you anyway?"

"I am Szymon Tomzyk." He held out a torn and blistered hand.

"He is a friend, Shwili, and my brigade leader."

"Brigade leader, brigade leader ..." said Shwili, but then his voice changed and it became quite normal, as if the crazed, cursing chicken-clucking wild man, who bestrode the kitchen and anyone who dared enter it, was just an act. Was there a difference, anyway, wondered Wolf, between an act and reality in this place? If someone could maintain an act, did that not then become reality?

"I like you, Wolf puppy. I can see you have something, some intelligence. Maybe not intelligence of great learning – I don't suppose you spent many years at school?"

"No," said Wolf. "Szymon and I were talking about this the other day. I went away to work."

"That makes sense," said Shwili. "But intelligence up here."

He tapped his forehead.

"I was taught both."

"How do you mean?" asked Wolf.

Shwili patted a log that lay beside the kitchen fire and the three of them sat down.

"I will tell you. My father was a scholar and a teacher in Armenia. It is a beautiful country a long way South of here, but Stalin has ruined it. I grew up under strict moral rules and strict learning. I studied with my father and twin sister as well as attending school. I loved the mountains and in my spare time I would roam the hills and hunt.

"My father's brother, Uncle Zikan, was a bachelor and a mountain-man — a legend in our district. He was self-sufficient and a great hunter. We thought alike and there was a great rapport between us. Zikan made sure that I learnt how to defend myself in all circumstances. He taught me to throw a knife as well as he did — you have seen how well! And he taught me to fight using skill rather than physical strength. During one summer holiday, when I was fourteen years old, Zikan left me alone on a remote mountain. He said he would be back, giving me the impression that it would be the next day.

'You've got the knife and you know how to use it, so you'll not go hungry,' he said.

"The next day came but Zikan didn't. For seven days and nights I was alone with the elements. Four times I attempted to find my way back to my uncle's cabin and four times I eventually abandoned the idea. I won't go into details about the seven days – it would take too long. The mountain goat I killed and ate, the crevice in the rocks I found for shelter, the water drip I discovered accidentally and the poisonous snake that ran off with my knife in it. It took me a whole day to track him, following the blood stains."

Shwili stopped to make tea. He poured two mugs and put a large piece of sugar in each. This was a treat, a luxury, that was so far beyond the norm for Wolf that he wondered if he was dreaming, until the lice began to itch and he looked down at the rags that counted for his clothes.

"I don't know why I am telling you all this," said Shwili. "I am a very impatient man."

"Please go on," said Wolf. "It is all we have – hearing the stories of others takes me away from all this ..."

He swept his arm around the encampment and the forest.

"How did you survive?"

"I started a fire near the entrance of the crevice and kept it going day and night. I was desperately lonely and very worried that something must have happened to Uncle Zikan. But at the same time, I sensed that he was safe and indestructible.

"For the first three days, I felt sorry for myself, but then I adjusted to the environment and found a sort of harmony with my surroundings. The mountains, the gorges, the gigantic trees and the animals — suddenly I felt part of them. I felt a sense of belonging, as if I'd been there before. Previously, I had loved the wonders of nature, but never felt part of it. Can you understand what I mean, puppy?"

Wolf thought of the fields outside Bledow. There were no bears or wolves there of course, but, hiding behind a hedgerow, running through the orchards or lying in the wheat fields, he had never questioned the movement of the seasons or the workings of nature. The thrushes would be there when the red berries came; the rats would scamper across the floor of Hela's father's barn. He accepted life as it came and went.

"I think I can, Shwili. Can I call you Shwili?"

"That's my name, but only when we're alone. Otherwise, you can call me what the rest of them call me – 'fuckin' cook schmuck' or whatever.

"Eventually I started talking to myself and to everything around me. I apologised to the hare for killing it and to the wild flower for treading on it. On the seventh day, at about sunset, Uncle Zikan appeared right out of the scrub, as if he'd just come out of a shop onto the street. He pretended to be surprised to see me there. I was overjoyed. He picked me up like a child, hugging and kissing me.

'You have passed the test of survival with honours,' he said. 'I am very proud of you. You will survive anything that life has in store for you. Remember, always adapt to the circumstances, irrespective of where you are. Use your hands, your brain, and listen to the inner voice of instinct. It's there if you know how to listen. During this last week, I was always around, watching you from a distance. Now, the next important lesson to prepare you for is how to enjoy the God-given physical pleasures between a man and a woman.'"

Shwili chuckled.

"'Tonight,' my uncle said, 'you will sleep in the cabin alone, but tomorrow you will sleep with a teacher.'

"The following evening while I was reading, my uncle returned accompanied by a gorgeous, smiling woman. My uncle left us, giving me a knowing smile, and said he would be back in three days."

Beneath the pallor of his skin and his stubble, Wolf felt himself blush. He had no experience with women or girls and yet the thought of them, the memory of the orchard in Lutsk, awakened in him from time to time, sometimes unexpectedly. He pictured Shwili with a naked woman in this mountain hideout.

"You were lucky," he muttered.

"I was," said Shwili. "I learnt something very precious in the mountains and in that cabin. Everybody noticed a change in me when I came back from my mountain schooling. When I got back, I went straight to my father and paid my respects. He was with his best friend Davidu the Yevrei. They studied together, discussed things and loved each other's company. Davidu's son was in the same class as myself at school and we were good friends. Both of us were ostracised for not belonging to Komsomol.

"We both finished high school with very good grades. I was hoping to be an architect and my friend, who was crazy about music and composing, thought of nothing else; but first we both had to enlist in the Air Force officers' academy. After nine months' training, we came home on leave to find a funereal atmosphere. My beautiful twin sister had been arrested.

"Apparently an NKVD officer had been pestering her. He would wait for her outside the school where she taught and escort her home. He would brag about being well-connected through his father in Moscow, and that she might consider herself privileged that he cared for her. Ilya, my sister, detested him and eventually she told him to stop pestering her. She told him that even if he was Stalin himself, she would not have him. At 2.30 am the following morning, Ilya was dragged away. No one in the family was allowed to see her; they said she was a socially dangerous element.

"Wearing my uniform, I ran to the NKVD headquarters only to be told, 'Sorry, comrade, we have our instructions.' I went crazy. I telephoned the C.O. at my camp asking for help, but he advised me not to intimidate the NKVD. 'You are one of our best cadets, with a brilliant future, so don't spoil it.'

"I could not leave the NKVD office without demanding to see the man who denounced Ilya. I was told he had gone back to Moscow. In my rage, I picked up a chair and smashed it on the officer's desk. He pressed a buzzer and two armed guards arrived and locked me up in a cell. During the night, I was taken for interrogation.

'Confess, you are a saboteur. We know all about you and your Uncle Zikan, a parasite and an enemy of the Soviet.'

"I saw red, I could not control myself. The stupidity, the fabricated insinuations. Diving towards the interrogator, I seized him by the throat and held on until he stopped struggling. I walked out nonchalantly. At the gate I smiled at the guard and told him I had to report back to my regiment. I ran home, grabbed my knife and some clothing and hastily made my way up to the mountains.

"Uncle Zikan was calm and collected when I told him what had happened and did not blame me for what I had done. He also loved Ilya dearly. Her arrest broke his spirit but there was nothing he could do. He too had enquired at the NKVD and was answered with threats and insults.

'You can't stay here,' he said. 'They'll be here soon. Go back to your crevice and hide.'

"A week later my uncle climbed up with the news that my mother and father had been arrested. 'They're looking for us. A whole platoon is guarding the cabin, we can't return there.'

"For days we watched them hunting us, realising that our freedom was short-lived. Uncle Zikan was caught, but managed to kill two of them. The third one emptied a whole magazine of bullets into him. I came up from behind and plunged my knife into the NKVD soldier. For four weeks, the mountains swarmed with troops. On three occasions, I was cornered but escaped. I think I killed two more and wounded many others.

"Eventually, I was completely exhausted and famished. My knife was gone, left in the chest of one of the bastards. I was caught and chained hand and foot. I could never understand why they didn't shoot me. I had a feeling that the NKVD officer in charge admired my resourcefulness and courage. At the following interrogation, I stood guarded and chained while I related my story. My gut feeling, from his behaviour and his remarks, was that he knew I was telling the truth. So you see, Wolfie puppy, here I am."

Wolf looked at Shwili with different eyes.

"You said that your father's best friend was Davidu the Yevrei."

"Yes," said Shwili. "Why?"

"Because I am Jewish too."

"No, puppy, you're Polish."

"I'm Polish by birth, but Jewish too."

"Well, I'll be damned. I see what you mean. Puppy the Yevrei. Hah! I thought you were different to some of these yobs and thugs."

24 THE SANATORIUM

13 January 1941

BLACK BOILS covered many of the prisoner's legs and ankles swelled. Gums turned white and teeth became loose and fell out. Sores oozed pus and blood, and liquid faeces ran down men's thighs. Scurvy. Tsinga is what the Russians called it – a lack of vitamins.

Viscerally, Wolf knew that things were not right in his own body and when he saw men grab handfuls of spruce needles and soak and boil them in water, he did not hesitate to do the same. The taste was bitter and sharp. Sometimes he would simply eat the needles raw, stripping the twig and chewing them, but still men were falling sick everywhere.

It was on leaving the bath house late in the afternoon that he found he could see only the dim shape of the hut. He had to hold on to feel his way. He could hear the voices of men and see vague figures, nothing more.

"Please! Help me," he called, feeling weak and exposed.

He was relieved to hear Andrei's voice.

"What's wrong, Wolf?"

"I don't know – I can't see."

Andrei took Wolf's arm and led him to the sick bay. The lek-pom took one look at him.

"Oh, it's just chicken blindness. Nothing to worry about. Everybody gets it. If we were in any kind of civilized place, I'd say take cod liver oil and eat plenty of vegetables and fruit. But there's none of that here. It'll probably go away."

But it didn't go away. Though he could see more in the morning, he stumbled through the day in an unfocussed world, Andrei doing much of Wolf's work. By the time they marched back to the camp in the evening, even dim shapes had gone and Andrei had to guide him back.

"Here, Wolf, take your soup." He held out his hand and felt for the mug. He drew it to his lips.

"Thank you, Andrei."

Tomczyk came and sat down beside him.

"What are we going to do with you, Wolf? You can't see enough to do your work. Andrei is not going to be able to work that hard every day and if you don't meet your quota, the engineer is going to start marking down your bread ration again."

"What can we do Szymon?" Wolf had never felt so helpless in his life. In his body he felt, if not fit, then fitter than most of the other men around him. But he could not see.

He had an idea.

"Cod liver oil — that's what the lek-pom said. I don't suppose there will be any of that in the cook house, but Shwili may have some sort of oil."

"Come on then," said Tomczyk , pulling him upright, and guided Wolf towards the cookhouse.

Shwili did not recognize them at first.

"Get out of my kitchen!" he roared. "What's the matter with you, mate. Got a case of the chicken blindness?"

He put his hands over his eyes and started squawking, stumbling around like a blind chicken this time.

"Blind chicken, chicken blind, can't see its arse behind," he crowed. "If you can bring me a woman, or mahorka, you can stay. Otherwise, get out of here. Go, get out!"

"It is I, Wolf the Yevrei, Shwili, and Szymon. I can't see. The lek-pom said I need cod liver oil."

Shwili stopped his antics suddenly and quietened.

"Wolf the puppy," he said. "I did not recognize you. Let me look. "

He held up his hand in front of Wolf's face.

"How many fingers?"

Wolf peered.

"Five."

"And now?" He folded his thumb behind his palm.

"Three?"

"Wait here, Wolfie. I will find something for you."

Wolf could hear clanking and rustling in the kitchen, and something being poured.

"Drink this."

He handed Wolf a wooden bowl. Wolf sniffed. It was an oily liquid, and stank of fish. He sipped at it.

"Urgh. That's disgusting." It was rank and bitter.

"Drink it all Wolfie. One gulp. It's good for you."

"What is it?"

"Fish piss," chuckled Shwili, walking away. "Come back tomorrow evening for another dose of Shwili's lovely medicine. I need to find something in the forest. It'll fix you, believe me."

******

3 January 1941

Shwili was right. Whatever the liquid was, and whatever the herb was that he found in the forest, Wolf's eyesight returned after a couple of days, but now he had a new problem. A big scar had opened on his left shin. It wept non-stop and would not heal and both legs ached.

Desperate for a pee, he went outside, but all that would come out was a teaspoonful of urine. It happened again and again and would not let him sleep. It weakened him, he could feel the strength, such as there was, draining from him.

Desperate to fulfil his tree-felling quota and not let Andrei down, he carried on until, late in the day, he crumpled to the ground. His legs refused to obey his brain and get up.

"I don't know that I can go on, Szymon," he said. "I just don't think I have the strength."

Tomczyk looked at him.

"You can, Wolf. Let's get you back and you can go and see the lek-pom."

Andrei hauled him upright, and put an arm around his shoulders, supporting him, but he collapsed again.

"Get up," shouted the guard. "Get up or I shoot."

Wolf knew that the choice, if he went no further, was being shot, or isolation with no food for not working, and death either way. He was not frightened of death. In this cold dirty world that they inhabited — starved, exhausted, and now sick — it did not seem like something to be frightened of. Welcomed rather.

"Go on then, shoot me," he said. "What are you waiting for?"

But at the same time, Father Lenkovski's words came back to him: 'Fight, hold on, trust, Wolf', and he raised his hand weakly.

The guard lowered his rifle. Tomczyk and Andrei took an arm each across their own exhausted shoulders to get him back. It was on his backside that Wolf shuffled and dragged himself along the line of men waiting to see the lek-pom.

******

February 1941

Wolf was not conscious when he was carried into the grubby tent that served as a hospital ward at the back of the lek-pom's surgery. He did not hear the pleadings of Tomczyk to get him away to a proper hospital. He did not know that he was taken back on the railway line that they themselves had built nearly to the Urals. He did not know that they had cut the clothes from him before he entered the sanatorium and incinerated them. He did not know that a woman had hosed him down and scrubbed him before he was lain on a metal bed.

When he woke, a man came to see him. He wore a white coat and had a gold-framed pince-nez. He looked like a doctor from a children's picture book. He put a stethoscope to his chest and asked him to breathe in and out and to cough. He felt around his penis and his testicles, then spoke to a nurse. She gave Wolf pills to swallow and applied ointment to his legs. He was given two meals a day – real meals. The soup had meat and vegetables in it and there was more bread.

Days passed slowly — it was not a place designed for things to happen other than slowly. Gradually his sores began to heal and his strength to return. He felt that he must be in some sort of dreamland.

He tested his legs and arms and found himself wondering about escape. But through the barred window, all he could see for miles and miles was a flat frozen landscape. Scrub trees no more than a metre high struggled out of the ground. Nearby was a concrete building that appeared to be linked to the sanatorium by a road. Otherwise there was nothing. The sanatorium, so far as he could tell, was made up of a corridor with wards for six people on either side, and at one end a room for the doctors and guards.

An orderly began to take him out in the afternoons. His name was Igor. Igor was not a tall man, but rotund. Though the food in the sanatorium cannot have been plentiful, even for the staff, it had not diminished him. His head was shaven and his face carried a perpetual grin. When he laughed, great swathes of his body shook, even after the laughter itself had subsided. It was not hard for Wolf to consider him his friend.

They walked round the building and every day, well wrapped, a little further into the tundra. Communication was slow because, though Wolf had picked up some rudimentary Russian at the camp, Igor spoke with a different accent and had no Polish. But what they lacked in meaning they made up for in good humour and gradually, with a combination of speech and sign language and scribbled drawings, they made each other understood.

"We get some bad people in here," said Igor. "Crooks, people who would not give two pence for your life, but you – I like you Wolf."

Wolf nodded.

Igor pulled a paper bag from his pocket. From a different pocket he pulled off a strip from a sheet of newspaper. On the newspaper, Wolf could see a photograph of the man he knew to be the leader of Russia – there were pictures of him everywhere.

"You are tearing Stalin's head," he pointed.

But Igor shrugged his shoulders.

"He's a bastard; he deserves to burn."

He drew some tobacco from the bag and rolled it into the newspaper, then lit it. He drew on it deeply and, with a satisfied sigh, handed it to Wolf.

"Mahorka," he said.

"What is that?"

"It's tobacco. People in the countryside grow it and mix in some wild herbs. It's very good."

Wolf had seen a few of the guards at the camp smoking something and had caught the acrid smell. He inhaled and immediately coughed. It tasted bitter and burnt the back of his throat. The smoke swirled in the air around them. He felt a little light-headed. He drew again and coughed again. Igor laughed.

"You will get used to it," he said.

"How do you get it?"

"There are ways and means," said Igor. "We have things in this sanatorium that people want. They have the mahorka that I want. It is the way the world goes round."

Every day, Wolf looked forward to his afternoon walk with Igor. The mahorka warmed him and he liked to watch the smoke curl in the cold air. Sometimes Igor would inhale deeply, filling his lungs with smoke, then let it out in little rings. When he was done he would slap his thighs.

"Ha ha, Wolf, I am the champion smoke-ring blower of the tundra."

One day a fufaika and valenki, a hessian shirt and hat, were laid on Wolf's bed. He knew what this meant and he knew that it would come but still the order for him to leave the sanatorium came suddenly and without warning. He looked around for Igor to bid him goodbye as a guard hurried him on.

Igor came rushing out. He embraced him in a huge bear hug, then held out his hand to shake Wolf's. Wolf felt something being transferred into his palm. Clasping Igor's hand between his own, he closed his palm around the small package.

Wolf waved, moving his right hand swiftly into his newly issued jacket pocket. He did not dare look at the package until he was well away from the sanatorium and on the bus that took him on the first part of his journey back. Surreptitiously, he held it up to his eyes, then to his nose. As he suspected, it was a block of mahorka. Enough to make perhaps twenty cigarettes. Gold dust.

25 SUGAR LUMPS

2 March 1941

BACK AT home in Bledow, on a corner shelf in the kitchen that was built into the wall, Wolf's mother would put flowers in a vase, whatever wild flowers or crops were growing in the fields around them at the time.

Beside it, in late 1938, she had stood a postcard. The photograph was in black and white and a corner was creased and slightly torn. The postcard was of a scene around vineyards in Palestine. It came from Wolf's Aunt Mocheved, who had left Poland with her husband Yitzhak and their children when things started to become bad.

The photograph showed men working on the vines, their tops off, belts loose around their waists. It represented some far-off land that seemed, to Wolf, an unattainable dream. But it was this photograph that suddenly came to his mind as he arrived back from the sanatorium to the outskirts of the camp. Not the smiles of the men working on the vines or the dream, but the black and white and the crease. The grey landscape. A destroyed landscape, a destroyed people.

He saw with new eyes the gaunt faces of the men, their sunken eyes, their teeth sticking like tent pegs in bare gums, the rags that they called clothes, the squalor of the place, the empty rusting tins and the smell that lingered of sweat and torpor and malignant creeping death.

He vowed to himself again, as he walked in with the guard, that he would do whatever it took to escape this place. He would use whatever guile was in him to survive. He would use his wits, other people, anything, to get to Palestine or, if not Palestine, then somewhere where people respected each other. Recovered from the sickness, his stomach at least half-full and a new energy within him, he did not doubt that he could do this.

It did not take long for his resolve to be tested.

"Shwili," he called out, as he passed the cook house on the way to the camp office.

"Quiet," said the guard.

"He's gone," said a voice from inside.

The office clerk muttered something to the guard and he was marched towards a different hut. Tomczyk was nowhere in sight. Wojciech was the name of his new brigade leader and he knew immediately that he was in trouble.

"Why are you bringing me this lazy Jew?" Wojciech moaned to the guard.

"Orders."

"Orders maybe. I'll make sure he obeys orders."

He pointed to another man.

"Krogulski, this is your new partner. Have fun," he sneered.

Krogulski was of medium height, with broad shoulders and an olive complexion. Though his head was completely shaved, his hair was clearly black. His deep-set, black-brown wizened eyes confirmed the impression in Wolf that the man was a gypsy. He could feel the jealous eyes of both Krogulski and the rest of the brigade on his new clothes, as yet unsoiled. These would be prize possessions and he knew he must stay on guard.

They marched with the rest of the brigade to the area of the forest they would work on that day. Krogulski was sullen and merely grunted when Wolf tried to chat.

"How come a Jew speaks such good Polish and works so hard?" asked Krogulski eventually when they broke at midday for a few minutes.

"I don't know," said Wolf. "How come a gypsy masquerades as a Pole?"

Krogulski's face reddened. He was livid. Sweat broke on his forehead.

"I'll kill you like a rat, you Jew dog," he said, raising his axe.

Wolf stood his ground, tensed, ready to strike back. Krogulski froze, suddenly hesitant.

"If you want a fight, you can have it," said Wolf. "This is a Jew you cannot intimidate."

"I'll be buggered!" said Krogulski, a grin breaking out across his face. "Jew dog, you're all right."

He held out his hand ready to shake Wolf's. Wolf was wary, prepared for a trick, but Krogulski persisted.

"Come on, shake my hand. You're a Jew, I'm a gypsy – we'll work together."

The arrangement made sense. To native Poles and, Wolf had observed, to Ukrainians, gypsies were on the same rung of the ladder as Jews, or one only marginally higher. They, too, were treated like dirt. In the days that followed Krogulski told Wolf of the taunts he had had to endure as a boy.

'Hey Krogu, is it true your mother was raped by a filthy gypsy?' That was the most common.

Wolf wondered how some people could be so blind to others of different birth or faith, why they should be of any less value than themselves, where such prejudice came from and why it existed. But it did exist and it existed, especially, in Wojciech. The man was mean to the core. He was the leader of the brigade; he was supposed to carry all of the men with him to reach their appointed quotas. But when it came to the allocation of soup, for which the brigade leaders were now responsible, he did not stir the pot from the bottom to ensure that a piece of meat – albeit the meat of some worn-out horse that had hauled its last rail and finally collapsed – was included in Wolf and Krogulski's portion. They received only the top, the liquid, with just the occasional piece of vegetable floating in it.

******

It was not enough.

Wolf could feel the strength and energy begin to drain from him again. He knew he had to do something different. One day, on marching back from a different area of the forest, he saw that a new shed had been built to one side of the camp. Sacks were being unloaded into it from a wagon.

"That must be food of some sort," he said. "How can we get to it?"

Krogulski looked at him.

"You mean it, don't you?"

Wolf nodded.

They studied the position of the shed. It was outside the perimeter fence, but, as the crow flew, not far from the back of their own hut. Between the back of the hut and the fence was just scrub. No one ever went there, except, perhaps, to urinate.

After eating their evening bread and soup, the two men slipped round there. They moved along the fence, inspecting it. It was around three metres high — too tall to scale without drawing attention; anyone attempting it would be visible to a guard who looked that way. In one section, however, the planks of the fence bridged two small mounds between the supporting posts. There was already a small space beneath them.

"Here," said Wolf.

Over the next evenings, exhausted though they were, they developed a system, taking turns to increase the size of the gap. Two coughs were a warning signal and one the all-clear. With the hand axe and shovel that they used to clear the forest, bit by bit they enlarged the gap. The ground was too hard to dig, but they could break it up and slice off another layer. At the end of each evening's work, they camouflaged the gap on both sides with the dead shrub wood that was scattered around the camp. They prayed that the guard on the other side would not be studying this section of the fence too closely.

"Done," said Wolf after a week of digging. "I think we can go under tomorrow evening."

He felt the excitement throughout the next day. It was a risk, he knew, but he was willing to take it.

If I get outside the camp, he thought, I will be free. That thought did not linger long. He might be free, but he would be in the middle of a huge forest miles from anywhere. There was nowhere to go except down the railway line, and that would lead only to another camp and more guards. The goal, the purpose of the break-out, was food — survival.

"Do you want to go first?" he asked Krogulski. "I will look out on this side."

His partner hesitated, weighing up the options.

"No, you go," he said.

Wolf listened for a minute in the darkness, then slithered through the gap on his stomach, peering tentatively through the scrub as his top half edged through on the other side. There was no sound. He could not see anyone, not even the tell-tale glow of a cigarette.

Resting his folded arms on the ground, he pulled the rest of himself through. He stopped again. As far as any guard was concerned, this was an escape. At best he would be locked into the isolation cell, his feet bare on a floor of cold water or ice for days — very few came out of there alive. At worst, or perhaps in fact at best, he would be shot on the spot.

Still there was no sound or movement. He stood up and, crouching, ran the few metres to the shelter of the hut. He felt his way round until he came to the door. His hands touched something metallic. It was a latch. He tested it, expecting it to be padlocked. To his surprise, it lifted. As he pulled the door towards him, there was a loud creak. He froze, listening. Still nothing moved. He crept inside. The floor was boarded and the hut smelt musty and dry; rough hessian and tar lingered in the air. He felt his way around. There was a pile of big sacks. He tried to lift one; it was perhaps twenty-five kilos – a dead weight that flopped in his arms. Flour he guessed. He could lift it, but it was too big to get back into the camp. He moved on around. He came to a pile of smaller sacks that rustled. Something lighter and more formed was inside. He worked his finger in. Sugar lumps! Perfect.

He took two bags, then inched the door, centimetre by centimetre, closed again.

"Krogulski, I'm back," he whispered as he reached the outside of the hole.

There were two coughs. Wolf heard a man's voice and then a stream of urine against the inside of the fence, several metres down. He held his breath, his heart pumping so loud he thought that the man peeing must hear it. Then the single cough came, very quietly.

He passed the first bag through, pulling the other behind him.

"It's sugar lumps," he said, tearing at the string that closed the bag. They were large lumps. He took one and stuffed it into his mouth, then gave some to Krogulski and briefed him on the shed.

While his partner was outside, Wolf pondered on what he could do with the sugar. He could not take it into the hut. He could not leave it where rain or snow might melt it. He did not want to leave it all in the two bags. For one thing, if it was found, that would mean he would lose it all at once. For another, it would be too obvious that it had come from the warehouse rather than sneaked out of the kitchen.

"Don't tell me what you are going to do with yours," he said as Krogulski came back through the gap with his own supply, "And I won't tell you what I am going to do with mine."

First, temporarily, he hid his two bags back under the scrub. Next, he went to the kitchen tent. Those who worked there would throw out the hessian sacks that carried the flour that made the heavy black bread when they were empty. These were prized possessions. A neck hole could be cut in the bottom and arm holes at the sides to make an additional vest.

Wolf was lucky. A large sack lay discarded on the ground and he could not waste it, but, for the sugar, he needed something different. He looked around the back of the tent - though caked in mud, some smaller sacks lay half-buried in mud.

Wolf took these and went back to the bags of sugar lumps. With a blunt knife that he had found previously near the kitchen, he cut the hessian into smaller sections. He transferred into each ten sugar lumps, then tied the little pouches with the twine that had been left in the top of the sacks.

By now, most men were on their bunks or asleep. Wolf moved around the camp like a squirrel preparing for winter, placing the little bags under stones, beneath shrubs, in the crook of a tree's low branches – any place that he knew he could get to easily and where they would not be easily found.

Finally, he took another lump of sugar from the first bag and put it in his mouth. The sugar was coarse and a dirty brown in colour, but to Wolf it was a taste of a sweet life that he was determined to reach. The few remaining unbagged lumps he stuffed into his pockets. He was relieved to find in there too, secure from predators, the block of mahorka that Igor had given him at the sanatorium and the grey stone that he had picked up at the Vistula river.

******

An uneasy truce developed in the brigade. Wojciech and others were, perhaps, just waiting for Wolf and Krogulski to fade and die, as others had before them. But they didn't, and Wojciech didn't know why. Despite the weak soup that they were given and the low bread ration, they were still working hard and achieving their quota.

"How come you are staying so strong?" Wojciech growled in frustration one evening.

"Oh, it's from the wonderful food ration you give us every day, Wojciech."

Krogulski's face was red with anger, but Wolf held his arm.

"Wait," he said.

"We'll see about what makes you strong," growled Wojciech and walked away.

******

14 April 1941

"These trees here," said Wojciech when they reached their appointed work area in the forest, "are yours. You two," he pointed to two burly urkis that Wolf recognised as men who had grunted in agreement with Wojciech the night before, "do those."

Wolf looked across. The two sets of trees were quite close.

"We will shout when they are coming down," he said.

"We too," said one from the other team.

Wolf and Krogulski began to hack off the branches of the first of their trees, in preparation for felling it.

Instinctively, Wolf looked up. A spruce was on the point of falling.

"Jump," he shouted to Krogulski and they leapt to the cover of their own tree just as the spruce came crashing down.

"What's going on?" shouted Wolf. "That was too close."

"Sorry, are you all right?" The other men carried on working.

Wolf, like all of them by now, knew how to fell a tree, how to make it fall to a particular line by studying the way it leant. Provided there was no obstruction, a tree would be felled into its leaning line. It took practice and experience and skilful cutting and wedging to fell a tree accurately against its leaning line.

He looked across at the next tree the other team was working on. It was leaning away from himself and Krogulski and he carried on working. This time it was Krogulski who saw it. There was no warning shout. The brushing of the top branches against the canopy like the onset of a sudden shower, the first crash of breaking branches, and then the roaring, lengthening tide of wood extending out from the trunk and smashing towards them.

Wolf dived again, the tree slamming into the ground all about him, a smaller branch whipping him backwards to the earth. Blood trickled from a wound on his forehead. His chest was bruised. He tested all his limbs.

"Krogulski!" he called. "Are you OK?"

There was no reply. A large branch pinned Krogulski to the ground. Blood seeped from a corner of his mouth.

"Krogulski, can you hear me?"

Wolf put his ear to his partner's mouth. There was no movement, no sign of breath. He went towards Wojciech, his anger filling him with a new kind of energy. Wojciech looked surprised to see him.

"You are behind this," he said. The guard was close by. "Those men tried to kill both of us. Twice, they felled a tree to land on us. They've killed Krogulski."

Wojciech shrugged and feigned innocence.

"I do not know what you are talking about. Why would one member of the brigade want to kill another?"

The guard came over. He looked at Wojciech.

"I saw it. This will be reported to the commandant."

Wojciech immediately began to whimper like a cornered animal.

"No, no there is no need to do that. I...I will make sure it does not happen again."

But the guard took no notice of him, ordering him and the two urki to dig Krogulski's grave at gunpoint.

******

To Wolf's relief, Wojciech's brigade was disbanded the next morning and he was assigned back into Tomczyk's. Tomczyk looked older and more gaunt than when Wolf had last seen him. His voice was frailer and the authority that he held in his person barely clung to him beneath the drooping rags of his clothes.

The work was no less arduous. The fact that Wolf now received his fair share of soup and bread did not make the rations remotely sufficient. Always he was hungry and desperate for more food. Every evening he would go to one of his sugar lump hiding places and replenish his pockets. He ate the sugar lumps surreptitiously through the day. They sustained his energy for a while, but they did not build it.

They had been in the camp for eleven months now and a fair distance of railway had been built. They had joined up with the rails laid by the camp to the West of them. To even get to the railhead to the East, to the area where they now worked, was a five-mile hike. The men of the brigade, run down as they were, dragged their tools and wheelbarrows there, barely able to raise one foot in front of the other.

Sometimes a train would come through carrying rails and other heavy equipment for the next section. Unloading the rails, even with rollers and the help of horses, was an exhausting task. Along the side of the rails was written ZIS – Zavod Imeni Stalina, the rail factory named after Stalin. It felt, to Wolf, as if he was in a nightmare that would have no end. He would slap the side of his face with his palm. Stay awake, Wolf, he told himself. Look out for the opportunities when they come.

One evening, a train stopped right outside the camp. Wolf could make out its tall funnel above the perimeter fence. He crept round the back of the sleeping hut, wondering if the hole that he and Krogulski had made was still there. With a bit of scooping and shoving, he got through. No one was guarding the train. He walked up the wagons on one side, but the doors were all locked. He slipped up the other side, feeling for any crack or hint of an opening.

On the third wagon, his hand felt a space. He leaned upwards, trying to ease the door further open. There was a creak and he froze. The sound seemed to carry for miles through the silent night air. He listened for footsteps or voices; the wagon was between him and the camp, but he could hear nothing.

He felt inside – it was sacks of flour again, but the gap was not wide enough to pull one out. He did not know if he had the strength, anyway, to carry a twenty-five kilo sack under the fence and through to the sleeping cabin. Would it be safe there, anyway, from rats and rain, let alone other prisoners? He had brought his blunt knife but he needed his bowl.

Hunger began to pound within him at the thought of extra food. Crouching low, he crawled back through the hole under the fence. Men growled and grunted as he reached for his bowl.

"Are you sleep-walking, Wolf? It's not soup time. What's wrong with you, mate? Go back to sleep."

He slipped out again.

He sawed away at the sacking with his blunt knife, each strand an effort, until he could feel a slit large enough to insert the bowl. He scooped the flour into it and picked up a handful in his fingers. The flour was so dry it clogged his mouth and stuck to his lips. It was impossible to eat this way.

On the far side of the track, under an overhanging rock, was some unmelted snow. He took this and, sitting on the rock, mixed it in with the flour until it became a sticky glutinous paste. He ate and ate ravenously, wiping his fingers, filthy with the dust of the rails and the day's earth, around the bowl to gather every last morsel, then licking them clean.

Vaguely, he remembered his mother telling him not to eat raw flour when he was a child.

"It will blow up inside you and give you a stomach ache."

He decided to come back the next night anyway.

.

26 BAND ON THE HILL

28 April 1941

WOLF'S new working partner was Herzl, also Jewish. He told him about the train and they spent the early part of the day wondering how they could cook the flour to make it more palatable. Herzl had lived in Ljublin and had joined the exodus east to Lutsk when the bombers came. He had been a builder and had made a good living. Though older than Wolf, he was still a young man, in his mid-thirties. His wife, Naomi and his daughter Sonja had escaped with him. He knew the ice cream stall where Wolf had worked the previous year.

"Sonja always chose the mocha," he said. "The ice cream would dribble down her chin and she would dance away from Naomi with the cornet in her hand."

There was a sadness about him, for he had no idea of their whereabouts. When the Russians had demanded he attend the library office, he had gone on his own.

'We'll only keep you for a few minutes,' they had said, but took him straight away. He had not even been able to kiss Naomi and Sonja goodbye.

"I dream about them," he said. "We will cook you a feast when we get out of here."

Though ribs protruded now from a mass of sand-coloured hair on his broad chest, Herzl was a strong man and threw himself into working with Wolf.

As they arrived at the rail head at the end of their five-kilometre trek, Tomczyk pointed ahead of them. The white-painted arrows that marked out the railway track rose over the gradient of a small hill, perhaps sixty or seventy metres at the highest point.

"We have to cut through this now," he said.

"You're joking!" said a man called Zvi incredulously. "You want us to move a mountain? There must be machinery that can do that."

It was clear to everyone that this would be more gruelling than anything that had yet been thrown at them, but Tomczyk shrugged his shoulders.

"I know, but this is what Zielinski says we have to do. Make a cutting through the hill. He must know how difficult it will be, but he has his orders too. It's the usual story – dig through the hill, meet the quota, and we get food."

The arrows climbed the hill in a double row ten metres apart and passed across the top. They had to dig and cut between these marker posts. That would give space for the tracks to be laid and a train and wagons to pass through. Tomczyk pointed out the area where each team should work and Wolf and Herzl set to — there was no point in delaying. All they had was a pickaxe, a wheelbarrow, an axe, a saw and a shovel. At least, Wolf thought, the hill was not too wide.

First the shrubs and trees that stood on top had to be cleared. This was the work that they had become used to. It began to rain again as they started to dig out the clumps of grass and stumps. As each team dug deeper, the path from the top of the hill to the pile where the earth and scrub and branches was left became muddier. Men slid and fell as they tried to get a loaded barrow down the hill or an empty one up it.

"I'm too tired to try to do anything clever with the flour," said Wolf as they walked back. "Let's just mix it with water."

The thought of the extra food filled them with anticipation, but when they got back to the camp the train had gone.

******

Day after day they returned to the hill. The mud caked their clothes and a certain camaraderie, an end-game resignation, developed between the men.

"We're like the men who built the pyramids in Egypt," sighed Herzl.

Wolf did not know where Egypt was — he knew it only as the country the Jews had escaped from after the plagues, the Exodus from Mitzrayim — but he had seen pictures of pyramids and the metaphor was not lost on him, the enormity of the task they had been set.

When they got back at night, those who had the energy played a game – lice-popping. An item of clothing was held up against the fire. The lice exploded in the heat like machine-gun fire or fireworks. Pop-pop-pop. The winner was the man who created the loudest, longest period of sound. The pop was louder, the hotter the lice became, but the risk was to set fire to the clothing. Many a man had his trousers or shirt scorched or burnt through where he had held them too close.

As time wore on, they became too exhausted to do anything back in the camp but eat their ration and fall asleep. Morning after morning Wolf looked at the scar in the hill and it looked no different. The loaded barrows now had to come out through the ten-metre wide cutting. Men teemed about   like ants – backwards and forwards, some stumbling and falling on the way, others milling around them, crowding over them, stepping bodies into the mud. In places, rocks and huge stones blocked their path. The only way to move them was with pickaxes and men and ropes. Twice a man was killed by a rock that, once it reached an incline, took flight.

Another man was struck in the eye by splinters of stone as others pounded a rock with their pickaxes. His scream tore through the forest. He clutched his hands to his wounded eye, stumbling around in half-blindness. He was held down by his colleagues as one of them tried to hold the wounded eye open and remove the splinter. His legs thrashed and beat the ground, but without any delicate instrument it was hopeless. Released from his colleagues' arms, he ran around in desperation until he stumbled and rolled off the hill. The guard's bullet was a merciful release.

Herzl did not suffer any of these injuries, but his complexion became greyer. His work-rate slowed and he sweated freely.

"I don't know what's wrong with me, Wolf. I just don't have any energy."

Wolf worked harder and harder to meet their quota.

******

Days at the hill turned into weeks. Through the haze of exhaustion, Wolf could now see a cutting. It seemed that they had actually done what they had joked about. They had moved a mountain, or nearly so. Behind them, the line of the railway track stretched westwards. The end of it was just 200 metres from where they worked.

"Leave the last three metres," ordered Zielinski one afternoon.

29 May 1941
In the morning, the commandant addressed them.

"Comrades, today is a special day. You should all be very proud of what you have achieved. You have cut through the hill. Today we will celebrate."

"Celebrate?" muttered Zvi. He was a tall, raw-boned man, even younger than Wolf. Early in life he had been sent out to work in a textile mill in Lodz, stacking the heavy bags or loading carts. It was August 1939 when the factory owner had told him to get out while he still could.

"Celebrate," he said again. "What with? Some brackish water and a piece of bread? Where is the wine? Where is the feast? What are we celebrating anyway?"

As they reached the hill, they heard the rumble of a locomotive behind them. It stopped well before the railhead, its tall funnel belching smoke. From the two carriages that it pulled, a motley array of men stepped out, looking gingerly about them.

They wore black uniforms with belts of white webbing, and triangular black hats. On a few of them, the belts were of polished brass, the white sash worn diagonally across the chest and shoulder. Two men carried drums across their waists. The rest carried, beneath their arms, a musical instrument – a trumpet, a bassoon, an oboe or a trombone. The instruments were highly polished, points of light in the gloom of the forest.

One man stood out. He did not wear black but red and the sash that ran across his chest was itself of polished brass. He did not carry a musical instrument, merely a thin stick. Behind him, labouring slightly, came a man with round spectacles and a moon-like face. He wore a fur hat and a long navy blue overcoat that dragged across the undergrowth.

Wolf looked on in astonishment. The commandant had come out and stood in front of the man in the red uniform, pointing. Those with instruments now split into two groups, and began to climb either side of the hill.

A man with a bassoon slithered on the wet muddy surface. In slow motion, his left foot went from under him; he held out his arm for balance and the bassoon went flying. He tumbled, rolling down the slope until a bush caught him. The man in the red uniform shouted at him and he picked himself up and found his way down to the bassoon. Wolf wondered if he was hallucinating. He had heard about mirages in African deserts.

Eventually, the two groups, six each side, had scrambled to the top. The brass of their instruments was less shiny now, mud spattered and smeared across them. Most of them had patches of brown on the knees or seats of their trousers or on their elbows where they had fallen, but they lined up finally on either side of the cutting, the man in red on the left, facing them, his arms raised. The commandant stood behind with the man in the wire spectacles. Two guards had escorted him up the hill by a different route, supporting him if he stumbled.

It was now that it began to rain. There was nowhere to hide and no shelter. The commandant barked an order to the men below in the cutting.

"Clear the earth," he ordered.

Wolf raised his pickaxe. He could see Herzl beside him barely able to lift his shovel. Behind the row of shovellers, the other members of the brigade held wheelbarrows, ready to haul away the final three metres of soil and rock.

The man in the red uniform raised his arms and music struck up from the top. The bassoons coughed and spluttered and the trumpets missed their notes, but the two drummers held their beat. Little did the men below know that this was the Internationale and that the words of the first verse alone, had it been sung, ran along the lines of:

Stand up, damned of the Earth
Stand up, prisoners of starvation
Reason thunders in its volcano
This is the eruption of the end.
Of the past let us make a clean slate
Enslaved masses, stand up, stand up.
The world is about to change its foundation
We are nothing, let us be all.

"Faster," the guards shouted at the ragged men. The music reached a crescendo, the drummers playing with such intensity it seemed the drums' skins, dampened by the rain, must break. The man in red kept glancing down and then across at the man with wire rim spectacles. Uniforms and coats hung limp in the rain.

Still the earth was not cleared. The man in red slowed his hands, palm down to indicate to the musicians to come to an end, but then, immediately, raised them again for a repeat.

This time, as the men below, urged on by the guards, worked in a frenzy and the musicians reached the climax, the final shovelfuls were cleared. The drummers played a final note and for a moment, there was just silence, broken only by the beat of the rain.

The man with the wire spectacles took them off and wiped them with a clean white handkerchief. He looked down at the cutting and along the line of the railway, waiting only now for the rails themselves to be laid. He looked down at the bedraggled men who were standing back now in exhaustion, leaning on their pickaxes or shovels or wheelbarrows, waiting for the next order, and across at the band, and began to clap. The commandant began to clap. The man in the red uniform began to clap. The band members, bending their arms around their instruments began to clap too and the guards below in the cutting began to clap.

"Clap," they shouted at the prisoners.

Reluctantly, wearily, Wolf put his hands together, though he could not raise a sound. He did not know what the clapping was for. The music out here in the forest, the completion of the cutting, the presence of this man, whom he supposed to be some sort of dignitary, meant nothing to him. He did not care.

He looked across at Herzl. His eyes were closed and his body slumped against the side of the cutting. A trickle of muddy water ran down the earthen wall and onto his shoulder but he seemed unaware of it. Above him, he could hear the dignitary speaking, shouting above the noise of the rain.

"This is great work you are all doing for the people. The commitment and sacrifice you are showing is an example to us all. Comrade Stalin himself has sent me to view your efforts and to report back on his project, this great railway line which will transform our Soviet Union. All you men are part, now, of this great movement."

Wolf kept hearing the word 'great' and wondered what the man was talking about. All he cared about was his own survival and to help Herzl.

As the band and the dignitary negotiated their way back to the train that was hissing and belching once more behind them, Herzl slumped to the ground. The other men in the brigade were already shuffling back to the camp through the pine. The guard shouted at him to get up and move on. Wolf bent down to his partner.

"I'm not leaving you here," he said.

Herzl's face was the colour of the rain clouds above them. Wolf glanced back. He did not have much time. He knew the guard's orders: 'If they are too sick to move, leave them to die there; if they try to escape into the forest, shoot them.' Many *had* died out there and many, too, had offered their backs to the guard's bullet.

"Come on, Herzl, you can do it. I'll give you a sugar lump, when we get back. The lek-pom will write a note for you — you'll have time off. Maybe Tomcyzk will be able to persuade them to send you to the sanatorium."

Herzl's eyes glimmered slightly and, leaning all his weight on Wolf, he stood and moved forward, step by straining step. The strip of tyre, strapped with a piece of filthy cloth around the bridge of his foot and his ankle, that was all he had for a left shoe, slap-slapped against his bare sole, catching sometimes in the scrub.

Wolf's energy was draining out of him when Herzl collapsed again. He knew that he could not carry his partner all the way back. It was only when Tomczyk returned and took Herzl's other shoulder that he could summon the strength to move ahead.

"Thank you, Szymon."

"I need you both," said Tomczyk. He looked even more frail himself. "I will speak to the lek-pom."

They passed under the sign at the camp gate and walked Herzl to the fire. That, at least, burnt well as men stoked and fuelled it, trying to warm and dry themselves. Wolf propped him up against the edge of the cook-hut.

"I will get your soup," he whispered.

The cook ladled the watery soup into the two rusting cans.

"Here you are — drink this." Herzl's eyes were closed. Wolf lifted his head to the can, but it lolled back. Tomczyk came over.

"I don't think he's going to make it, Szymon."

This time Tomczyk lifted Herzl's head and held the can to it. Again his head lolled back.

"I am sorry, Wolf."

Wolf drank his partner's soup in one, long impoverished draught. He drank his own more slowly, clasping his hands around the warmth of the can. He muttered the Kaddish where he sat and left others to steal the lice-ridden clothes and bury the naked body.

He sank, exhausted, onto the rough-hewn planks of his bunk. He pulled the sharp grey stone that he had picked up at the Vistula river — back, it seemed to him, in another lifetime when Hela was still with him and Bledow was still close — from his pocket. He had clung to it through everything, but now had barely enough strength to scrape another notch in the wood above him. He did not know why he did this. He had lost count of the number of notches he had left. He had scraped them in each of the places where he slept, his message. In this hut, it was notch number 58. That was the number of nights since he had got back from the sanatorium.

He considered the men he had known since leaving Bledow – Chaim, Josef, Nikolay, Andrei, Igor, Krogulski and now Herzl. They were all like dreams, broken scenes, friendships suddenly interrupted as he had to say goodbye again. He could barely picture Rywka's face now.

27 MAHORKA

7 July 1941

IT WAS Tomczyk himself that Wolf had to worry about now. The gauntness and listlessness that he had noticed in him seemed to have redoubled after Herzl's death and he had been admitted into the medical tent.

Wolf went to see him in the evening. He spoke to the lek-pom.

"I have come to see my friend Tomczyk. How is he?"

"He is not well. He is sinking. He needs the sulpha powder but I have very little of it. My orders are to keep it for an urgent need."

"This is a Polish officer. Surely he is an urgent need?"

But the lek-pom shook his head.

"There is nothing I can do."

Wolf went into the grimy section at the back. It stank of urine and canvas with a tinge of something medical. Six palliasses lay on the ground, stained and fraying. Tomczyk was in the far corner. He lay on his back, his eyes staring wide at the ceiling. He tried to turn his head to speak to Wolf but could not make the muscles work. Flies buzzed about him.

Wolf put his hand on Tomczyk's forehead as he remembered his mother doing back in Bledow on the rare occasions he was sick. It was burning.

"I don't think I am going to make it, Wolf." His voice came out in a hoarse whisper. "This dysentery has got me. I feel so weak. My bones and muscles don't obey me."

"You are going to make it, Szymon. You are an officer in the Polish Air Force."

A fleeting look of pride passed across Tomczyk's face.

"We need you, the brigade needs you and I'm going to help you. You need food and you need medicine."

Wolf pulled from his pocket a sugar lump. His hand touched the pouch of mahorka that he had kept there safely since he had left the sanatorium.

"For a start, eat this."

He placed the sugar lump in Tomczyk's fingers, then held the mug of tepid kipiatok that stood beside the palliasse to his lips. He had, in reality, no idea how he was going to help him, but something told him that he had to try.

As he walked away, he saw the lek-pom and Sado, the one-legged man who had recently taken over in the cook-hut, sitting on a log. In their hands were coarse-made cigarettes, rolled in pieces of rough paper. Reams of smoke filled the air around them, keeping the mosquitoes at bay. The smell took Wolf back to the sanatorium. Mahorka. An idea came to him.

"How much do you want for a smoke?" he asked.

"Nothing," said Sado. "There is no more. We are smoking the last of it. I don't know what I am going to do without it."

"Maybe not," said Wolf. "I have some."

The two men looked at him open-mouthed.

"But you have to help me. I will give you both enough for one cigarette a day but you, Sado, have to give me extra food for my friend Tomczyk in there." He jerked his head towards the medical tent.

"And you," he looked into the eyes of the lek-pom, "have to give him that sulpha powder you say you have, whatever it is."

"How do we know you have the mahorka?"

Wolf fished in his pocket and pulled out the grimy pouch that held the precious tobacco. He held it up.

"We can start now if you like."

Both men nodded. Then Sado said, "I need two cigarettes a day if I am giving you extra food for yourself and your friend."

The lep-tok chipped in too. "If the NKVD find out I am giving the sulpha powder to Tomczyk, they will put me in isolation. I need two cigarettes a day as well."

Wolf held up the pouch again.

"This is all there is. There is not an unlimited supply. If you have two cigarettes a day, it will not last long enough for him to get better."

He drummed his fingers on his knees, thinking.

"Here is what I will do. One cigarette a day for each of you until he gets better. There is enough for about twenty smokes here. So enough for ten days. If he gets better before then, you can have the rest."

"That is fair."

Deftly, on his one good leg, Sado moved across the darkness to the cook-house. He came back with a thick slice of black bread and a small piece of salted herring.

"Take these and give me my mahorka."

Wolf measured out the dried and crumbled leaves. They were a dirty green, and their aroma burst like a hungry tiger from the pouch. He wanted a cigarette himself, but steeled himself. He measured another portion for the lek-pom.

"I will come with you back to Tomczyk and you can give him his first dose."

He knew that the lek-pom would do it. He would not get his fix the next day if he didn't. Wolf went to

Tomczyk's bedside. He seemed to be asleep, his breathing shallow.

"Szymon, you are going to get better, believe me. I have arranged it."

Tomcyzk struggled upright and stared at him vacantly. Wolf could hear something being stirred in the next room, then the lek-pom came in with a small cup of liquid. Wolf sniffed at it. It smelt, anyway, like medicine.

"Drink this," said the lek-pom. He held the cup to Tomcyzk's lips as Wolf tilted his head back. Most of the liquid went in.

"That will do you good."

"Now, eat this," said Wolf, handing the piece of herring to Tomczyk. He watched him eat, his jaws moving slowly. Then he passed him the other half of the bread.

As Wolf left the medical tent, he noticed a large jar of dark brown glass on the bench. Inside there appeared to be a white powder. The label read 'sulphaguanidine.'

******

The next evening, after he had given Tomczyk his food and medicine, Wolf sat with the two men as they smoked.

"If you don't mind me asking," he said to Sado, "what happened to your leg?"

"He is a miracle," said the lek-pom.

"No problem," said Sado. "I like hearing people's war stories too – it passes the time. We had been assigned that day to cut the long grass in the clearing…" he pointed generally in the direction of where some new huts were being built. "…with a scythe. The Commandant wanted to extend the camp as you can see so that more and more prisoners could come here.

"I am Czech. I am from Prague, I am not a country boy. I had never seen a scythe in my life before, let alone had reason to use one. Its curved wooden handle, as tall as my neck, its two hand grips in strange places and its long curving blade like an Arab's scimitar were completely alien to me. No one showed me how to use it, how to sweep it in arcs horizontally over the ground. No one else in my brigade knew any better.

"In a ragged line, we moved across the scrubland until I came across a particularly obstinate tuft. My scythe, blunted after a morning's hacking, and with nothing to sharpen it with, stalled at the tuft. I braced myself and raised the blade over my right shoulder as if it was an axe. I swung, but the curves of the thing foxed me. The blade smashed into the bottom of my left leg, at the back of my ankle, driving through the sinew.

"I can remember up to there. I collapsed to the ground, people told me later, screaming in agony. My foot was held only by the skin and a final piece of bone and blood poured from the wound. Other men ran over, ignoring the curses and warnings of the guard. One of them tore a piece of cloth from my shirt and tried to tie my foot back onto the leg. 'Get up!' shouted the guard.

"I pushed up with my right leg, but, of course, as soon as I applied any weight to the left, I crumpled to the ground again. I screamed and screamed. The foot hung from my leg as if it belonged to some altogether different body. The guard had raised his rifle, but when he saw my foot he lowered the gun. 'Carry him back to the lek-pom,' he ordered two men. 'Quick.'"

The lek-pom took up the story.

"Sado's foot hung loose, like a sandal attached only by its ankle strap. He screamed at every jolt and pull. They carried him into the tent and laid him on the nearest palliasse that was itself still stained with the blood of the last man to lie there.

"He fainted, his face a deathly white. I inspected him and as soon as I touched the injured leg, he woke and screamed. He looked down. 'Cut it off,' he shouted. 'You cannot mend that here. Cut it off.'

"I looked at him. I think I was as shocked as him. 'I cannot cut it off,' I said. 'I have nothing to cut it off with. I do not know how to cut it off.'

"Sado looked at the two men who had brought him in. They were now taking a little rest, nosing around for my supply of water and bread. 'Cut it off … please,' pleaded Sado. 'Use the axe.'

"Neither of them could bring themselves to do it. 'We'd make it worse,' one of them said.

"Sado, summoning whatever life and energy was left in him, leant across and took the axe. Sitting up, he began to slash at his leg, trying to finish the job. But he could not get the right angle. He screamed and screamed each time he made contact, violent gashes appearing on his shin, blood spurting. He subsided onto the mattress, the axe falling to his side. Sweat dripped from his forehead. I poured water on his face. He sat up again and reached for the axe. The guard came in. 'What's going on? Can you not see that he cannot do it himself?' He cocked his rifle. 'One of you two do it, or I will finish him off. I should have finished him off out there in the forest.'

"One of the men took the axe. 'I am sorry, Sado,' he said, tears rolling down his cheeks. 'I will do it.' The man positioned himself as he would to split a log. He swung first to make sure he had a clear arc. He placed a plank underneath the ankle for a clean cut. 'Are you ready, Sado?'

"Sado closed his eyes, clenching his teeth and grasping the side of the mattress. The man swung. There was a loud crack. It was like a butcher's shop. Sado screamed again but this time the foot and the bottom of the leg fell apart.

"Sado had gone very, very pale. A look of bewilderment mixed with relief hung on his face as he stared at the stump of cleaved bone and gristled flesh. Blood poured from the wound.

"Instinctively, one of the men grabbed a piece of twine and tied it round the leg. He tied it first below the knee but it did not stop the bleeding. He moved it above the knee and turned and turned and slowly the flow of blood became a trickle. 'Now what?' he said.

"I was completely out of my depth. 'I need a bandage – anything,' I said. 'Give me your shirt – just a sleeve will do.' He tore off the sleeve; it was no more than a filthy rag. I dipped it in the pot of water, and squeezed it out over the wound. 'Bring me the salt,' I said, pointing to a hessian sack in a corner.

"I dipped my hand in the salt and sprinkled it against the wound, pressing it in, then tied the shirt-sleeve around it. 'I will make a crutch for the poor bastard,' said the man who had used the axe. 'If he lives.'"

Sado chuckled, raising the amputated leg for Wolf to see and blowing a smoke ring.

******

Religiously, each evening, the three men followed their routine. Sometimes Sado would produce a piece of cabbage instead of fish, but always the extra bread. The lek-pom's medicine cup was always well-filled and Tomczyk drank it down lustfully now. In turn Wolf would measure out the tobacco, enough for Sado and the lek-pom to roll a cigarette each.

By the fifth day, Tomczyk, though still weak, was talking. His eyes were brighter and a new energy had entered him.

"You are good to me, Wolf. I do not know how you have worked this medicine and this food, but I am feeling better. I had a proper shit today."

As if to illustrate it, he released a loud fart.

"That's good," said Wolf. The behaviour of their bodies was a regular subject of conversation between the men, if any conversation there was. "It will take a few more days to get you up and walking. Take it easy while you can."

When he arrived the next evening, Tomczyk was trying to stand up. Holding on to the side of the hut for support, he took a few steps before subsiding again onto the mattress.

"He is better," said the lek-pom. "It is time for the rest of our mahorka."

"Better, yes, but not recovered," said Wolf. "Not ready to lead the brigade again. Two more days perhaps."

Forty-eight hours later, as Wolf recovered from the day's work, Tomczyk came into the hut. He was a little unsteady on his feet but there was a firmness about his person. He went over to Wolf's bunk.

"Thank you," he said simply.

They walked together to the cook-hut. A plume of smoke rose from the back and Wolf took in a great lungful. The lek-pom and Sado were arguing and gesticulating. Mosquitoes whined in the air nearby but, as if paralysed by the smoke, did not venture closer.

"Aha — the patient and the mahorka man!"

Wolf pulled the diminished pouch from his pocket and divided the remaining tobacco in two.

"You are all right, Jewish," said Sado.

For the last time, he went into the inner recesses of the cook-hut. This time he brought back two pieces of bread.

28 RELEASE

15 August 1941

THE SLANT of the light was different when Wolf was woken that morning. And it was not the voice of the normal guard, barking at them to get to work; it was an NKVD man.

"Albert, Wolf," he called. By dint of his surname, Wolf was the first. He eased his emaciated legs from his bunk and stood. The NKVD man motioned him outside. More men were called out.

"What's going on?" they muttered to each other — only Polish men were being selected. Wolf was relieved to see Tomczyk join them.

They were directed to the office hut.

"Disc!" said the clerk, holding out his hand.

The metal disc, stamped with the number 317, that he had been given on his arrival at this place still hung grubbily around his neck. Wolf pulled the leather thong over his head. The number was barely visible now, smeared in grime and dirt. He was apprehensive. His ID was being taken from him. But then the clerk leafed through a sheaf of papers and handed Wolf a document. It was curled at the edges and had four fold-marks, but at the top was his name in capital letters with 317 circled in blue ink beside another number — B167. It was the document that he had been given at the prison in Lutsk.

Morozov came up to the line of men.

"Excuse me, sir, comrade sir Commandant, please can you tell us what is happening?" asked Tomczyk.

Instead of the tirade of abuse or harsh orders that they had come to expect, he spoke politely.

"I heard news a few weeks ago that Hitler has invaded Russia. Russia is now at war with Germany. Yesterday, I received orders to release all Polish people at the camp. You are free to go."

"What do you mean?"

"You can go. You can join the Russian army if you wish or simply go, leave here."

Some men let out a muted cheer. Others, too weak to comprehend, stared vacantly out towards the endless trees. Wolf returned to the hut and picked up his torn jacket that, at this time of the year, he used as a pillow, his wooden spoon and his tin can. He walked out into the morning air. No one was forcing him to cut down trees and dig. He shook his head, trying to think.

He was not going to join the Russian army, that was his only certainty. He collected his ration of bread and pocketed it. He would need it later. He collected the little bags of sugar lumps from their hiding places around the camp and secreted them in his pockets.

He walked up to the railway, the line that they had built, that had stolen so many lives. He looked to the right to the North-East, the section that ran up to the cutting through the hill; he looked to the South-West – a clear, narrow corridor through the dense forest, stretching, it seemed, beyond the horizon.

Tomczyk was standing with a group of men outside the cook hut.

"They say that we can stay here one more night, Wolf," he said, "while we plan what we are going to do. But we think we should leave today."

Already Tomczyk had taken on the authority of an officer.

"We have to get to a train," he said. "The NKVD man told me a Polish Captain will meet us at the station in Kotlas and take care of things from there. Apparently there's a railway stop fifteen kilometres down the line now. From there we can get to Kotlas."

"I'm ready," said Wolf.

Poles from other brigades joined the group, some faces that Wolf had not seen since the journey on the barge to the camp, others missing. Some men were hesitant, like budgerigars frightened to leave their cage though the door was wide open, others followed Tomczyk purposefully. Wolf looked around as he approached the gate, wondering if this was some trick, if the NKVD were going to double-cross them or worse. But nothing happened. Nothing. No one told them anything as they left, no one gave them a map or money or directions, no one said goodbye.

They dragged themselves forward, a haggard band of men, a band of scarecrows, some missing noses or ears, most of them missing teeth, the shaven scalps and stubbled chins pitted with sores. The track, such as it was, beside the railway line seemed to go on forever, but there was only one way forward. A bitter wind rose and some men began to complain.

"It's too cold, we need to rest in the shelter of the forest. I'm starving."

But Tomczyk led them on.

"We are too close to freedom now, whatever is going on. When we get to the station, we can shelter. Perhaps we will find food."

Gradually, in the distance, they made out a mix of drab colours that shifted and wove. As they got closer, they saw that people from other camps — some Jewish, some not, but all Polish — were gathered at the rail stop. They looked no different to their own group, clothes hanging limply from starved bodies.

A queue formed behind an urn of hot water. Two Russian guards looked on. Tomczyk went over and spoke to them, then moved around the groups of people from other camps. He had some information when he came back.

"Apparently General Anders is mustering a Polish army in Uzbekistan," he said. "The train out of here will take us to Chibyu and then to Kotlas. There will be more orders of where to go and what to do when we get there. How we get clothed and fed."

As they waited, seeking whatever shelter from the wind they could find behind bushes or trees or the small concrete constructs of the station, Wolf heard a shout. It was Maurice, one of two Jewish brothers that he recognised from the barge journey to the camp.

"Help, I need a doctor, my brother is dying."

He would not leave his brother Isaac's side, but turned in every direction, repeating his plea.

"Good job," said a Pole. "One less yid."

Maurice was livid. He picked up a large stone and smashed it into the Pole's face. Wolf went over.

"Good for you," he said quietly to Maurice, as the Pole slunk away, his face like a burst tomato. Wolf had learnt over the months in the camp that it did not pay to simply ignore the Jew-baiting.

"When the Nazis entered our town and led us away," said Maurice, "I promised my father that I would protect Isaac. I have done so all this time. That is all I am doing."

Wolf nodded. He looked at Isaac, but there was nothing he or anyone else could do – the walk to the railway stop had drained him of the last vestiges of life.

From somewhere, one of the guards produced a pickaxe and, to warm himself from the icy wind, Wolf attacked the hard ground. He could barely dig deep enough to cover the body, but his muscles were used to the swing of the tool and Zvi came to help him. They laid Isaac in the grave and with Maurice recited the Kaddish.

29 LEAVING KOTLAS

WOLF watched, through a crack in the timber side, the graveyard path they had forged through the forest receding behind him. The wagons were still cramped and stank of urine but this time, they were heading towards a kind of freedom, not imprisonment. Though he had never in the past contemplated it, the idea of joining the Polish army excited Wolf. If he could do something to avenge the overrunning of his beloved Bledow, and whatever else he did not dare to contemplate, then he would be happy to do that. And if that meant, too, clothes and food and an ordered existence, then that was worth fighting for.

He smiled across the wagon at Tomczyk.

"Did you ever think we'd get out of there, Szymon?"

"When I could even think straight," he said, "I told myself that this was just an awful storm, and that every storm has an end. I had to force the thought out of my head that we'd just live that sad life until we died; that I'd never have a chance to return to the Air Force.

"I don't know how we managed to survive. I couldn't believe it yesterday when the NKVD man came in and started calling our names. I still can't."

He knocked his knuckles against the metal side of the wagon.

"What about you?"

Before Wolf could respond, a Polish voice broke in.

"I don't know what it is about you and that Jew, Tomczyk. You're so matey with him you might as well get married."

"What exactly are you saying?" asked Tomczyk, fixing the man's eyes with his own.

"Well, he's Jewish."

"And...?"

"Well... you know what Jews are like. My father always said Jews cannot be trusted and ..." His voice trailed off as he stuttered for words.

Tomczyk continued to look at him, without speaking. Eventually, he said:

"I do know what Jews are like. This man saved my life."

"And he saved mine," said Wolf.

******

19 August 1941

The train creaked and groaned into Kotlas station and disgorged its motley band of men. The milling crowd pushed and shoved and shouted on the platform. Some men had pouches of belongings knotted in sacks or sheets, others, like Wolf, had nothing. No one, it seemed, knew where they were going or what to do next.

He looked around for Tomczyk. Over heads, he saw him. He was pointing towards an exit. A throng of men poured in the same direction. The perimeter fence of a labour camp ran very close to the station outside. Russian soldiers barked orders, pointing them through the gate towards a huge tented area. Wolf was hesitant to go in and for a moment he faltered. But he was tired and hungry and he could see Tomczyk still ahead of him.

Bread and soup were handed out as they filed in. There appeared to be no logic or order in the tents, just lines of camp beds, a single blanket on each. Wolf subsided gratefully onto one of these. It felt almost like luxury.

He woke early and refreshed. He was impatient to move on. The camp, now that he could see it clearly in daylight, oppressed him. It reminded him too clearly of where he had so recently been – the watch towers that were placed at intervals around the perimeter, surrounded by barbed wire, the rotting wood of the structures, the rats that skittered underneath them. He felt that, at any minute, guards would secure the gate, give him a pickaxe and order him into a work group.

He looked around for Tomczyk, but there were too many tents. There were far more people here now – Poles from different camps in every direction. He found some water. Snippets of conflicting information came through. 'Hitler's troops are advancing on Moscow,' 'Hitler has taken Moscow,' 'When we meet up with General Anders we will take back Poland.'

The whereabouts of General Anders was the subject of wild speculation – Tashkent, Turkmenistan, Uzbekistan, Alma Ata, Samarkand, all were mentioned. None of these names meant anything to Wolf. He did not know where they were – he had no map in his mind of the vast expanse of the Russian or central Asian region to be able to visualise. He knew that he had come to Kotlas from the North-East direction and that he had no desire to return there.

He walked out of the open gate of the camp onto the streets outside. The road was busy with trucks and carts heading south out of the city. On the back of some of the carts were men who had been prisoners like him, their ragged clothes telling the tale.

"Where are you going?" he shouted to one of them.

"Who knows? Far away, I hope," he said, holding on to the side as the wheels jolted over the rutted road. Wolf remembered the uncomfortable ride on the way to Lutsk.

He walked over to the station. He saw a man there whose bearing carried the same authority as Tomczyk, though he wore the dishevelled, filthy clothes of a camp inmate. From somewhere, he had found a white eagle. Rough lines of thread attached it to his shirt.

"Is there any news? When can we expect to join up with General Anders?"

He looked at Wolf. Speaking man to man to a Jew was not, it seemed, something he was used to.

"I don't know that they will let Jews into the army," he said. "Anyway, I have received a message that they are sending up special trains for us; but it may be some days, even weeks, before they get here. The whole Russian railway is tied up moving war material and ammunition to the army further south."

That was enough for Wolf. He decided to take the next train out of there, wherever it was going. He had no money, no ticket, no food and no water – he simply had to escape from Kotlas. It was too close to all the pain. There was no time to find Tomczyk and say goodbye.

A train wheezed and smoke poured from its funnel like an angry man. He saw Zvi and Ezra, another man from Tomczyk's brigade, enter the station.

"I'm getting out of here," he called over to them. "There's no future for us here."

Hurriedly he explained what the officer had told him.

"I don't know. At least we have a bed here and they are giving us more food," said Ezra.

"Your choice, but you need to make a decision quickly," said Wolf as the train belched again.

"Where's it going? How do we know it's not going to take us back where we came from?"

Wolf shrugged his shoulders.

"The sign says Kirov. There is a sign for Chibyu on the other platform. That's where we came from."

He started to move towards the train.

"How are we going to get on without a ticket?"

The guard had slammed the doors shut and already blown his whistle when the three men ran down the platform. Wrenching a door open, they dived inside as the train inched forwards.

.

30 KIROV

20 August 1941

OTHER passengers edged along their seats. Wolf was aware of the rags they wore, and of the filth and odour that they must carry with them, but they were on their way. The countryside sped by faster and faster outside the windows.

It was some time before a conductor appeared. He looked at the three men distastefully.

"Your tickets?"

"We have no tickets. We have been freed from a labour camp. We are going to join the Polish army and fight the Germans."

"That may be, but you still need tickets. If you have no tickets, you will have to get off at the next station."

"Where is that?" asked Wolf.

"Kirov."

It was a day's journey away. There was nothing the conductor could do.

Wolf slept fitfully. He was hungry and thirsty. A woman sat on the bench opposite with her husband. Wolf had seen so few women over the previous fifteen months, it was as if he was looking at a museum piece, a new and peculiarly attractive form of life. Even through his own stench, he could pick up an aroma from her. She asked where they had been, what had happened to them – but then her husband woke. He nudged her in the side with his elbow and she became silent. Occasionally, she would look up and her eyes would meet Wolf's.

Kirov was a large and busy station and the three men tumbled quickly out of the carriage. He threw one last glance back at the woman before they merged into the crowd. People looked at them strangely, backing away.

Wolf took stock of the station. At different points, there were kiosks and stands selling doughnuts, rolls of bread with sausage or cheese, bottles of lemonade and water. The food was displayed in front of the kiosk, which had a little door to the side. Above it was a window, where payment was made.

"I'm going to find something to eat," he said.

"But we haven't got any money," said Ezra.

Ezra was a quiet, earnest man, the stubble on his face grey. A strange bedfellow for the impetuous Zvi, Wolf thought.

"No. I'm just going to take it."

Wolf chose his target kiosk carefully. Coming in from the side, setting his eyes on a bread roll, he suddenly broke into a run. He grabbed the roll and raced on, merging quickly into the crowd on the other side. In the seconds it took the kiosk owner to come out and shout, anyone who had seen him had moved on. 'There in the grey shirt,' he heard, but he was already well ahead. He slipped into a large group of people, slowing and walking with them, several of them between him and his pursuers. He saw the pursuers come to a stop and look around, then shrug their shoulders. He couldn't see Zvi and Ezra anywhere.

He moved through the station until he came on the goods train area. He slipped down onto the track behind a wagon and bit into the bread roll, then looked at it. It was sausage. It was probably not kosher, but he did not care –

he was ravenous. Unspoken reasoning told him that his religion allowed this. He had to stay alive. He climbed back up onto the platform. He had no idea where the other two had gone. He might be safer on his own anyway, he thought.

Carefully he scanned the destination boards, giving the food kiosk from which he had taken the roll a wide berth. He saw a board that read PERM. On the opposite platform, the sign read KOTLAS. Perm, he reasoned, must be the direction he needed to go. On the track side was a barrier. It was not high and, though his legs were weak, he was able to clamber over it quickly. Now, he moved down the outside of the train until he was several carriages down. He could hear the guard shouting on the platform and the train up ahead wheezing like a fat uncle. He climbed onto the coupling between two carriages and, checking that the guard was looking the other way, jumped down. As confidently as he could, he walked up the platform and opened a carriage door. Inside, he slumped onto a bench.

"Sholem aleykhem," he heard someone say. "Peace be upon you."

He looked up. In front of him was a group of Jewish people, some of them young, barely teenagers, others adult. Their clothes were bare and worn, but not filthy and lice-ridden. Knotted sheets of possessions sat beside the parents on the seats or in the luggage racks.

"Aleykhem sholem," he said. "I am sorry."

He pointed to his clothes and his entire person as the train set off.

"I probably stink and if I were you I would not sit near me."

It was then that he noticed that one of the children held a mandolin. She began to strum it gently and picked out a tune. It was Bulbes – a Jewish folk song that they used to sing as children:

Sunday potatoes
Monday potatoes
Tuesday and Wednesday potatoes
Thursday and Friday potatoes
But on Shabbas, something special
A potato kugel!

Wolf began to sing along and the others joined in too.

Bread with potatoes
Meat with potatoes ...

"You poor man," a woman said. "What happened to you?"

"I escaped from my home town of Bledow in Poland when the Nazis came," said Wolf. "I got to Lutsk, but the Russians sent me to a labour camp in Siberia. They made us build a railway. Now I have been released and I am joining the Polish army."

"The Polish army?"

"Yes. Apparently General Anders is gathering an army from all the Polish people who were imprisoned in Russia. Then we can fight the Germans."

The woman passed Wolf a water flask. He took a few sips.

"No, no," she said. "Drink."

This time he took great draughts of the water. He laid his head back. One of the adults now picked up the mandolin and played a jaunty tune:

A young lad stands, and he thinks
Thinks and thinks the whole night through
Whom to take and not to shame
Whom to take and not to shame
Tumbala, tumbala, tumbalalaika
Tumbala, tumbala, tumbalalaika

A teenage girl danced in the aisle of the carriage, her toes tapping and her dark pigtails flying to the music.

A huge tiredness came over Wolf and his head lolled against the side of the bench seat. He could hear the mandolin play on behind his dreams. He felt at home with these people who spoke his language and played his childhood songs.

******

"You have slept for fifteen hours," the woman said when he woke. He stood and stretched. He was hungry again. He could not ask these people for more food. He would fend for himself.

"What happened to all of you?" he asked.

"We were in Lutsk too," she said. "The NKVD came. They hammered on the door one night and told us to pack our things."

"They put you on one of those awful trains?"

"Yes."

The woman's eyes filled with tears as she described their camp. To Wolf it sounded luxurious. Though the men were set to work cutting down trees, the children attended school in the local village and she was able to join a craft group and work as a seamstress. The family lived together in a wooden hut with a stove at one end.

Wolf heard a change in the engine's tone; he felt the train slow and brake. It was dark outside but he sensed a chance for food. He moved towards the door. Every twenty yards or more on the lighted platform, there were kiosks – the same kiosks as in Kirov — selling food and drinks. Steam from a samovar of tea or soup swirled around some of them.

The thought of a mug of hot soup was like a dream to him but it would have to wait. He picked out the kiosk he wanted before the train had even come to rest. Emboldened by his previous success, he jumped out. A bulky woman swathed in a thick coat, scarves wrapped around her neck, was being served in front of him. This time, using her as cover, he grabbed a bread roll and a bottle from behind and sidled away into the throng of people jostling to get on the train. The shouts came, but already the train was moving.

It was not theft in Wolf's mind. He did not steal sweet cakes or goodies. It was simply survival, just as a bird will take grain from a farmer's barn. It was the fault of Russia that he had no money and was starving. He had built a railway for the country and nearly died. It was only fair, therefore, that he should take from the country what he needed. He knew, of course, that it was Stalin, not the people, who had put him in this position. He apologised, inside, to those he took food from.

31 BREAKDOWN

WOLF recognised the Ural mountains as the train crossed them, heading Eastwards. He remembered the helplessness when they had crossed the range in the other direction. This time, they came to a huge station, Sverdlovsk.

From there, weeks passed in a blur of railway stations and railway carriages – Troitsk, Kartaly, Orsk, Chelkar. Sometimes his sixth sense, sometimes just the flow of people, moved Wolf forwards. Some conductors turned a blind eye to him, others, frightened for their own position, went only by the rule book. Some fellow-travellers took pity on him and offered him food, others moved away.

27 September 1941
The train rumbled slowly for hours through an open sparse landscape – Kazakhstan, someone said – until, unexpectedly, it shuddered to a halt. Wolf looked out. There was no station; a few huts stood on the steppe a kilometre away. Occasional wind-whipped shrubs punctuated the grassy expanse.

He leant out of the window. The driver and the guard were inspecting the track. The engine was still steaming and creaking as if its metal skin would burst. The guard went back and returned with a huge spanner. The two of them shoved and heaved to no avail, then shrugged.

They reversed the engine back up the line for two kilometres to a tiny station, no more than a concrete hump in the flat land. The guard came down through the train.

"I am afraid there is a problem with the track and we are going to have to stop here until it is fixed. We have called for a line maintenance team to come."

Wolf decided to act. They were going to be there a long time – that was obvious. He climbed down from the carriage and made his way across the grassland to one of the shacks in the distance. As he came closer, he saw that one side was for human habitation, the other for animals. A corrugated roof, rusted and with moss growing on top, covered both sides. Pigs grunted and snorted and snuffled in the ground nearby.

Rounding the edge of the building, he saw a large woman. She seemed almost to have been born from the earth. Her skirts and her smock were the colour of the soil and a green scarf was swathed around her head. She carried one leg stiffly, as if it would not bend or carry weight and her face was riven with deep contours, in defiance of the flat countryside. She was bending over a metal bathtub washing some clothing. To one side, two large logs smouldered in a fire.

She did not seem surprised to see Wolf. He held his palms together and put them to his cheek, the sign of sleep. She nodded and pointed to a section of the animals' house. A wooden ladder leant against a raised platform, a man's height above the ground. On it was laid some hay.

"Spasevo," he said. "Thank you."

She said something in a language he did not understand. He looked at her blankly. She pointed to his chest, then picked at her own smock and pointed this time to the bathtub. The shirt that Wolf wore when he left the labour camp still hung in filthy folds around his body. He pulled it over his head, his pale skin and thin frame exposed.

She let out a squawk like an exotic bird as she saw his protruding bones. She held the shirt open, studying it. Seeing the lice, she put it to her mouth and ran her teeth along the seams, nipping and chewing as she caught them as if they were a delicacy. Wolf blinked – he had seen prisoners eating rats, but never lice.

When the woman was satisfied that she had eaten all of them, she plunged the shirt into the water and worked it vigorously. Then she wrung it out and hung it on a contraption of wooden posts that stood by the fire to dry.

She pointed to Wolf and then to the water. It was tepid and had a strange tar-like tang about it, but to Wolf it was luxurious. He splashed it over his face again and again, then filled his hands and rubbed it over his chest. He looked across to her and pointed to his trousers.

A smile passed across her craggy face. "Da, da," she said.

She didn't bother to look away as he took off his trousers. He stood in the water naked, then lowered himself in. With his legs tucked in towards his chest, he could just sit in the tub. He washed the water over his feet and rubbed his legs. He sluiced it over his genitals and ran the side of his index finger up and down the cleft of his bottom.

Finally done, he stood and shivered. He walked over the bare earth to the fire and the woman cackled with laughter. He allowed his legs to dry before he put on the trousers again. She handed him a grey blanket, then disappeared into the dim light at the back of the hut. When she came back, she was carrying a piece of black bread and a sliver of smoked fish.

******

Wolf woke early. A loud banging came across the steppe. A team of men with hammers and pickaxes were working on the rails. The sight of them filled him with dread — as if he would be called upon to go with his brigade to cut down more trees or lay more rails.

The woman was already about, chattering to the pigs as if they spoke the same language. He held his hands together to her in gratitude.

"Spasevo," he said again.

She handed him his shirt, now dry and Wolf felt a tinge of youth flow through him as he re-boarded the train.

32 NINA

29 September 1941

THERE WAS a salt tinge to the air around the concrete shelter in which Wolf slept the night outside Aralsk station. He had judged that, from here, he could cross the track and climb onto a train without any problem. Usually there was time to do this, but the train that came in in the early hours of the morning seemed to be in a hurry. It set off again almost as soon as it had stopped. Wolf ran, scrambling up the coupling of the last carriage, and grabbed at the handle of the rear door.

A grey-uniformed guard stood there behind the glass. An awful apprehension filled Wolf – the spectre of imprisonment again, another camp, more trees, more rails. But the train was already speeding up – it was too dangerous to let go now. The guard frowned, uncertain, it seemed, whether to let Wolf in. He glanced towards the front of the carriage, then relented and opened the door. He leant out an arm to haul Wolf in as rails and sleepers sped by beneath him.

"What are you doing on this train? Show me your papers."

"I am going to join the Polish Army."

He studied the papers for some time.

"But why are you not in the main part of the train?"

"I nearly missed it. I had to race to catch it."

"You can walk up to the front. You will have to pass through this carriage and the next one. These are special carriages."

Wolf's eyes passed over the seats behind the guard. They were all filled with women. Some had babies with them. The smell in the carriage was different to the smell he was used to – the body odour of men, dirt, sweat and faeces. This smell was softer. There was a hint of perfume and the warm smell of the babies and their nappies and their urine. The sight of a woman was still a novelty for Wolf. To see so many all at the same time unsettled him – and excited him.

The guard pointed up the aisle.

"When you see the guard up there, tell him I sent you. He will let you through."

A huge body of water stretched to the horizon to the right of the train. As Wolf moved through the carriage, holding the top of the bench seats to keep his balance with the roll of the train, women looked up at him curiously. Some were facing the back of the train, some the front.

He glanced behind him, expecting the guard to be prodding and pushing him forward, but he had stopped and seemed to be chatting to two of the women.

At the far end, a woman with a baby stared at Wolf intently. Her clothes looked rumpled, but expensive. She was, perhaps, thirty, and wore a red-patterned scarf around her auburn hair. Her face was fresh and vital, but carried a look of hurt behind a half smile. As Wolf approached, she widened her legs a little, invitingly, her skirt riding above her knees.

Embarrassment was his first reaction, embarrassment mixed with desire. But he had no tools for dealing with the opposite sex, no experience, and he walked on, his cheeks burning, to the end of the carriage.

The guard there looked up in surprise.

"Who are you? What are you doing here?"

Wolf pointed to the guard at the back.

"He sent me up to you. He said you would let me through."

The guard relaxed.

"The problem is that you cannot get to the front carriages until the train stops; there is no interconnecting door on the next one."

He pulled out a packet of tobacco and handed it to Wolf with a paper.

"Have a cigarette, tovarish."

Wolf was astonished to be greeted as a comrade.

"Spasevo," he said and began to roll a cigarette as Igor had taught him in the sanatorium.

"So why is this train carrying a carriage full of women and children under armed guard?"

The guard shrugged.

"No idea. Orders."

"And where are they being taken?"

"I don't know. I did hear someone say Alma Ata, wherever that is. But that might just be speculation."

There was a toilet cubicle to one side next to the door. People had been going back and forth into it while Wolf and the guard had been talking. He took the opportunity to go in himself. As he came out, the woman with the baby was at the door. She was so close he could breathe her fragrance. She did not have the baby with her and she did not step out of the way. Instead she gently pushed him back in, and fixed the latch on the door.

She pulled him to her. He could feel her breasts against his chest as she pressed her pelvis into his. She was breathing fast. Briefly, she nuzzled his neck, her breath coming now in short gasps. An indistinct picture of Rywka's face passed in front of Wolf; he wished it wasn't all happening so quickly. He did not know what to do, but he didn't need to.

Leaning against the back of the cubicle, the woman released Wolf's penis from his trousers and for a few moments, stroked it. Then, raising her skirt, she guided him in. She held him by the hips and moved him against her. Involuntarily, he grasped her breasts and felt the wild pleasure of the movement. With a gasp, he climaxed and she held him inside her as the spasms rushed through him.

In no time, it was over. She looked at him with her wide, grey-blue eyes, a mixture of sadness and gratitude. She kissed him on his lips.

"Thank you," she said and re-arranged herself.

The woman who was waiting at the door of the cubicle as they left looked at them strangely.

"That's the way the world goes round," said the guard and winked.

The woman came back with the baby. She handed a piece of cheese to Wolf.

"It is all I have, I'm afraid."

Wolf noticed, now, her long elegant fingers – it was not a hand used to manual labour.

"Thank you, but please tell me – what is going on? Where is the rest of your family? Why are you being taken away with these other women?"

She looked around, as if worried that the guard would overhear her, but he was busy playing a game with a little girl. Holding the baby in the crook of her arm, she stroked Wolf's face with her left hand, running her fingers over the stubble.

"My name is Nina. My father is a well-known surgeon at the Faculty of Medicine in Moscow. My husband is a doctor too. We were married in Moscow a year ago. We had one week's honeymoon and then he was ordered to the front. Other than one heavily censored letter, I haven't heard from him since. Three months ago, little Misha was born. It was a difficult birth. If it were not for my father's help, I would not be here today."

She looked around again.

"A few days ago, the NKVD called and ordered me to pack some things for myself and the baby. They told me I had two hours. I asked them why and they just shrugged – said they were obeying orders. I made frantic phone calls to my father but his telephone was constantly unobtainable. About ninety of us, all mothers with children, were assembled at a local cinema. We kept asking why, what have we done? One rumour was that our husbands had been captured by the Germans and so had been classified as enemies of the state. I don't know, none of us knows, but then they put us on this train."

She slipped away as an NKVD man headed down the next carriage towards them. Wolf felt a kind of sadness encompass him.

33 BREAD

30 September 1941

THE TRAIN stopped at Kzyl Orda. Its destination, Wolf learnt, was Alma Ata, many kilometres to the East, the place the guard had heard the women were being taken to.

The platform was crowded. The flow of people gathered here included not just Poles and Jews released from the labour camps, but also Russians, Ukrainians and Kazakhs escaping South from Hitler's armies. There was no official information, but rumour and hearsay told Wolf that he needed to get further South and West to join up with General Anders army. That meant heading for Tashkent, a different train. Wolf caught a glimpse of Nina's face in the last carriage as her train left the station. He waved, but she was feeding the baby and did not return his goodbye.

The temperature dropped overnight and Wolf shivered as he climbed on board the Tashkent train the next morning. For hour after hour the train meandered across the gaping countryside. Wolf ate only red watermelons. He did not even have to steal them from the barrows that were lined up at the stations where they stopped. He could just dive into the fields next to the stations and pick one from the ground.

The landscape turned to desert; there was a copper colour to the sand. Hungry for solid food, he looked out for bread at the next station. One particular barrow held entire loaves and it was this one that, like a hawk eyeing its prey, he targeted. He had perfected his technique. Swarming off the train in the throng of passengers, he lifted a loaf in the air.

"How much is this one?" he asked the barrow owner, then put the loaf down and raised another one.

"And this one?"

Then he let the next customer past him and, as more people jostled by, he slipped away. He was lucky this time. An entire loaf of fresh white bread, round, the crust nicely tanned, was in his hands. The smell of it tantalised him and he could barely contain himself from tearing off a piece. Safely away from the barrow owner, he mounted the steps to the train and sat down.

He pulled off a large piece and began to eat. He heard footsteps approaching from behind. His heart lurched as he saw a police uniform. He tried to remain calm, continuing to eat. The policeman sat down. With relief, Wolf realised he must be off-duty. For a time, neither of them spoke. Then Wolf held the loaf out to him, pointing to the bread. He nodded and Wolf handed a generous piece across, then watched him chew on it contentedly.

Wolf slept and when he woke in the early morning, the train was coming into a large station. The policeman waved to him as he left. Men, women and children spilled out onto the platform, whole families running from the German advance. Thirty or forty men in dark suits and carrying briefcases descended from one of the carriages further down. Wolf wondered if they were party officials.

He walked out of the station building onto a large square. People were congregated there, some bustling this way and that, like chickens, with their luggage, some retreating silently into the corners, looking on quietly.

******

7 October 1941

There was a vibrancy about Tashkent and something told Wolf that, for the moment, his journey would end here. Roads led off in different directions from the station square. To one side there was a park. People slept on the benches and around the edges and under the trees, huddled, some alone, some in groups, their clothes in tatters.

One road led to the centre of the old city. Foreigners, Wolf quickly learnt, were not allowed into the old city at night. He decided to test the lie of the land and followed the signs to the centre through tree-lined streets and pavements pitted with pot-holes. Though he knew nothing of architecture, he could see that the buildings were old and beautiful despite the faded paint and flaking plaster. The shops had food, proper food, on display, not just bread and water melons.

He walked back to the new town. A lot of people had gathered in a market square. He stood and watched for a while. He could hear Polish voices and others speaking in Yiddish. A long queue snaked around one side of the market stalls. He noticed two men who seemed better dressed than many others. He thought that they were probably Jewish.

"What is this queue?" he asked them after a while.

"It's for bread."

"I'm starving but I have no money." He had already established that this was not a place where he could easily steal.

The two men looked at each other. One of them stroked his beard thoughtfully.

"I tell you what," he said.

"I will lend you twenty rubles. The cost of the bread at the kiosk is two rubles; the black market price is three. You can queue and sell the bread and then queue again and pay me back. When you pay me back I want twenty-two rubles."

"OK, I will do that," said Wolf.

For hours he stood in the queue until he reached the front. He bought the ten loaves and it did not take him long to sell them. One he kept for himself, eating it slowly through the long wait as he rejoined the queue. Again, hours passed until he reached the front. This time he bought thirteen loaves. He walked around the edges of the market place, in the dusty corners where people had set up temporary shelters – sheets of red and tan silk stretched to the ground, held down with stones or lumps of concrete. He would look for those with old or young or sick family members, those who could not queue for hours for the regulation bread.

"Do you want bread? It is three rubles."

"We cannot pay that, we have no money. That is more than the Government bread."

"It is cheap," Wolf said. "It is one ruble more – that is my charge for queuing for you for four hours."

Most people, if they were hungry enough, would buy. This time, he kept two loaves, one to eat and one to keep for the next day. He saw the two Jewish men returning and counted out their money. He found that twelve rubles were left over. He had not had money, had barely even seen money, for so long that he looked at it in disbelief.

He was preparing to queue again when the police came. A man was with them, pointing Wolf out.

"Do you have a permit to sell bread?" one said. Wolf shook his head.

"I am just trying to survive, get some food for myself and help other people."

"Only government-authorised outlets can sell bread," the man said dispassionately.

They took him by both arms and marched him to the police station. They led him to an interrogation room and indicated an upright wooden chair, worn with years of use. Waist high, metal-framed windows looked out onto the back of another building.

"Wait here," said the policemen.

Wolf kicked himself. How could he have been so stupid — to have taken one risk too many? He had got so far. He could not face the idea of imprisonment again or even … he could not bring himself to contemplate another labour camp.

He heard footsteps approaching and looked up. To his surprise, it was the policeman who had shared his loaf of bread on the train. The policeman looked at him and asked for his papers. He did not show any sign of recognition. He studied the papers for a few moments.

"What are you doing here?" he asked.

Wolf had learnt that, to show that he was part of the fight against the common enemy, Germany, made friends.

"I am going to join the Polish army, to fight against Germany," he said.

As he spoke, the policeman moved around the room and opened one of the windows, then nodded.

"I will be back in a couple of minutes," he said.

Wolf needed no further invitation. Nimbly he lifted one leg over the window-sill and pulled the other through. He was in an alley way of bins and empty cans and boxes. It stank of rotting vegetables; it must be at the back of a restaurant, he thought. A dog barked. He glanced behind him, running, and quickly merged into the crowd on the street.

34 SICK IN TASHKENT

17 February 1942

THE NURSE came in with a pile of clothes stacked in her arms.

"Here you are, Wolf. These should fit you."

Wolf took the clothes; they carried the odour of another man. It was the grey serge uniform of the Russian army - a shirt, a jacket, trousers and boots. He put them on. He had to force his feet into the boots and the sleeves of the jacket hung below his wrists, but they were clothes and they meant he could finally leave.

He walked out of the hospital feeling like an impostor. He went to the market-place – he knew he would find some of his acquaintances there, if they still remembered him. Poles who, normally, would have made some snide remark about Jews, did not recognize him, only looking at him quizzically. He reached the group of Jews.

"Hey, look, a ghost has come to see us. Careful, we might be ordered out to cut down trees!"

Wolf laughed.

"What happened to you, Wolf? We haven't seen you for weeks, no months. Eventually we thought you must be dead."

"I will tell you. "

He sat on the edge of a fountain. At that moment, he heard a shout and two men approached.

"Wolf! Amazing! I never thought I'd see you again. How long have you been here? What the hell are you doing in a Russian uniform?"

It was Zvi and Ezra. Wolf stood again and embraced them.

"I looked all over the station for you in Kirov after I'd nicked that bread roll," he said. "But you were nowhere to be seen."

"No, we made ourselves scarce when we saw people going after you."

"In the end I decided I might be better off on my own. Don't ask me how I got here – I just kept taking trains. I ended up in Tashkent somewhere around October time."

"You've been here all this time? So what did you do? Give in and join the Red Army? I can't believe that."

"No way!" said Wolf, turning to the whole group. "No. Here's what happened. Did you ever meet Natan? He found a room, a tiny room. It was only about two metres by two metres. He said I could share it with him. It had clay walls and just straw on the floor. There was one window – not really a window, just a hole. You filled it with loose bricks to close it. It was cold, very cold, but a lot better than the benches in the park and it was dry too. We stayed there through the winter, made a few pennies carrying luggage for people at the station – anything we could do. Then Natan got sick, they said it was malaria.

"I walked with him to the medical centre. I tried to help him but he was in a really bad way and after a few days he died. Then I got it, whatever it was. I had a raging fever. I went to the medical centre – they said take vodka and pepper. I tried that. I had to queue for hours for the vodka. I stole some pepper and took the bottle and the pepper back to the room. It must have been three or four days that I lay in that straw – not eating anything, just pouring pepper into the vodka glass and drinking it. I don't remember much about it. I know I had to go out and get more vodka. My temperature was raging, burning, but I wasn't getting any better.

"One morning, I decided that this so-called medicine was not working so I found my way back to the medical centre. They looked at me and said, 'You have to go to the hospital.' They couldn't help me get there. They just said, 'It's two kilometres down that road.'

"I was so sick I couldn't stand up properly. I had to hold onto buildings, where there were buildings. Where there were no buildings, I had to crawl on all fours. I didn't know what I was doing. There was a Russian guard outside the hospital with a gun. I lay down on the floor like everyone else.

"The next thing I knew, I woke up in a metal-framed bed with a nurse standing over me, trying to pour boiled water into my mouth. The water was pouring down my shirt. I don't know how long I was there – it must have been weeks. It took a long time for the fever to go down, they had no medicine for it, but gradually I started to get better and they started giving me some bread with the boiled water. It wasn't much better than the bread at the labour camp, but it was food.

"Eventually, they said I could leave, but sometime when I was delirious, someone had nicked my clothes. I had nothing. So the nurses said, OK we will have to wait for someone to die. And, well, there was a military section in the hospital, and you can see who died."

Zvi raised his arm in a mock salute and the other men followed.

"Tell me, anyway," said Wolf, "what is happening here?"

Zvi shrugged. "We are waiting. We don't know anything. More and more people are arriving in Tashkent. Jewish," he swept his arm around the square, "Polish, Uzbeks, Kazakhs , Ukrainian."

A group of Polish men walked past them.

"Hey, my friend here is asking — what do you know about General Anders army? How do we get there? When do we join up?"

The Poles looked across. One, perhaps seeing Wolf's attire, responded.

"We are waiting for orders. Supposedly there are trains coming from the North with Polish soldiers."

"They are not going to have Jews joining up, anyway," said another with a sneer. "I wouldn't bother worrying your big nose about it."

Wolf stood, ready to retaliate with more than words, but his feet were unsteady.

"Don't bother with the ignorant bastards," said Zvi. "Let's find some new clothes for you."

35 THE TRAIN TO SAMARKAND

EARLY IN the morning, carts would arrive in the vegetable market from the villages outside Tashkent. It reminded Wolf of his childhood, when he would go with his uncle to Warsaw with plums or pears and butter.

They had abandoned the big market near the railway station square as their main haunt. So many people had come into the city now and were doing as they were doing — just trying to survive, sleeping on benches or under any shelter they could find, taking food where they could get it. The vegetable market was deeper into the city and less crowded. Local farmers brought their produce here — strings of onions, cabbages, beetroot and potatoes. Chickens clucked around the stalls and under the wheels of the laden carts.

Usually, if he had not been able to earn a few kopeks from odd jobs, Wolf could steal enough food from this market to survive the day. Sometimes, if there was produce left over, the farmers would leave it for them before they returned home. With Zvi and Ezra he would build a small fire beside the wall where they slept and cook the food and share it.

29 May 1942

At first light, Russian soldiers appeared on every side of the small square, closing the entrances. They moved in, ordering the men to line up behind the statue of a soldier on horseback.

"Shit! What's going on?" Zvi asked.

"No idea. I don't feel good about this."

The previous day, Zvi had befriended a man named Chremino. He wore a navy blue suit that was stained and filthy but once must have been expensive, and round his neck was a gold chain. He was sick as a dog.

"He reminds me of my father," Zvi had told Wolf and Ezra.

He had put a blanket over him in the evening and had given him some of the food he had scavenged from the market.

"Bless you," Chremino had murmured.

"It's hard enough looking after ourselves, let alone someone else," Ezra had said.

Now Zvi helped Chremino to his feet and supported him across the square to the statue.

"Can you take his other shoulder?" Zvi asked, turning to Wolf, as they were marched under guard in the direction of the railway station.

The image of the last day in Lutsk came to Wolf – the serried rows of people at the station, the screaming children, the knotted sheets of possessions, the cattle wagons in the siding, the clang as the doors slid shut. But they passed the station and moved on to the hospital. More groups, native Poles and Polish Jews, arrived from different parts of the city. A stout woman in a blue uniform addressed them outside. Her hair was tied in a bun under a white cap. She had a loud no-nonsense voice.

"You are here for a medical," she said. "You will come into the cubicles in here," she pointed to a door, "when called. Numbers one to four."

Four figures in white coats, stethoscopes hanging round their necks, filed inside. The doctors were all female.

Wolf looked across at Zvi.

"I don't know how he's going to get through this," he whispered, nodding towards Chremino.

"Three!"

Wolf had reached the front of the queue and stepped forward into cubicle three. The doctor could barely have been more than twenty-two herself. Her eyes were bright.

"Shirt off," she said.

She pressed the stethoscope to his chest.

"Deep breath in."

"Now, out slowly."

"Trousers off."

Wolf lowered his trousers. The thought of Nina came to his mind. The doctor pushed at his stomach and felt around his penis and his testicles. He could not hide his gorging erection. She looked up at him with amusement, but she was business-like.

"Clothes on ... Pass," she said loudly.

He joined the group of men declared fit. He was astonished to see Chremino stagger towards them.

"I'll never make a soldier." Chremino's voice came out in a whisper. "I expect they just want to get rid of us out of the country."

It was back to the station that they were now marched. Wolf's gut churned. Surely, they were not being passed fit just to go back to the camps. He could feel Chremino's strength ebbing against his shoulder. They were led onto a platform at the far side of the station. A Russian officer addressed them.

"This train will take you to Chardzhou. There you will join up with the main trains of the Polish army."

"Thank heavens for that," said Zvi. "I thought for a moment ..."

"So did I," said Wolf.

******

"I know I stink," Chremino said weakly. "I have had diarrhoea for two weeks. I am sorry."

Wolf took turns with Zvi to sit with him in the train, giving him water from time to time and cooling his face with a wet piece of cloth. His dark greasy hair, greying at the temples, flopped across his forehead. Wolf could not understand how this man could still be wearing the suit and the gold chain.

"How did you manage to hold on to your suit and that chain?" he asked. "In our camp, they would have been nicked a long time ago."

"Ah," said Chremino. His voice faltered as he spoke. "I was in what they called a compulsory resettlement prison in Achinsk. They did actually return the possessions we arrived with when they released us. Even my suit and my gold chain. There used to be a pocket watch attached, but I swapped it for some bread and fish and mahorka." He bent over, convulsed with coughing. Sweat poured from his brow and Wolf wiped it again.

He leant back, breathing heavily.

"What did you do before you were imprisoned?" Wolf asked.

"I was a professor of fine art in Warsaw," he said. "I was known as a Dadaist. I kept Dadaism going in Warsaw. A small circle of artists and writers would come to my house and we would talk and smoke and drink."

Wolf nodded. He had no idea what the man was talking about – his childhood and youth before the war had allowed no space for art and culture, but he understood that Chremino must have led a wealthy and refined life. He understood too that here, in this railway carriage, all that counted for nothing. They were all equal under the twin swords of health and hunger.

"That chain must be worth a fortune," whispered Zvi.

Other men, hanging back from Chremino's stench, eyed it across the carriage. By the evening, Chremino had a high fever. His eyes were closed and he did not respond.

"I think he's dying," said Zvi. "If he does, I'm going to take that chain and you can help me sell it. We'll go halves on the proceeds. We should make enough to buy some decent food."

"No, that is theft," said Wolf. "I don't want anything to do with it."

"Don't be such a prude," said Zvi. "You know very well that if we don't take it, someone else will. And it's us who have been putting up with his stink and talking to him. He wouldn't have got this far without us."

Wolf did not say anything. He knew that Zvi was right. Others would take everything from Chremino if they didn't. He dozed off, his head lolling against the back of the wagon. He woke to a blow from Zvi's knee in his thigh.

"I think he's dead," he hissed.

Wolf felt Chremino's forehead; it was still warm. Zvi began to raise the man's chin, feeling for the chain. A low moan came from him.

"No, you can't," said Wolf. "He may be on the way out, but he's still alive."

"He isn't," said Zvi. "I held my ear to his chest. He's not breathing, there is no heartbeat."

Wolf looked away. He dozed off again until he heard Zvi's voice raised above the general hubbub.

"Who nicked the gold chain? Come on, own up. Chremino said I could have it; it was me that looked after him, none of you bastards."

Chremino's body, bare and stripped, lay slumped against the seat back. One man wore the suit jacket, another the putrid trousers.

"How can we get rid of it?" said Ezra. "We'll all stink like that if we let it fester in here."

He put a blanket over the body.

"That's no good," said a Pole. "It doesn't make it stink less."

Before anyone could do anything, the Pole strode across and grabbed Chremino's ankles. He dragged the body towards the door.

"Wait, we need to bury him properly."

"You can jump out with him and bury him if you want," said the Pole. "That would be one more Jew gone."

He turned the tarnished brass door handle and to Wolf's surprise it slammed open. Holding onto the carriage with one hand, the Pole eased the body out head first. The last they saw of it were two legs crashing down onto the rails below.

No burial prayer came from the Poles in the carriage but Wolf, Zvi and Ezra bowed their heads and recited the first section of the kaddish.

.

36 CHREMINO'S CHAIN

31 May 1942

THE TRAIN slowed and pulled into Samarkand railway station. It was early morning.

"This train is going back to Tashkent," said one of the guards. "Another train will come in at 6 p.m. this evening and take us on to Chardzhou. Until then, do not leave the station."

"Come on, let's explore this place," whispered Zvi as soon as the guard had passed. "We can make some money."

Wolf looked at him.

"What do you mean? You did take it yourself?"

Zvi showed him a corner of the chain hidden in his pocket. He turned to Ezra.

"We're just going to have a look around," said Zvi. "Want to come?"

Ezra shook his head.

The guards stood smoking on the platform in front of the low white station building. It was not difficult to evade them. Outside, Wolf and Zvi found a city like none other they had seen. Towers and minarets and turquoise domes rose from an ancient wall. Many of the buildings were lined in exquisite patterns of tiles. Loaded camels stood tethered to trees, chewing, and donkeys pulled small two-wheeled carts carrying sacks of grain or vegetables. A few lorries, battered and dusty, were parked in narrow streets.

They saw a shop selling food. Sausages and bread were displayed in the window.

"We'll come back here when we've made some money," said Zvi as they approached, but, when they got closer, they saw that the sausages and bread were dummy — just painted cardboard.

A man approached from the other direction. His trousers were tucked into knee length leather boots and he wore a white fez. He looked wealthier than some of the other people they had passed. Holding the chain in one hand and gesticulating with the other, Zvi indicated that they wanted to sell it. He looked at them, the thin starved racks of their bodies, their odour and uncleanliness, and turned his back on them. Another man did the same and they began to lose heart.

"Give it to me," said Wolf.

The next man showed a little more interest. He wore a jacket that might have come from Paris or London and braces over his check shirt. He studied the chain carefully.

"These are hard times. All I have is seventy-five rubles," he said.

Zvi was on the point of accepting, but Wolf elbowed him.

"Forget it," he said, as if enjoying the man's joke.

He turned.

"One hundred," said the man.

Wolf kept walking.

"One hundred and fifty," he shouted, but Wolf knew now that they had a valuable commodity on their hands. As great a fortune as one hundred and fifty rubles sounded, he knew now that they could get more.

"We need to find the jewellery quarter," he said.

He remembered that back in Warsaw, when he worked there, the jewellers and shops that sold watches and clocks were clustered in one area. They came to an intersection of narrow streets.

"Please can you tell us where the jewellery quarter is?" they asked a man.

He looked them up and down.

"Why do you ask?"

"We have an antique gold watch chain to sell."

"Ah," said the man. "The jewellery quarter is that way, but I know someone who may be interested. He is a dentist and a collector."

He directed them to a house on a wealthy street ten minutes walk away.

"Number 21," he said.

Number 21 was shrouded in purple and yellow bougainvillea. The woman who greeted them did not seem disturbed by their appearance.

"Come in," she said and ushered them into a waiting room, smiling all the time. "I am afraid my husband is out at the moment, but he will not be long. I will see if I can get him on the telephone."

She disappeared and Wolf could hear a telephone conversation in the next room.

"…but hurry up, they're here now."

He leapt up. A window opened from the room onto a garden. There was a gate at the back. He straddled the window and climbed out, with Zvi close behind him.

"What the hell are you doing?" hissed Zvi when they got through the gate – we were close to selling it."

"I don't think so," said Wolf. "I had a really bad feeling."

They heard a shout from the direction of the house and a car drew up outside with a squeal of brakes, then men's voices. They raced down a narrow alleyway, looking for an escape route.

"What is the problem?" came a voice from a small courtyard. The woman's hair was dressed in a bun and she wore a red and white-patterned apron that burst around her ample waist.

"Some men are chasing us, they are trying to steal something from us."

Instinctively, Wolf felt that he could trust the woman.

"Please," he said breathlessly," can you tell us where to find the jewellery quarter."

She looked them up and down. Then she pointed down the alleyway and in a combination of Russian and Uzbek and hand signals, conveyed the route.

They reached a small watchmaker's shop set into a crumbling clay wall and rang the brass bell. They could hear movement inside, but it was a long time before the door was opened by a wiry, grey-haired man, stooped at the waist. His wire-rimmed glasses sat on the end of his nose and he wore a short leather apron. Inside the shop, there was little visible in the way of merchandise. On the walls were some posters of pocket watches, the paper yellowed at the edges, and in one corner, a small safe.

The man looked at them with a kindly smile.

"How can I help you?"

Wolf held up the chain.

"We want to sell this gold chain. It is a very valuable item that came with us from Poland; we managed to hold onto it in the labour camp where we were imprisoned but now we have no money and no food. We have been offered six hundred rubles for it, but I know it is worth much more. Can you better the offer. We are in a bit of a hurry, as our train is leaving soon."

Wolf had no idea where the six hundred rubles came from. The man picked up a magnifying glass and inspected the chain. He tested the gold with a liquid.

"It is gold," he said without lifting his head. "I will give you six hundred and forty rubles."

Wolf was speechless for a moment. Zvi trod on his boot, mouthing him to accept this time.

"Sir," he said, "thank you. I will accept your offer if you can provide us also with two loaves of bread and some fat." The man looked knowingly at him. He placed the chain on a small table and went out of the room.

"What the hell?" said Zvi. "We could have got our own bread and be out of here with six hundred and forty rubles by now."

"Yes, and bump into whoever was in that car."

The man returned with a bag of coarse grey cloth. Inside it were two round and crusted loaves that smelt freshly-baked, and a small piece of fat.

"I do not have much fat," he said. "But to compensate you I have also put in some sugar."

The man then went over to his safe and pulled a key from his belt. He counted out the six hundred and forty rubles carefully and handed the notes to Wolf. Wolf counted them himself, his hands shaking. He had not seen so much money since he worked for the handbag manufacturer in Warsaw in 1938.

"Thank you," he said eventually. Zvi was fidgeting impatiently beside him.

"Sir, please could we impose upon your hospitality and eat some of the bread here – we have not eaten for twenty-four hours."

The man looked at them again, clearly trying to weigh them up. Then he leaned his head towards the brown inner door and ushered them into the room behind the shop. It was small, but warm and clean. Two wooden chairs sat against a rough-hewn, blue-painted table. A kettle sat on the hob and he made three cups of sweet tea as Wolf and Zvi tore off chunks of bread, spread the fat over it and bit into it with hungry mouthfuls.

The door-bell rang.

Calmly, the man pulled himself upright against the table and went into the shop, closing the inner door behind him.

Wolf tensed, his jaw poised in mid-mouthful. He looked at Zvi – there was no other way out of this room.

They could hear voices from the shop. For several minutes, the voices went on; one of them began to shout, but the watchmaker did not react. Wolf could hear that, in his slow deliberate way, he was refusing to be cowed by these people, whoever they were.

Eventually, the outer door banged shut and the man came back in.

"Tell me one thing," he said, "and please give me an honest answer. Is this chain stolen?"

"It is and it isn't," said Zvi. "It hung round the neck of one of our colleagues from the labour camp. We had been looking after him for the last two weeks - he was very sick with dysentery. Other ex-prisoners kept eyeing the chain. Our colleague eventually died on the train last night and yes, I took it from round his neck. If I hadn't, someone else would have done so just as they took his suit – his jacket and his trousers were gone barely before he had taken his last breath."

"I understand," said the man. "That is not really stealing to my mind – it does not belong to anyone else now. Those two men who were at the door, they told me you have escaped arrest and are wanted for theft."

"I think they realised we had something valuable and were trying to steal it themselves," said Wolf. "I had a bad feeling when we were up the road at what was supposed to be the dentist's house."

"What number?" asked the man.

"21."

"Ah, and did you meet the woman?"

"Yes."

"You were lucky then. She is a nasty piece of work. She is the dentist's helper and an informer. A lot of innocent people have gone missing as a result of her."

"Time to go," said Zvi.

The watchmaker picked up the chain, spreading it over his palms and admiring it for a moment, then placed it in the safe. He pulled a large key from his pocket.

"I will guide you back to the railway station via a safe route. Those two men will not be in a good frame of mind – you do not want them finding you out in the streets."

With that he led them through the alleys and market stalls of the old city, under arches and through mosques and ancient buildings, stopping every now and then to scan the area and listen for the car.

"Where are you going?" the watchmaker asked before he left them.

"We don't know. Only that we are joining the Polish army to fight Hitler."

"Well, safe journey, wherever it takes you."

"Thank you, sir. It has been an honour meeting you."

It was not difficult, once back at the station, to merge in with the other ex-prisoners. Most of them were outside on the platform, milling about. Secretively, in one corner, Wolf began to count out Zvi's three hundred and twenty ruble share.

There was a shout at the far end of the station building. The dentist woman was with two men in shabby black uniforms. Wolf half-turned his back but she was pointing to an altogether different man.

"How dare you accuse me?" they heard the man say. "I have been here all day. You ask these people."

Other men nodded, cursing the newcomers. The woman looked around helplessly.

"They all look the same," she wailed. "Scarecrows, with rags hanging off them. Could be that one, or those two, or those two…"

"You stupid cow," said one of the men, "taking us on a wild goose chase. Get away. Don't call us again unless you have real information. We're not paying you for running us around in circles."

And with that, they drove off, leaving the woman stranded.

"Where the hell have you been?" said Ezra. "I was getting worried."

They took him aside and told him and shared some of their rubles with him.

******

The train came to a halt in Chardzhou. They could see another train on a different line, packed with people. Nothing happened and there was no information, no food and no water. It was very stuffy inside the carriage and the stench of Chremino lingered. Wolf opened the same door from which the dead man had been thrown.

On the platform, a man wearing the uniform of a Polish general moved back and forth to an office where senior NKVD men appeared to be entrenched.

"What's going on?" asked Zvi of a Russian soldier, leaning out of the window. He offered him a cigarette and the power of the tobacco worked again. The Russian rolled his cigarette thoughtfully and looked around to check that no one could hear him.

"That is the main Polish army train," he said, pointing. "It is going to Krasnovodsk and you are supposed to be going with it, but, as far as I can understand it, the Polish general does not want Jews in the army. They don't want to let you or any other Jews on this train board that train. But our people have food for everyone – they will not release the food until you are all allowed on the train. That's what all the fuss is about."

Hours passed.

As Wolf walked back from the toilet on the platform, he passed the Polish general. He seemed to be addressing a radio man, conveying a message.

"The instructions that were given by General Anders himself were that Jews should not be allowed to join up in any of the recruitment centres, wherever they were. That is unless they were already in the army before the war, or were doctors or highly qualified. The Jews that came to this same place, Chardzhou, by boat up the Amu Darya river – they're not being allowed in."

The general listened for a while to a message that was being sent in response.

"The problem is that the food and all the supplies are on this second train. They won't release the supplies unless we take the Jews too."

He listened again.

"Well, they'll have to fend for themselves then," he said.

Wolf went up to the man.

"General, sir, I am Jewish. I am a Polish citizen. I can assure you that we want to fight the Nazi bastards just like you do."

The general looked at him. Unprotected by other soldiers, he did not seem to know what to say.

"I see," he said eventually.

"Was that the general you were speaking to on the platform?" asked Zvi, when Wolf got back to the carriage.

"Yes. I told him we were Jews and we were ready to fight."

"Good on you."

It was some hours before there was a lurch. The train moved a short distance forwards, then shunted to and fro, couplings banging and shuddering.

An officer came over from the main train. "You can move to this train now, Jews in the rear carriage."

"My name is Dowgelo, Second-Lieutenant Dowgelo," he said once they were on board. "If I had my choice, I wouldn't have any of you Jewish bastards on the train or in the army. But you scheming rats have worked it so that none of the real soldiers can get any food without you here. So I'm going to keep you under my thumb."

******

It was eight days before they reached Kraznovodsk. A vista of sea opened out in front of the train as they passed through a gap in the hills behind the town. The station building was long, low and white, discoloured by the weather and neglect. In the corners of the building were little towers. The platform thronged with people, but the train moved slowly on through to the port itself. Ships of all shapes and sizes, large and small, some with masts, some with funnels, crowded the water, anchored just offshore or tied to huge bollards at the dockside, coils of rope like twisted serpents tethering them. Some were fishing boats, some freighters, some oil tankers, some coasters and a few passenger vessels.

Russian guards led them off the train to a huge warehouse that lay between the railway line and the sea. It was a relief to be free of the taunts of Dowgelo and his mates for a while. The smell of hot food — cabbage and stew — greeted them as they entered. The building was the Russian Army's canteen. Wolf took the bowl of stew that was handed to him and bread from a basket on the table and fell on it. He could not remember the last time that he had eaten such a meal.

37 THE AGAMALI OGLI

12 June 1942

HE WOULD have eaten another bowlful of the stew but they were directed to the back of the canteen. There was an announcement over the loudspeakers.

"Attention, attention — boarding is about to begin. Any possessions that cannot be accounted for will be confiscated and treated as a criminal offence unless they are given up to the officials at the border…"

A murmur went through the lines of men. People were looking around.

"Does that mean they're going to take any money we have?"

It did not smell right to Wolf. Part of him said, give up the money – you are so close; and another part said – you have this money, you deserve this money, take it with you, you must be able to use it.

Zvi nudged him, a worried look on his face.

"Follow me," said Wolf, leading him towards the toilets, Ezra behind.

They crammed into one cubicle and Wolf began to take off his boots. He pulled out the inner sole, counted out two hundred rubles and put them inside. Zvi did the same.

"I'm not going to risk it," said Ezra. "I'll hand it in or you take the money back."

"Come on, Ez, I'll look after it for you," said Zvi and took off his boots again.

They waited their turn. Wolf watched as men went through the line one by one. Some gave up some money, some had nothing. Some were told to step aside and were searched. Wolf's heart thumped as he was called forward. He pulled the remaining rubles he had, sixteen, from the inside pocket of his jacket, making a show of getting every last one.

"That had better be all," said the official. He was Polish, confirming Wolf's suspicions.

Zvi joined him outside. They looked behind; Ezra had been pulled aside. He stood naked as one guard searched his anus and another rifled through his clothes and shoes.

"Phew, I think we must be crazy," said Zvi.

"Yes, but that's some bloody racket going on between those Poles and the Russian guards. Why should they have our money?"

On the dockside, ships were moored side by side, horns blaring; crew bustled about working the ropes. Long lines of people waited patiently to board – thousands of them. It was not just men; there were women and children too. Some had suitcases and boxes. How on earth, Wolf wondered, had they managed to hold onto these possessions? Some were there, it seemed, simply to escape the country, some to fight. A girl of barely sixteen wore the badge of the Polish armed forces – a white eagle, its head turned to the right, with gold beak and talons over a red shield – roughly, but proudly, sewn onto her coat.

They were led towards a large ship. The name Agamali Ogli was painted in white on the bow. The black funnel carried a red band at the top; unusually, it was positioned towards the back of the boat. In the centre was a white structure that must, Wolf thought, house the better cabins as well as the bridge. The sides of the boat dipped in the centre from bow and stern, leaving a deck area protected only by metal rails, the sea just feet below. From a distance, the Agamali Ogli looked impressive, but when he got closer, he could see pockmarks of rust burgeoning from the metal hull like suppurating boils.

The wooden gang plank creaked under the weight of the continuous flow of men that poured over it. Onboard, they looked around for somewhere to base themselves. Dowgelo ordered them towards the stern, but it was already thick with bodies.

"This way," said Zvi, ignoring the Pole. He had spotted a space below the lifeboats in the centre section. They moved together, forging their way through the throng. Dowgelo disappeared inside.

"Thank heavens for that. Hopefully that's the last we see of him for the journey."

"Where are we going?" Wolf called to a sailor.

"Don't know," the man said, shrugging his shoulders.

Wolf looked up towards the prow and then to the stern. The entire boat was crammed with people. It seemed to creak with the weight of them and the responsibility. It slumped low in the water and the tugs that pulled it out into the open channel laboured with the effort. Zvi waved to Krasnovodsk as it receded and the Agamali Ogli turned onto its course. Wolf judged they were heading south. That meant to him nothing in terms of geography but hinted at a warmer place.

A bitter sea wind bit through their skimpy clothing. As the boat began to roll and buck in the angry swell, Zvi turned ashen. He rushed to the rail, vomiting into the water.

"I don't know if I can make this," he said.

"Of course you can, Zvi. It's just the waves, you're not ill. You'll be fine once we get to where we're going."

"Wherever that is."

The seas grew rougher still. The ship poised for sickening moments on the crests of the swell before hurtling down into the troughs. The deck became a broiling mass of vomit and excrement. The stench was so strong that even the wind could not move it – it was as if the boards themselves were imbued with it. Men were hunched, shivering and grey, clinging to railings or any piece of structure they could find.

No one came with food or water, no one checked on the sick. Water washed over the lower section of deck and Wolf watched in horror as a man who had lain down near them, clearly sick, was suddenly dislodged by a more violent wave. Before anyone could reach an arm out to catch him, he was sliding down the slippery deck. As his legs tipped over the edge, he grabbed the last piece of railing, his body flailing against the side of the ship. Wolf fought his way across. Wedging himself against the railing and holding on with one hand himself, he reached for the man's other hand.

"Swing towards me," he shouted through the spray. The man seemed to summon one last effort and swung his body towards Wolf. Perhaps his arm was weakened by the dysentery and the months of starvation for, as the one arm moved towards Wolf, the other let go and he disappeared into the waves.

"Lifebelt, quick!" but Wolf could not be heard amongst the hubbub of men and sea. The ship moved on and the man's head disappeared from view.

******

Still the storm built. Waves lashed the lower deck, spray pouring down on them. Above them, hung between stanchions, were two lifeboats. A metal ladder led to them, its thin rungs leaning left and then right with the roll and pitch of the boat. Ezra looked across at Wolf.

"We'll be safer up there," he shouted.

Wolf nodded.

"I'll go ahead of Zvi, you go behind."

They began to scramble up, fighting to hold on and somehow ease Zvi upwards. It was a precarious hold at the top — a final leap of faith into the lifeboat. Ezra, already in, held his arms out but Zvi, retching and looking down at the swirling waters, froze.

"Go on, you can do it," shouted Wolf. "There are other guys behind us."

Zvi jumped. He landed, arms and legs flailing, on top of Ezra and crawled towards the bow. Wolf followed and more men piled in behind them. How these lifeboats could rescue even a tiny proportion of all the people on the Agamali Ogli if it went down, Wolf could not imagine. He was shivering from the soaking the waves had given them as they battered the ship.

"See if there is anything to put over us," he shouted. "Feel in the front and the back."

"Here!" shouted Ezra.

He was pulling something out, yellow and shiny. A tarpaulin.

"Thank God!"

They dragged it over themselves. The sides of the boat at least prevented anyone rolling overboard and the tarpaulin provided some protection from the water. Wolf thought of the barge that had taken them part of the way to Siberia. That journey had been a luxury compared to this. He could see ashen, resigned faces around him, people close to the end of their tether. His teeth chattering, he summoned a renewed determination. Come on, Wolf, he told himself. You are on your way to freedom, away from Russian soil. You are joining the Polish army. This boat journey cannot last long. You have lived without food before. Just hold on.

Suddenly Zvi pushed the tarpaulin away and moved onto his knees.

"I have to shit," he said, lowering his trousers.

"You can't just shit in here, man."

He lifted himself weakly, hanging on to the sides of the boat, leaning his buttocks out over the angry water. The ship pitched and for one frozen moment, his torso swayed outwards, his arms flailing. Ezra grabbed him from the right, another man from the left.

Wedging themselves against the side of the boat, each holding an arm securely, they allowed Zvi to reposition himself. A liquid, farting eruption mixed with the sound of the storm. The wind caught the stream of urine and faeces and swept it back through the spray, showering the tarpaulin. At the stern, men spat and wiped their faces clear.

Zvi fell forwards. There was no way of cleaning himself. He pulled his trousers up, tightened the belt and curled up under the tarpaulin.

It came to Wolf's turn to defecate. Supported on either side, he looked between his legs at the foaming sea below. For a moment he felt the water calling him, as if calling him home: you will be warm here, comfortable, there will be no more pain, no more hunger.

He felt a tug on his arm.

"Get a bloody move on," said Ezra.

As he landed back on the boards, Wolf felt a kind of gratitude to these men who had held his life in their hands. They shared a bond built on the foundation of the long months in the camps. They were his travelling companions on what felt like the final leg of the journey, protecting each other, their bodies cramped together under the tarpaulin, salt water swilling about in the bottom of the lifeboat.

Wolf sank into a kind of purgatory world, neither awake nor asleep, neither alive nor dead.

For hours he lay like this, a murmur or a groan sometimes punctuating his torpor if they could be heard against the wind.

******

It was in the early morning light of the third day that Wolf poked his head above the tarpaulin, sensing that the seas had quietened. He saw the misty form of a shoreline ahead of them and a few lights shimmering.

"We're close to land," he shouted into the tarpaulin and suddenly, as the men stirred and grumbled and pulled themselves upright, the horror of the journey receded. They looked up into a clear blue sky and the air itself carried a different tang.

38 PAHLEVI

THE AGAMALI OGLI cast anchor some way short of the port of Pahlevi in Iran, joining other larger ships also moored offshore. Smaller boats swarmed across the sea, ferrying the thousands of occupants to land.

Wolf could not believe that he was finally out of Russia. Until he got off the boat, he was terrified that it would turn around and take him back.

He could barely stand up when his feet touched dry land. He could feel the rolling and pitching of the boat still swaying in his legs. It was hard to keep his balance. Some men subsided onto the hot fine sand, kneeling and kissing the ground or scooping up great handfuls of it and spraying it over themselves. The scent of spices and charcoal mingled in the air with the salt of the sea and the docks. Lines of men stretched out across the long beaches. Beyond them lay a sea of tents.

Khaki was dominant at the port-side, the neat and efficient colour of British battle dress a stark contrast to the limp rags that covered the new arrivals. Officers barked orders and soldiers directed the motley, dazed crew of men in broken Polish.

Dowgelo had reappeared. He did not look as if he had got away lightly with the rough crossing of the Caspian Sea himself.

"ID?" asked a British officer.

"Army – but Jews," said Dowgelo.

The British officer ignored the last two words and directed him to the Polish Army Reception area. It was a warehouse just behind the beach. As soon as they were under Polish command again, Dowgelo spoke to a more senior officer.

"This is the bunch of Jews that we had to bring with us on the train to release supplies for everyone. The Russians insisted on it."

They were ordered into a cordoned-off section of the warehouse and told to wait. A Polish soldier guarded them. Stinking still of the vomit and excrement of the boat, starving and thirsty, Wolf had not expected this. He was angry. He had seen, as they came in, the tidy encampments of the British army and, beyond it, another where the Polish flag was flying.

He turned to Zvi and the others.

"I don't know what the hell is going on but we need to get out of here. They have no right to detain us here. We're not prisoners now, we're joining the army."

Dowgelo and the guard were talking, out of earshot. Seizing their opportunity, Wolf, Zvi and Ezra, along with seven other Jewish men, slipped out through a small door at the back of the warehouse and made straight for the main town.

As they reached the centre, they could see a line of people, the canvas of a tent and a pillared building beyond. Smoke curled upwards from the vicinity of the tent and a stench of burnt wool and hair filled the air. Pahlevi folk stopped in their tracks and stared at the straggle of Jewish men. The Iranian faces did not carry the pain and fear that was written on Russian people's faces; though they might have been poor, there was a calmness and friendliness about them.

With sign language, they explained that the building in front of them was the public baths. The British had organised disinfection and bathing of the newly arrived. Wolf and the rest of the group joined the queue and, as they got closer to the tent, Dowgelo suddenly appeared. He approached the British officer nearby and pointed to them.

"These men have escaped from Polish army detention," he spat. "They are Jewish filth. They should not be here. They do not deserve disinfection or a bath."

The British officer had no idea what he was talking about.

"Jews," Dowgelo said again, holding his nose.

This time the British officer did understand him. He was a big man. Muscles bulged from his khaki top and shorts. He grabbed Dowgelo by the neck.

"What the hell are you talking about?" he shouted, centimetres from his face, then kicked him hard in the backside. "Get out of here."

Dowgelo picked himself up from the ground and slunk away, defeated.

Outside the tent were large cases marked 'A.L. 63 Anti-Louse Powder.' A soldier was taking cans from the cases and tipping the powder into a large container. The container was attached to a stationary engine that sat on the flat bed of an army truck and powered a pump. A hose led from the container under the side of the tent. On the truck door was stencilled in white: '25th Field Hygiene Section – Royal Army Medical Corps.'

The British officer beckoned the men forward. On entering the tent, they were told to remove any possessions and put them in a bag, and to remove their clothes. The clothes were taken immediately to the incinerator outside. Wolf removed the rubles from his pocket. For a second he searched for his stone from the

Vistula river until he remembered that he had lost it, along with the clothes he had then, at the hospital in Tashkent. He had nothing else. He was told to sit on a chair. He felt a razor cutting through his hair.

"Stand," the soldier said in poor Polish.

"Close your eyes."

He could feel the powder being sprayed on him. It smelt strongly of disinfectant.

"Rub it all over yourself, over your scalp, into your pubic hair and under your armpits," the soldier said.

They were ushered through the baths like sheep through a sheep wash, but there were large bars of soap and the water was warm. A pile of towels stood at the end and beyond it separate piles of clothing. A soldier selected a battle-dress, a shirt, a blanket, an overcoat, a khaki webbing belt, a cap and a pair of plimsolls and handed them to Wolf. He could not believe it. Real clothes! Clean!

Night was beginning to fall and the temperature was cooling. Zvi joined him.

"There were two Polish soldiers outside the baths. I overheard them talking. They are expecting a No. 32 Company at the main camp tonight. I suppose they are on another boat."

The Jewish men conferred together.

"Worth a try," they agreed.

They had worked out where the main entrance to the Polish camp was and, as darkness fell, approached it.

"32 Company, sir," said Ezra, who had been selected as the most officer-like of the group. The sentry peered at a list with a torch.

"Ah yes, got you," he said. "You made it early."

A soldier led them through a network of tents, all marked with letters of the alphabet. He stopped at a catering tent and waited while they were each given three slices of corned beef and some round hard biscuits. Then he led them to a large tent and pointed to an area laid out with mats on the sand.

Wolf chuckled to himself as he ate. Bath, clothes, food and a bed!

He was awoken by shouts and a torch being shone across them.

"Get up! Get out! Who are you? "

The real No. 32 Company had arrived.

******

Thrown out of the Polish camp, they made their way back towards the centre of Pahlevi in the early morning light. The road took them through a wealthy area with modern villas surrounded by bougainvillea, hibiscus and sweet-smelling roses.

In the distance, they saw dust rising as two cars approached. The cars slowed and then stopped at the sight of this group of men, British battle-dress hanging from their skeletal frames. An officer got out.

"What the hell is going on here?" he asked. "Who are you? What is your unit?"

Wolf had picked up a few words of English.

"Polish army," he said. "Jewish."

Then he made a shoving movement with his hands. The officer was Jewish himself. He spoke very little Yiddish, but, between Wolf's English and his Yiddish, they established what had happened. The officer instructed them to go back to the camp. He had already demanded the presence of the Polish C.O. by the time they got there.

"You will enlist these men officially into the Polish army," he ordered.

******

15 June 1942

A long queue of men waited on the sandy path that led to the Recruiting Station No.3 (Teheran Command) tent. The canvas flapped slightly in the warm lazy breeze. A

Polish soldier sat on a wooden chair behind a folding table. He looked disgruntled, but a British soldier beside him waved Wolf in.

"Come on in."

From Wolf's best guess, he was a sergeant. From a cardboard box, he pulled a khaki booklet. Glued to the front was a sheet in English entitled: 'POLISH ARMY – Soldier's Name and Description.'

"Name?"

"Wolf, Albert."

"Date of birth?"

"June 1920," translated the Polish soldier in heavily accented English.

'15 June 1920,' the sergeant wrote.

"Happy Birthday, mate."

Wolf was twenty-two. The Polish soldier took over the questions.

"Parish, county, region?"

"Bledow, Grojec, Warsaw."

"Occupation at enlistment?"

"Metal locksmith apprentice."

Wolf had no idea why he said it. Perhaps it was a subconscious response to being there enlisting in the Polish army, to having a clean uniform on his body, to having food in his stomach, to all that he had escaped from – the bombing, the hunger, the illness, Siberia, Russia, the never-ending journey.

'Locksmith,' wrote down the British soldier.

Wolf was directed to a set of scales. The needle stopped vacillating at 160 lbs – 11 ½ stone. Another British soldier held a tall post against his body.

"Stand up straight, mate."

He brought a horizontal marker down the post and called off his height.

"5ft 10, sir."

Wolf sat down. The sergeant looked into his eyes.

"Eyes – brown. Hair - black. Distinctive Marks and Minor Defects …"

The soldier looked him over.

'None,' he wrote, then consulted the page again.

"You are Soldier number 25403," he said, adding the Letters 'AP' after the pre-printed military number.

He handed the record book to the Pole and folded his hands. It took another twenty minutes for Wolf to answer all the remaining questions in the Polish Army record book that lay beneath the outer sheet. His parents' names, his mother's maiden name. Under 'Comments', the Polish recruiting officer wrote: '04 – 05.42 – Transport from USSR to OX WPSW.'

He opened a tin revealing an ink imbued sponge and pointed to a square on the page. Wolf wetted his index finger and placed his mark as directed. The man flicked the pages back to the first page of the book.

"Sign here," he said, the look of distaste still lingering on his face, as if he was touching something unclean.

Wolf signed, the bold flourish of the W ebbing to a wavy line. The man now picked up a stamp, plunged it into the ink and thumped it down onto the page.

'3 POL F ALLY RECRUITING STATION' read the stamp.

"Dismissed."

Wolf felt an immense sense of pride. He was ready, when he left the tent, to lay down his life for Poland.

39 IN THE ARMY

THE POT-HOLES, ankle deep mud and dirt of Russian streets was replaced in Pahlevi by tarmac roads and modern buildings. The shops were nothing like the bare-shelved shops in Russia and Uzbekistan. Freshly baked flat breads and long breads stood on the counters. Great piles of fruit – pomegranates, figs, melons, peaches and grapes – overflowed from wicker baskets. Dates and walnuts were heaped on barrows with halva and sweet biscuits.

A Jewish doctor came to talk to the newly enlisted soldiers.

"All the food that is here is very tempting, no doubt," he said. "But do not eat too much in one go. Remember, your bodies have been starved for a long time and have adjusted to this privation. And eat slowly. If you don't, your body may revolt and you could have all kinds of serious problems."

It was good advice. The temptation for Wolf to gorge himself was ever-present, animal hunger driving him to eat like a dog, as if every new meal was the last meal that he was ever going to be served; some men, unable to restrain themselves, swelled up like balloons.

Vodka was brought to the camp each evening, a measure per person. It was a difficult time, a time when Polish soldiers, their tongues loosened by the alcohol, would kick off with their snide remarks.

"What are you doing in the army, you group of long-noses?"

Wolf found a way of toning it down. A Polish soldier whose bed was not far down the row from his own was not eating his dates.

"I tell you what," said Wolf, ignoring the taunts. "I'll swap you my vodka for your dates."

It was a good deal all round and other men adopted it. For a while, the promise of the next day's extra vodka secured the peace.

******

A lull followed in Wolf's life as military routine was established in the new recruits. In the mornings, drill — left turn, right turn, left wheel, right wheel, about turn. The Polish two-fingered salute was practised to perfection with the stiff and attentive turn of the head, more in the German manner than the British. The Polish army took great pride in ceremonials, and so formation marching and even singing were practised daily.

The N.C.O.'s were brutal to their fellow Poles of lower rank, but they reserved their real hatred for the Jewish soldiers. Out of sight of any British officers, Dowgelo would come up to them, so close they had to wipe his spittle from their faces.

"Do you not know your left from your right, shitface?"

"Stand up straight, Jesus-killer," he screamed at Wolf one morning. Wolf's every instinct told him to punch the man but he held back. He pictured the guards at the camp in Siberia. After those men, this abuse was tame. He looked Dowgelo in the eye until he ran out of his anger.

In the afternoons it became part of the routine to go to the bath-house. Soap and water were plentiful and they could wash, or rather scrub, the unclean stench and filth of the months of incarceration out of their bodies.

******

It was, still, a raggedy troop of men that was inspected on the beach by General Kwasniewski after two weeks of drill. Men who had been starved or sick for months – how could they be expected to stand ramrod straight to attention or to march smartly, their bodies still weak and acclimatising to food? The general looked quizzically at this band of soldiers, their uniforms baggy, hanging off their bodies, trousers so long they hung over their boots or so short they did not reach them. He stepped onto a dais and someone handed him a megaphone.

"Soldiers," he said. "You have escaped the God-forsaken country that is Russia. Soon you will depart Iran too. You will know that Germany started this war, invading our country from the West; you may also know that Russia joined in and invaded from the East. You will go now, by different routes, to England or America to receive new training. When you reach England or America, tell them everything. Tell them how you were treated for the last two years — about the starvation, about the labour camps, the prisons.

"You know what the Russian government is like, but you have already defeated it. You have experienced the worst that they could throw at you and you survived. Through the vagaries of war, you will be fighting, when you reach your new units, not only on the side of the British and the Americans but also on the same side as the Russians. You will be doing this for one very good reason – to defeat our common Germany enemy and return, eventually, to a free Poland. Therefore, I am not saying goodbye to you, only farewell. Long live Poland!"

The opening notes of the jaunty tune of the Polish national anthem struck up from a piano that had been brought out onto the beach. The general and other senior officers on the dais stood to attention. As they began to sing, the massed soldiers joined in:

Poland has not yet perished
So long as we still live
What the foreign force has taken from us
We shall with sabre retrieve.

A great wave of patriotic sound, the words no longer audible, rose to a crescendo and swept across the Persian sands.

Rank was not something that meant much to Wolf. To him, after Siberia, men were defined by their words and actions, not by their insignia or title, but this speech filled him with hope. One day soon he would get back to Bledow.

******

It was as he was leaving the beach after this gathering that Wolf saw a familiar face. The man wore the uniform of a Kapitan in the Polish Air Force and walked with the air and purpose of someone in authority.

"Szymon!" Wolf called out. "How did you get here?"

Tomczyk came over, ignoring Dowgelo's frown, and the two men embraced.

"I never thought I'd see you again, Wolf. How did *you* get here, more to the point?"

"It was a long journey. I don't really know – I just followed my nose." Wolf tapped his nose and both of them laughed.

"You are lucky. Most of the other Jews who stayed with my group at Kotlas didn't get into the army. The recruitment people wouldn't take them, though I tried to persuade them."

Tomczyk looked across at the men with Wolf. He waved to Zvi and Ezra.

"Where are you going now?" he asked. "Do you know?"

"No idea. Someone said Palestine but it might be just rumour."

Tomczyk walked over to Dowgelo and spoke to him.

"I must leave now, Wolf, but I will see you there."

He took his hand warmly. Dowgelo was scowling as he walked away.

"I don't know what a decent Polish officer wants with you people," he muttered.

"I saved his life in the camp," said Wolf. "And he saved mine."

40 FAMILY

2 July 1942

THE BUS had bounced and jolted along the dry road across Jordan for hours. As it rounded a bend, Wolf could see the other buses and lorries following — a great convoy of Poles throwing up a dust cloud behind them. They had left Amman behind the previous day. It seemed weeks since they had passed through Baghdad and before that had left Pahlevi.

At a checkpoint in the desert the bus came to a halt. Soldiers in the khaki shorts of the British army held their hands out for the driver's documents and those of the soldiers inside. They took them into the tent that bordered the road.

"Look," cried Zvi. "See the writing on the sign over there. Half of it's in Hebrew. This must be the border into Palestine."

The Jewish soldiers craned their necks to see. Palestine was a name that conjured up dreams. It was a name that was spoken of with reverence at home in Bledow, but as if somewhere not quite real.

Our land, the land of our fathers, remembered Wolf. That was how Yocheved and Yitzhak, his aunt and uncle, had described it. They had left Poland in 1936 and gone there. They had joined the people striving to make it a reality – a true home for Jewish people. Wolf felt a kind of reverence for the concept of it, and now he was here it was as if he had stepped into a mirage. Unexpected emotions passed through him.

Others, too, clearly felt the pull of this land.

"We could join the Haganah or the Irgun," said Ezra. "Be done with these bad-mouthed Poles. I heard that Poland has always supplied weapons and training to those groups. It has always supported the creation of a Jewish state in Palestine, so why don't we join it?"

There were murmurs of agreement.

"You'd be fighting Arabs instead of Germans," said Zvi. "You want to live in this?" He waved his arms towards the desert outside the bus window, "or back at home in Poland?"

There was silence for a while, everyone lost in their thoughts and hopes. Wolf studied the land outside and the people he could see. They had left Dowgelo in Pahlevi; their new platoon sergeant was Wilek. He stepped out onto the sandy road and joined in with a discussion between other Polish soldiers and the British. There was a heightened air of watchfulness about him when he returned.

At a nearby railway station, everyone was ordered to disembark from the buses with their kit bags.

"Come on, Wolf, what are you waiting for?" said Ezra as he lined up to get off.

Sergeant Wilek did not move. He waited until Wolf and other stragglers were off the bus before getting off himself.

"What's got into you, Wilek?" asked Wolf as he watched him eyeing the men up and down.

"You'll find out."

On the platform, vendors were calling out 'Eggs a' bread, eggs a' bread.' Wolf handed over some coins and took the two hard-boiled eggs and piece of dry bread that were on offer, then boarded the train with the men from the other buses and lorries.

It did not take long for a rumour to run through the carriage. Two Jewish soldiers had slipped away at the border.

"You see," said a Pole, "you Jews cannot be trusted. You're unreliable. How can we fight with people like that on our side?"

He looked at Sergeant Wilek.

"Sergeant, please let them go, we're better off without them."

Wolf glanced at Ezra. It was no doubt true that the pull to leave the army here in Palestine was magnetic. He himself did not know which way to turn.

******

The camp at Rehovot was run with British precision. Jeeps raced everywhere. Discipline was tighter here and in the Polish section even more so when it was learned that five more soldiers had left to join the Zionist movement.

Wilek was fanatical. Blankets had to be folded to perfection on the thin army mattresses, and uniforms had to be spotless – free of the smallest grain of dust or sand.

As polite and deferential as he was able to be, Wolf went to the entrance of the Captain's tent.

"How can I help?" said the orderly scornfully.

"I've come to request a pass," said Wolf.

The man sighed, but ushered him in to the inner section. Wolf saluted the Captain in a movement which he felt he had now mastered.

"Sir, I have an aunt who lives near Haifa. I would like to ask your permission to visit her."

"I cannot do that. I do not have the authority to allow that. And, you know, a lot of Jewish soldiers have been leaving."

"But sir, she is the only member of our family that I know is alive. She is my mother's sister. She will be heartbroken if she finds that I have been in Palestine and not visited her. There is word that we may soon move on from here."

"I see," said the Captain, brushing his hands through his wavy black hair. He thought for a moment, then picked up a notepad with carbonised duplicate sheets.

'POLISH ARMY Second Corps — LEAVE PASS' was written at the top.

"This is very irregular," he said, "It is not entirely official, but it may get you somewhere. How long do you expect to be away?"

"Three days, sir."

The officer completed the chit: 24.7.42 – 27.7.42, and handed it to him.

"Wait," he said. He went through a flap at the back of the tent and came back with a pair of desert boots.

"Take these. See if they fit — you'll need them."

******

24 July 1942

With Ezra and some of the other men, Wolf walked out onto the road. They thumbed down an obliging British army truck that was heading into Tel Aviv, only twelve miles away. Wolf did not have a plan. His money had nearly run out and the Polish authorities were not paying them. A synagogue, he thought, was the best bet.

"Can you tell me where the main synagogue is, please," he said to the driver as he dropped them off at the bus station.

"There's a big one over there," said the man pointing. "Allenby Street."

Wolf nodded. "Thank you."

"Good luck, mate."

He turned to his colleagues.

"I'll see you back at the camp in three days," said Wolf.

"Not me," said Ezra. "I talked to some people here a couple of nights ago. They're meeting me at the railway station. I'm joining a different fight."

Wolf sighed. "Maybe you're right," he said, "maybe I'll join you sooner or later."

He headed towards Allenby Street.

The Great Synagogue was a modern building, with a central dome rising above the two tiers of the exterior. Narrow arched windows looked out from the walls and balconies and fifteen steep steps swept up to the great doors. Trees had been planted in the wide plaza around it. Inside, the bright Palestinian light poured down from the dome into the tall space and an air of calm enveloped the place.

It was Friday and Wolf waited until the Ma'ariv service began at sundown. It was, for a few moments, as if none of the pain of the last three years had touched him and he was sitting in the synagogue in Bledow.

"Bless ye the Lord who is to be blessed," said the Reader, opening the service.

"Blessed is the Lord who is to be blessed for ever and ever," came the response.

After the Shema prayer, the Reader led the congregation in reciting the Kaddish. Wolf's mind went back to all the men over whose bodies he had recited this prayer, picturing the shallow graves in the frozen earth of Siberia. He was reminded, too, of the lines that he had never been able to remember.

At the Kiddush at the end of the service, it was no doubt obvious to other members of the congregation that Wolf was on his own; he cut a strange figure in his British army fatigues. Some people nodded to him in greeting, then a man approached. He was tall, with round spectacles and a kind face. He carried a tallit and wore a delicately embroidered kippah.

"Can I offer you food tonight?" asked the man in Yiddish.

"That would be very kind."

"Then please follow me and, when we get to the house, you can meet my wife and children."

The Shabbat candles were already lit in the house and, as the wife busied herself with the Friday evening feast, the man poured Wolf a glass of wine. Two children, of perhaps ten and twelve, came downstairs for the meal. The whole family listened, rapt, as Wolf told his story until his eyelids drooped.

"Thank you very much for your kindness," he said.

The man led him to a small ante-room where a mattress lay on the floor.

"Tomorrow, we will get you on your way."

******

Though it was the Shabbat, the man pressed some Palestine pounds into Wolf's hand as he left him at Jaffa bus station.

"Leich l'shalom," he said. "Go towards peace."

The bus to Haifa was an ancient yellow contraption, encrusted with dust, a dirty white showing through the colour in places. Inside, there were more Arabs than Jews, the Arabs instantly recognizable from their keffiyehs. Though Wolf knew of the occasional fighting between Irgun and the Arabs, as well as the British, he did not feel threatened. It all seemed far away. The bus passengers were, perhaps, anyway, silenced by his military uniform.

As the engine coughed and strained over the uneven road North up the Eastern Mediterranean, Wolf took in the landscape outside. From time to time, he'd see a kibbutz, a patch of green with citrus trees, or a group of Bedouins in the sand dunes, tending to their goats. As they drew closer to Haifa, orange groves dotted the landscape.

He drew in his breath when he saw the mountain range to his right.

"Mount Carmel", somebody said in the seat behind him.

Haifa's bus station was bustling with people and suitcases.

"Kfar Ata that way," pointed a man, and it was not long before Wolf was on a second bus. The journey was short and soon he had arrived on a palm-lined street.

"Can you tell me where I would find a family named Betzeig?"

The house was little more than a wooden shack. A shaded balcony stood at one end. Purple irises lined the path to the door. Wolf knocked.

A young girl opened it. Her eyes widened to see a soldier standing there. She was coloured by the sun to a rich tan and her hair was tied behind her head. She wore a pale blue dress and her feet were bare.

"Can I help you?" she eventually stuttered.

"Judith!" he said, recognizing her. "Don't worry. It's me, Wolf, your cousin from Poland. Your Aunt Chana's son."

The girl looked at him.

"I don't understand. I ... I thought ..."

"Are your parents here?"

"No, they have gone to the synagogue, but I will get them."

She slipped into the house and pulled on a pair of sandals.

"I will bring them back," she said and skipped off down the street.

Wolf sat down on the edge of the balcony. Bees worked the orange marigolds that lined the side of the house. The flowers were carefully tended. He remembered the marigolds at Aunt Yocheved's house in Bledow before she left. How strange, he thought, that they should be here too, at the other end of the world.

He heard footsteps hurrying down the street behind and stood.

Aunt Yocheved and Uncle Yitzhak and his other cousins, Avraham, Nechama and Yisrael, rounded the side of the house. Aunt Yocheved ran to him, her arms outstretched.

"Wolf, my dear boy!" She hugged him, sobbing.

"How on earth did you get here? How did you find us? And look at you – in uniform. Is that a British uniform?"

Questions bubbled from her like a spring and it was some time before her face grew serious.

"And your mother?" she said. "Do you have news? Your father?"

They were still sitting on the edge of the balcony. Wolf shook his head.

"Nothing. I have no news of anyone. I have not received any letters and have not been able to write any. The last I saw of my family, I said goodbye to my mother before we fled Bledow. I could not find any of the others and there was no time."

Yocheved's face was quiet. Wolf could see that she was stifling tears.

"We have not heard anything either. I have written countless times to the family, everyone I could think of in Bledow, but have heard nothing back."

They were all silent for a while. Wolf picked a blade of grass from the ground and turned it in his fingers.

"Anyway," said Yocheved eventually, "Come inside. I will make a special meal to celebrate your appearance."

She led him into the cool of the house.

"Do you remember Wolf, children? You were only small when we left Bledow. Sometimes Wolf would come to our house and play games with you out in the field?"

Nechama shook her head shyly.

"Of course I remember him," said Avraham, "but he looks different now."

******

Two days passed in the warm arms of his family. As Wolf climbed the ladder to the small loft where he slept, he wondered whether the whole experience of the labour camp had just been a long and awful dream. On the last evening, before they ate, his uncle beckoned him outside onto the balcony.

"So what will you do now, Wolf? You have seen how happy we are here in Kfar Ata, how happy your cousins are."

"I have to get back to my company. My pass is only for three days. Already I am going to be a day late."

"That is, I suppose, if you want to go back. Do you know what is planned for you, for the Polish army? I don't suppose you will stay at Rehovot for long."

"I am in two minds," said Wolf. "It has been wonderful staying here with you. I had almost forgotten how wonderful it is to be with family. But something is also calling me back to Poland. I want to get back to Bledow, to help make Poland free again."

"I understand," said Yitzhak. "But if you ever reach a point where you want to consider other things ... well, let's say I know some people. I can put you in contact. You know there is the Haganah, defending us, trying to work with the British to establish a proper Jewish state. There is good training with them, they say; Avraham cannot wait until he's old enough. And then there's the Irgun, they are more radical."

"Yes," said Wolf, "I know. Some of my colleagues, other Jewish soldiers, have already joined them. In fact my good friend Ezra joined in Tel Aviv on my way here."

"You know where I am now," said his uncle, ushering him into the house for dinner.

******

By the time he got back to the camp in Rehovot, Wolf was two days later than his pass allowed. He had been reported as a deserter. The captain who had given him the pass was nowhere to be found.

"You are a deserter and you will suffer the punishment for desertion," said the officer who took on his case.

"I did not desert, sir," Wolf pleaded. "I visited my only family as my pass allowed. It was just that the journey took longer than I expected."

"The punishment for desertion in the Polish army has always been the same," said the officer. "There are no variations. You will stand in the midday sun for two hours with the items given to you and you will not move. If you move, then further punishment will follow. Dismissed."

A guard led Wolf to a square, shade-less section of the parade ground and told Wolf to wait there. He returned with a steel helmet and a heavily-laden kit-bag. He prodded Wolf from time to time over the two hours, but he refused to flinch or move.

"I'll give it to you, Jew, you are made of quite something," said the guard at the end.

Wolf stumbled. He could barely stand. His shoulders ached and he dropped the kit bag to the ground. He pulled the helmet off his head, rivulets of sweat pouring down his face. He was disoriented and dizzy, his clothes soaked. Zvi and other members of the company had been watching helplessly on the side, but now they rushed over. Two took his arms and supported him, while another poured water over him. He drank for what seemed like an hour and then slept.

41 THE AQUITANIA

5 August 1942

THE FOUR funnels of the RMS Aquitania loomed proud above Port Tawfiq. Wolf could see her on the skyline from the huge British camp in Suez.

In land-locked Bledow, his knowledge of boats and ships came from photographs and paintings, or the occasional play in a small dinghy on a pond. His recent experiences on the water he had no wish to recall – the barge that took him to Siberia, the Agamali Ogli that took him across the Caspian Sea.

But this ship made those two seem like dinky toy playthings. She was huge. He did not know that this battle-grey monster had had, in her glory days of the '20's and '30's, a black hull with a white superstructure and red funnels; that she had been known as The Ship Beautiful; or that she was two hundred and seventy-five metres long.

"Bloody beautiful, she was," said a Tommy. Wolf was picking up English words and phrases quickly. This soldier was just back from a visit to Suez town. Wolf soon realised that it was not the Aquitania he was talking about.

"Should've bloody seen her mate. Boobs the size of melons. Some bloody cross-eyed sailor had 'is eyes on 'er, but I 'ad 'er. Took me up the stairs, shaky ol' stairs. Couldn't get enough of 'er. If this is war, mate, get in there."

He paused for a moment, feeling his pockets.

"'Ang on a minute, where's me wallet? Who's taken me fuckin' wallet? Oh shit, no!"

******

Wolf was on guard when he entered the town with most of rest of the unit. Beggars squatted by the roadside. 'Bakshish', they cried. 'Bakshish'. As if he had any money to offer, as if he had not himself been in those same circumstances so recently.

As they got closer to the centre, even children lined the streets.

'Dzhig, dzhig,' they called, both boys and girls, thrusting their hips back and forth and tugging at his sleeve. A woman stood at the fork between two streets. She raised her top as the group of men approached, a bare comely breast revealed.

Outside bars Arab men beckoned them inside. 'Beer, wine, baba ghanoush,' they said. 'Nice time.' Photos of half-clad women lined the entrance.

"Looks good to me," said Zvi, and, with other men, headed inside. It was not that Wolf was not aroused by this place, but vague images of Rywka and Nina came to mind. He was curious, too, to see more of Suez.

"I'm going to explore further down," he said.

"Oh come on, man – it's all here."

But he walked on. He walked as far as Port Tawfiq where the Aquitania lay at anchor. From the North, other ships came in at intervals, their bows forging through the still waters of the canal as if ripping fabric.

******

Zvi and several of the other men were hung over in the morning. They were all called out on parade by Sergeant Wilek. He was accompanied by a British officer.

"Today you will embark on RMS Aquitania, the big ship you can see in the distance. She arrived here on 8 July with one thousand nine hundred troops from Great Britain who have joined the fight here in the Middle East.

"From here, she will carry five thousand German prisoners, who are in this camp, to the USA. Your task is very simple – you will be guarding them. To this end, you will be issued with rifles and ammunition. These are rifles taken from captured Italian soldiers. "

He held one up for them to see. Wolf admired the smooth, polished wood of the stock.

"This is the Carcano Model 91 bolt action repeater carbine with an en bloc recharge clip. The clip carries six rounds."

He held a clip up, the six bullets clearly visible. It dawned on Wolf, suddenly, that he was required to hold one of these guns and that these bullets, if fired, carried lethal force. He did not wish to think about that.

"It is very simple to use," the officer went on. "You place the clip in here … and pull the bolt up and out, like this, then in again. Now you're loaded. If you need to fire, you pull this trigger."

He pointed the rifle to the sky. A whiplash crack smacked through the air.

"And then, to re-load, you simply pull the bolt up and out, and then in again. You will be issued with multiple clips. If you've fired six rounds, you simply push in the next clip and the empty one falls out. Is that clear?"

The soldiers looked at him blankly. What the officer was saying made little sense to Wolf. This most elementary introduction was surely not weapons training. He needed to get his hands on the gun and try it for himself.

The officer called Wilek forward.

"Demonstrate again, Sergeant."

Zvi looked at Wolf and shrugged.

"You should not have to use the weapon. Once the ship is on the move, these prisoners have nowhere to escape to; but there are five thousand of them and there will be far less of you. Use them as a last resort in case there is trouble."

******

Wolf gasped at the murals on the walls and ceilings, the pillared columns in the halls, the ornate cornices, the intricate metalwork on the balustrades and the domed window above the grand staircase, as they were directed to their accommodation. The plush carpets, worn now by the tread of thousands of troops and prisoners, nevertheless still showed their original glory at the edges.

The brass fittings around the portholes in his cabin and the bathroom were tarnished now, but once they would have been polished by a crew member. Wolf could not imagine life in such opulence.

"This is a Second-Class cabin," said Zvi. "Imagine what First must be like."

They dumped their kit bags on the bunks.

"Fall in behind me," shouted the British officer. "I will now show you the areas where the prisoners will be held."

He led the way to the lower decks with Wilek. Each new deck was accessed by wide wooden staircases with carved bannisters. Some were just wide open spaces; from others, doors opened onto a corridor of four-berth bunk-bed rooms.

"And this is a prison?" said Wolf aghast. "If we'd ended up in a place like this, I would have called it a palace, not a prison."

As they climbed up again, the officer pointed to the stairs.

"These are our problem," he said. "They are wide and they are not easy to defend. Those Boche are going to get bored down there. They may try to rush the stairs. That is why two of you will be posted at the top of each set of stairs at all times. More soldiers will be posted higher up and round the bridge. Your role is to be the first line of defence, to nip any problems in the bud. Your orders are to shoot if there is any sign of trouble. How will you know when to shoot? The prisoners will be instructed not to set foot on the stairs, any stairs. If a prisoner comes round the angle of the stairs below you, they have already come too far. That is when you shoot. You do not wait until they are on top of you. Any questions?"

Wolf shook his head. It seemed strange to him, though somehow exhilarating, that finally he should be tasked with an actual soldiering duty.

"The prisoners will remain under British Command until they are installed on the different decks by their escort. Once that is done, you will take over guard duties. Until then, wait for further orders on the top deck."

******

"Look over there," said Zvi. A cloud of dust hung in the air above the desert, a dark line snaking across the sand beneath it. There was a distant sound of marching. As the line drew closer, it took shape — a long column of prisoners, still in German uniform, closely guarded by British troops.

Wolf almost pitied them. He knew what it was like to be marched, helpless, to an uncertain future. He had to shake his head to remember that these men, or their friends and fellow soldiers, were the ones who had driven him out of Bledow, who had killed his fellow Jews. And so he put his pity away.

******

The Aquitania passed through the Red Sea and left Diego Suarez and Madagascar on its port side. It stopped for two days in Capetown to pick up provisions.

"Next stop Boston Massachusetts," said Zvi as they left Freetown. "That's what I've heard. As long as the U-boats don't get us first; but I don't suppose they'd want to sink five thousand of their own people."

U-boats were part of the myth of the sea journey, the threat to be most feared. Wolf had heard of the Atlantic Ocean and, as the seas got rougher as they headed North-West, excitement and fear gripped him – excitement to be heading for the United States, the great land of fame and fortune; and fear that the ship might be targeted and sunk.

It was with such thoughts gripping his mind that he realised that the general hubbub of the prisoners on the floor below had turned into something louder. One man was shouting louder than the rest, taunting him; he put his foot on the lower step of the stairs.

"Haha, Jewish. Go on, shoot me. I'm not allowed to put my foot on the stairs."

Wolf looked behind him. His back-up was some way back, but he called anyway. He raised his gun. He still had not fired it, even in training.

"Come on then Jewish. Show us what you're made of."

Wolf held the gun to his shoulder, trying to remember what to do. The German did a little tap dance – on the step, off the step, on the step, off the step. After a little while, he seemed to get bored with this game.

"You know, prisoners have taken over ships before. Big ships like this. We could just pour up the stairs and you wouldn't stand a chance."

"Maybe not," said Wolf. "Nor would you against the machine guns up there." He jerked his head back.

"Hah! They didn't stop the soldiers who escaped in Capetown. I saw what you have when we came on board," the German said. "We are well-trained German infantry. Today, we are the captives, tomorrow it may be the other way round. So if you are not nice to me today, I will not be nice to you tomorrow. Heil Hitler!"

He stepped onto the second step of the stairs.

Wolf felt for the trigger. As the man's weight moved forward to take the third, he raised the barrel a little, then fired. There was a sharp crack as the bullet ripped through the wall, splinters of wood flying. Wolf stumbled backwards with the recoil, catching himself before he fell. There were shouts from behind him and soldiers came running.

"What happened?" asked Wilek. "What the hell's going on?"

"German was coming up the stairs, sir, on the third step. I fired as instructed. I missed."

The German had, of course, disappeared from view and Wolf lowered his gun with relief. He had seen enough people dying - the thought of actually shooting someone was anathema to him.

42 GALASHIELS

10 September 1942

ABBOTS MILL was a large austere stone building in the heart of Galashiels in the Scottish Borders. At the back of the building the River Tweed ran. It was cramped, damp, dark and draughty. The building was squeezed between Huddersfield Street to its South side and the River Tweed to its North, the railway line running parallel with the river on the North bank.

It was home to the 10th Battalion Dragoons of the Polish Army and a far cry from the US Army camp in Brooklyn where the Jewish unit had spent nearly two weeks after the Aquitania docked. The journey back across the Atlantic on an Italian ship overloaded with American soldiers had been rough. Wolf had been relieved to see Liverpool Docks ahead of them through a dank mist after five days at sea. At least now, he thought, they could get involved in fighting against the Nazis proper.

"What? All yids?" said the C.O. when they arrived at Abbots Mill. There had been no Jewish soldiers in the battalion previously, and the Poles looked at them as if they were a different life-form.

"I don't know what you bastards are doing here," said the corporal who led them to their quarters. "This bloody war was your own making. Without you we'd be back at home leading a peaceful life."

They were used to the taunts and jibes, but they did not expect it here in the army. Abbots Mill was not a comfortable place. Scores of men slept on each floor on double bunks with just a blanket, mice and rats tickling inside the walls. Heating was impossible in so large a space. The huge buffets that the Jewish soldiers had enjoyed in Brooklyn were a thing of the past. Here, the food that they were given was the left-overs. They were always the last in line.

The saving grace was in the training. The British army ran it, supplying the uniforms, the weapons and the equipment, and the prejudice of the Poles had no place in it. It was tough and hard training, live exercises taking place on the hills and moors of the Southern Uplands.

The British army now controlled the soldiers' pay too. Fifteen shillings a week was the pay of a rifleman in the 10th Dragoons, Wolf discovered, and now he was receiving it.

"We should have had this since we were enlisted in Pahlevi," said Zvi. "These bastards have been holding onto our money for months."

But there was no one to turn to. There were no Jewish officers – no one to review their conditions, to inspect their barracks or to carry out health checks.

43 CHAIM SIERADSKI

2 October 1942

THE WAVERLEY Hydropathic had been built as a spa hotel in 1871 to provide water cures for its guests from the River Tweed which ran behind it. It was a tall castle-like building, constructed of concrete. Square towers rose from the front and bow windows looked out over unkempt gardens. It was in Melrose in the Scottish Borders, just four miles from Galashiels. It was the headquarters of the Polish Signals Squadron, part of the 1st Armoured Division of the Polish Army and it was to this unit that Chaim Solomon Sieradski reported.

He shook his head, wondering at his new surroundings – the gentle hills and tree-lined river. He felt a close affinity to Scotland – it reminded him of his birthplace in Nowy Sacs in Southern Poland.

He thought back over the last three months. He had no wish to go further back – to the years before that in the prisons and camps and the journey away from Siberia.

******

He had arrived at the enlistment point in a small town near Chardzhou in Turkmenistan, frozen and starving. He was directed to a dilapidated old community hall where one hundred and fifty Polish citizens, both native and Jewish, were gathered. At one side, women stood behind trestle tables doling out soup with large wooden ladles, and bread. He had not eaten for four days since he left his billet with villagers way out in the countryside and wolfed the food down hungrily.

He looked up from his bowl to see Kmiec, a fellow-inmate in the Siberian camp. Kmiec had been a Lieutenant in the Polish army at the start of the war. Though he was not Jewish, the two of them had forged the sort of friendship in 50th Karny Lagerny Punkt camp that only the shared experience of life in such a place could forge. When they were released, he had stayed with the group led by Kmiec on the long journey to join General Anders army.

"Ah, Henek," said Kmiec. "It is good to see you after these last two weeks. How was your billet?"

"It was ... I survived," he said.

Kmiec beckoned him to a corner of the draughty room.

"Now please hear me out," he said. "I strongly advise you that when you are called up for interview for enlistment, you do not tell them you are Jewish. I have learnt that Polish citizens of the Jewish persuasion will not be enlisted into the Polish army. They are only going to take those who were already in the armed forces before the war, or else those with professions, like doctors or lawyers or dentists.

"Sieradski is a good Polish name and everyone knows you as Henek, which is short for Henrik – another Polish name. And ... your Polish is perfect. Please believe me – if you want to get out of Russia, this is what you need to do."

He had nodded. "Thank you, Tadek. I understand what you are saying, but I will have to think very hard about this."

He went outside to warm himself beside the fire. Logs and branches were being brought in from every side and thrown on the flames. A Polish officer, somehow already in uniform, pushed past him.

"Get out of my way. What are you doing here, anyway? They're not going to let Jews into the army."

He was outraged. He was proud of his Jewish heritage. He thought of his family. He thought of their large house in the town of Nowy Sacs where he'd wrapped jewellery and rings in linen cloth and hidden them behind the brickwork of the cellar when the Nazis invaded. He thought of his father's factory – the sweets and cakes and pastries that they made and sold in the shop.

He made his decision.

He was called forward to the enlistment area. A doctor sat at a table inside and examined him. He asked him to breathe deeply, in and out. He held a stethoscope to his chest. He bent and flexed each limb.

"A1 Pass", the doctor said. "You are a skeleton, but a skeleton with an iron core. Nothing that a few weeks of good food won't cure. Pass along."

He moved across to a table where two Polish officers sat, a Russian major on the far side of them.

"Name?"

"Sieradski."

"First names?"

"Chaim Solomon."

The Pole's face reddened into an angry grimace. He turned to the doctor.

"Doctor, there seems to be some mistake. You have passed this man A1."

He pointed to the first names written on the sheet and the two men conferred.

"I am sorry, you will have to report for another medical tomorrow morning. There has been a mistake. Dismissed."

He stood his ground.

"I am a Polish citizen by birth; so were my parents and my grandparents and generations before them. I passed the medical examination A1. I want to fight the German murderers. Please do not refuse me this chance."

The two Polish officers began a heated discussion. He walked over to the Russian major and, standing his full six-foot height, addressed him politely. His knack with languages was never more helpful – he used the Russian he had picked up in the camp and on the journey.

"Sir, I have passed the medical A1, I want to fight our German enemy, but the Polish officers are trying to pretend that the medical was an incorrect result because I am Jewish. They do not want to enlist me for that reason."

The queue backed up behind him. The Russian called the Polish officers to the other side of the room. They gesticulated and argued but the Russian shook his head firmly. When they returned to the table, the enlisting officer picked a blank Army Record Book from a pile and, without looking up, filled in the details and stamped it.

Chaim Sieradski was now a soldier in the Polish army.
The onward journey had taken him to Krasnovodsk, Pahlevi, Iraq, Palestine, Suez and South Africa. From there, he had embarked on RMS Mauretania, the older sister of RMS Aquitania. She had docked in Cardiff on 28 September and now here he was, at the age of 21, in Melrose.

44 A MEETING

16 October 1942

"CROSS the road scum!"

Wolf, Zvi and the others ignored them and walked on up the street. With some money to spend finally, they could visit the cinema in Galashiels or drink coffee in one of the local cafes.

"Do you know why you've got long noses? Go on, talk to me. Why have you got long noses?"

"So they can smell shit," said another Polish soldier.

"No, so they can see in the dark."

The Poles all laughed raucously.

"I don't even know what they're talking about," said Wolf.

"It's just nonsensical crap," said Zvi as they finally passed.

It was a fine day and they sat down at one of the outside tables of the Tweed View Coffee House.

"What's wrong with them?" said Fiona, the waitress in the café where they sat.

"Nothing you need to worry about, my beautiful," said Zvi.

He had taken a shine to her and passed his hand over her bottom.

"Get off me, you naughty man," she said, pushing him away playfully.

When she came back with their coffee, he got down on one knee.

"Fiona," he said, "wilt thou accompany me to the cinema on Saturday evening?"

She blushed.

"Aye," she said. "Aye, I will."

"Aye," copied the other soldiers, falling about laughing.

"Hang on," said Wolf. He'd seen another group in uniform approaching up the road.

They braced themselves for more abuse. They did not recognise the faces. As they drew closer they heard them speaking. It was Yiddish.

"Hello," said Wolf. "Come and join us."

The three men sat down. One of them held out his hand.

"Chaim Sieradski."

He was a little taller than Wolf with brown hair, curling at the edges. There was a commanding presence about him and Fiona looked a little flustered as she approached.

"What can I get you?"

Chaim smiled at the Scottish girl.

"Now don't you be stealing Zvi's girl," laughed Wolf. "He's just asked her out to the cinema on Saturday night."

Fiona was still blushing when she brought the tray of drinks for the new group.

"I haven't seen you at the mill," said Wolf. "Where are you based?"

"The mill? Ah – is that where you are based, here in Galashiels? There seem to be groups of Polish soldiers all over Scotland. No, we are in Melrose, just down the road. It's within walking distance. We found out about the cinema here and the dances in the drill hall. There are some lovely girls there too. We're going again this Saturday."

"Sounds like a good idea," said Wolf. "May we'll join you there? It's nice to meet other Polish soldiers where we don't get all the anti-Jewish jibes all the time."

"I couldn't agree more," said Chaim. "It gets to you after a while, doesn't it? What sort of unit are you in?"

"Dragoons. Armoured Support they call it. The Brits train us. It's hard, but if we're going to take Poland back again, it's no doubt what we need. It's a whole lot better than building a railway line in Siberia. You?"

"Signals. You were all in Russian camps too, were you?"

They nodded.

"Shall we go on to the dance at the drill hall after the film, Fiona?" asked Zvi as she cleared the table. "All these lovely men are going to be there."

She looked around at the men and blushed again.

"Can you dance, Zvi?"

He stood and, raising his arms above his head, twirled his body.

"See you on Saturday evening then," said Wolf, turning to Sieradski.

45 MORTAR UNIT

29 April 1943

THE TEN-TON Bedford army truck trundled and bumped over the narrow roads North for what seemed like hours. The platoon sat on hard benches bolted to either side, facing each other. Wolf looked affectionately at the Scottish countryside receding behind them.

"You are being re-assigned to Gullane on the North Coast of East Lothian," the Captain had said. "It is close to Archerfield, where many of you completed the basic attack course in January and February of this year. Here we are better equipped to train you on mortars and beach warfare."

The Marine Hotel was their new billet.

"I wonder why they built such a big place here," said Wolf. "It seems pretty remote."

"It's at the end of the railway line," said Zvi. "And golf – I saw signs to a golf course."

"It's only eighteen miles from Edinburgh," came another voice.

Ten wide steps led up to the front door, a stone banister curving down on both sides. Either end of the building was gabled and in the centre was a square balconied tower. After the privations of the mill in Galashiels, a bedroom with just four bunk beds seemed like luxury to Wolf. From the upper of the four floors, he could see the sand dunes and wide beaches of Aberlady and Gullane bays.

It did not cross his mind that these beaches might be considered suitable for a German invasion landing from Norway, or a training ground for some future invasion of France.

******

"The three-inch mortar is a simple, lightweight, man-portable, muzzle-loaded weapon, consisting of a smooth-bore metal tube fixed to a base plate to spread out the recoil, with a lightweight bipod mount and a sight. They launch explosive shells – sometimes we call them bombs — in high-arcing ballistic trajectories. Mortars are typically used as indirect fire weapons for close fire support with a variety of ammunition," said the British officer, addressing them.

He pointed to a weapon that had been pre-assembled on the ground. He held up a shell in his other hand.

"This is a shell. It weighs ten pounds."

Wolf was fascinated by its bulbous, almost phallic, shape and its tail-fin design.

"The 3-inch mortar has a range of 2800 yards. This is the new version of the mortar. The old version, the standard Mark II, had a range of only 1600 yards. We are training you on the very latest version, as you will see."

He paused for a moment.

"Why do we need mortars rather than artillery? Because, in the progress of an attack, the forward companies may need quick support, particularly against machine guns and machine gun posts. The high trajectory of the mortar allows it to be brought into action almost anywhere.

"There are two types of bombs – the HE, or High Explosive, bombs which fracture into small pieces and are highly destructive, and the smoke bombs. Smoke bombs release white phosphorus which creates a curtain of smoke that smothers the enemy's view and allows adjustment of targeting or repositioning.

"You will now proceed with your companies towards the sea where the training will continue."

Wolf was excited. Something about the weapon's mechanism, how it could be applied in battle, appealed to him. A line of pine trees bordered the rough grass and shrubs that had once been the Archerfield golf course before the war.

"This is ideal training ground for mortars," said the training officer, pointing out the cover of trees, sections of scrub, small hillocks and copses of young trees.

"A mortar unit consists of five men," he said. "The No.1 and No. 2 targeters, two men carrying the ammunition, which is carried in three-packs, and the loader. But first, let us look at the weapon in more detail."

With the help of an orderly, he laid the component pieces on the ground. He pointed out the barrel, the base plate, the sight case, the bipod stand, the coil spring, the breach piece, the muzzle and the muzzle cover. To detach the breach piece, he pulled a heavy spanner from a canvas spares bag that was part of the assembly kit.

"The breach piece contains the striker stud," he said. "The striker stud is what fires the bomb."

The orderly detached it and held it up for them to see.

"It's all too much for me," said Zvi, as they stopped to eat a sandwich, his back leaning against a tree. "Too scientific. I could throw a grenade better than trying to work one of those things."

"No," said Wolf, before they spent the afternoon assembling and disassembling the weapon. "No. I think I could get the hang of these."

******

23 May 1943

Intensive training had gone on for days as the platoon mastered the art of moving forward to a designated position, assembling the mortar, then disassembling at speed and running quickly to a new location. Now, the training was to start on targeting and firing the weapon.

"You are now familiar with the assembly of the mortar. Next you need to understand the aiming and laying of the mortar; then you will become an effective fighting force," said the British training officer.

He walked over to a fully assembled mortar.

"Moving the elevation operating handle over and to the left raises the mortar and reduces the range; over and to the right lowers the mortar and increases the range. With the traversing gear, bring the handle towards you and the mortar moves towards you, turn it away from you and the mortar moves away from you."

The clipped British tones were hard sometimes to comprehend and the complexities of this new field involved technical terms that Wolf had not previously come across. He had picked up a good level of English — unlike some of his colleagues, who were not interested in, and had no aptitude for, the language — but he was glad of the assisting Polish Lieutenant's translation.

The training officer pointed to a shell on the table in front of him.

"The tail unit contains a primary cartridge and six secondary cartridges. When firing at longer range, all secondaries are left in and this is called Charge 2. For closer range, Charge 1 is used. This means removing three of the secondary cartridges."

Zvi rolled his eyes towards Wolf. He held up his arm.

"Permission to ask a question, sir. Why are the three …er … cartridges removed for … er … Charge … what was it?"

"Do you mean, why are the three secondary cartridges removed for Charge 1?"

Zvi nodded. The officer looked at him and hesitated before responding.

"To reduce the velocity of the mortar as it is not required to travel so far."

Wolf doubted that Zvi understood the meaning of the word velocity, but he seemed satisfied.

"In taking correct aim," the officer went on, "the aiming mark must first be selected by the No. 1. The eye should be three inches away from the sight. The top of the pyramid of light in the sight should be in line with the centre of the aiming mark. The barrel and sight will only point in the same direction when the cross-level bubble is central.

"It is necessary to keep this cross-level bubble central whilst the mortar is being laid, so the No. 2 is required to assist in the laying. The No. 1 must warn the No. 2 which way he is going to traverse, so that the No. 2 shall know which way to turn his cross-levelling spool.

"If the aim is above or below the aiming mark, it may be adjusted by the collimator adjusting spool. Elevation is obtained by first setting the required charge, and the range on the range scale."

As he spoke, the officer pointed out the different features and mechanisms on the mortar, leaving time for the soldiers to draw closer and understand what he was referring to.

"For instance," he said, "Charge 2, marked 4 on the side, 1200. The correct elevation is put on the mortar by raising or lowering it until the longitudinal bubble is central."

He paused, and looked towards Zvi.

"Are you following, soldier?"

Zvi's face was blank. His lack of education and an innate difficulty with numbers was evident in his stumbled response.

"I'm trying to, sir."

"I think," said the officer, sighing and turning to his Polish counterpart, "that this soldier would be best used as a bomb carrier."

"Bomb victim, more like," muttered Zvi under his breath.

"Let us take an example. Charge 1, red on the side, 600."

He waved the soldiers forward, pointing with his baton to the different marks.

"No. 1 gets a rough idea of how much he is off by hand angles and roughly corrects the direction with the traversing handle. No. 2 centralises the cross-level bubble whilst No. 1 puts on the correct elevation. Accurate direction is now obtained with both No.'s working together. The mortar has now been laid.

"Now, when the mortar is used in anger, in battle, there may need to be a correction after firing. The commander will observe the trajectory and landing point of the mortar through his binoculars and will then advise the correction needed. This is accomplished with the direction dial and drums. With these, it is possible to lay the mortar any number of degrees to the right or left of the aiming mark. For instance, 'Left, 99 degrees' would mean adjustment as so."

The demonstrating lieutenant adjusted the drum accordingly.

"This means that the mortar is laid 99 degrees to the left of the aiming mark."

Though his brain was buzzing with 'aiming marks' and 'direction dials', 'traversing gear' and 'collimators', Wolf grasped the gist of the weapon's mechanism. He was keen to get his hands on a mortar and to put the instructions into practice.

46 GENERAL MACZEK

23 September 1943

A LARGE staff car drew up outside Archerfield House. An adjutant, his uniform immaculate, opened the rear door. A lean figure stepped out, his polished belt drawn tight around his waist. His face was keen, chiselled and intelligent.

"Is it Maczek?" someone said.

General Maczek's name had become almost legendary following his exploits with the Polish 10th Armoured Cavalry Brigade in France in 1940. Since then, he had been in Scotland in command of a newly-created 1st Polish Armoured Division.

He walked to a small dais. The adjutant passed him a megaphone and he addressed the assembled Polish troops.

"Gentlemen,

You may wonder what you are doing here in Scotland. For those of you who were forced to spend time in Russian camps, then I am sure this experience is a lot better, but still you may be saying to yourselves 'the war is not here, we have done enough training, we want to get our hands on Mr Hitler.'

"Let me tell you that I understand that. Let me also tell you that all the training is not, and will not be, wasted. The tide of the war is slowly turning. We do not expect it to be too long before you can be back on mainland Europe and then fighting your way back to our own beloved Poland. Many things will have changed, but the Eagle will not be defeated.

"I am here today because we are undertaking an exercise that you will not have done before, but that will further prepare you for battle. You will be divided into forces – one with red arm bands, one with white. In this exercise, the red armbands will invade the coastline here, between Aberlady and Dirleton, while the white armbands will repel them. The key thing about this exercise is that you will use live ammunition. Further North of here, on the Scottish moorlands, we have conducted similar live exercises with the tank brigades of the 1st Armoured."

A wave of surprise spread through the ranks.

"This exercise has all been carefully planned. It is entirely safe for you, but it is important for you to have the unique experience of live fire. There will, however, be ambulances on hand from the British Medical Corps, just in case anything should go wrong or anyone get hurt in any way. Now, your officers will brief you on your role. The exercise will begin at 0900 hours. Long live Poland!"

The four mortar units in the platoon marched north in the direction of the sea.

"Fan out across this scrubland," said the Lieutenant, "Two hundred yards apart. Remain under cover until I call you forward with three sharp whistles. The red armbands will have occupied that wood between here and the sea. Our goal is to drive them back towards the beach."

"This way you lazy bastards," shouted the corporal leading Wolf's unit, waving them through nettles to a thick clump of brambles and wild elder that provided good cover.

Over the four months of training drills with mortar targeting and firing, it was clear to the captain of their company that Wolf understood the mortar and the intricacies of its targeting best in the unit. He had therefore been appointed as No. 1.

He now peered towards the woods in the distance. Autumn was still a month off and they were a mass of green; they would provide excellent cover for the red armbands. For themselves, the white armbands, there were a few clumps of larger bushes, such as the one they were in, which could provide cover, but they were singularly exposed.

At 09.00 precisely, there was a roar from behind them. The artillery had opened up and for five minutes they could hear nothing but the pounding of the guns and the whistle of shells way overhead. Wolf looked at the corporal. Uncertainty was etched on his face. He looked to the side. He could see the next unit two hundred yards away, camouflaged in a dip in the ground. The lieutenant was at the front of them, waving his arm forward, his whistle useless in the clamour of the big guns.

Wolf pointed him out to the corporal.

"Smart arse," said the corporal. "Of course I've seen him."

"Right, re-position to those bushes ahead. Now! At the double!"

This was an exercise that the unit had practised over and over again. Each person knew what he would carry – the barrel, the rest of the assembly, the ammunition three-packs — but this time, as they broke cover, the crack of rifle fire and then the steady staccato beat of a machine gun greeted them. Wolf could hear bullets spitting into the ground and ricocheting off trees. Everything in him told him to dive for cover.

"Keep going," shouted the corporal.

Out of breath, sweat pouring down his face, Wolf scrambled into the bushes.

"Come on, faster you bastards. Assemble the mortar."

The corporal pulled a sheet of paper from his pocket and studied it. He looked to his left to see if he could see where the lieutenant was, but there was no sign of him.

He pointed to a section of the wood where the band of trees bent eastwards, inland.

"Aim there," he said.

Wolf looked. His judgement had been honed by the months of training — it was about 2000 yards away. With the naked eye, he could see movement in the area and the occasional flash of red.

He squinted through the sight and selected his aiming mark.

"Traversing right," he said to his No. 2.

To the right of them, they heard the crack of a mortar being fired, followed quickly by the explosion. Earth spat up ahead in the scrub to the right of their own aiming mark. Wolf held his hand flat in the direction of the target. Again he saw movement and flashes of red.

"Charge 2, 1500."

"That's more than 1500," said the corporal. "Put it into the woods at 2000."

"There are men in that wood, I can't target 2000. People will be injured or killed."

"Listen, you long-nosed bastard, target 2000 – that's an order."

"No," said Wolf.

The lieutenant appeared suddenly from behind them in a loping run.

"Why are you not firing?"

"He refuses to obey my instruction to shoot. He says, if we fire into that wood, there'll be a lot of people hurt."

Wolf, Zvi and the other members of the unit looked at each other, an urgency in their eyes. Rifle, machine gun and occasional artillery fire were bursting all around them.

"Sir, we've seen in training how accurate Wolf is," shouted Zvi above the din. "He can drop a mortar on an individual tree. Some of those reds are bastards, but none of us want to kill them."

Wolf stood his ground. The lieutenant was on his knees, studying a map that he had spread out, tracing his finger over the marked wooded area. He looked at his compass and frowned.

"The mortar will never get that far anyway," he said.

"Sir," said Wolf, trying to remain patient, "this is not the Mark II mortar. That would not have made it that far. This is the new version. It will go that far and further."

The lieutenant looked at him, then back to his map. He raised his binoculars and scanned the woods.

"I can't see any movement. Target the wood as instructed."

"Sir …"

"No 'Sir'. No question. Just do it or I'll have you court-martialled."

Wolf sighed and looked through the site again.

"Charge two, red, 2000."

With his No. 2, he made the adjustments.

Zvi dropped the shell into the top of the muzzle. Instantaneously, there was a crack as it hit the striker stud. He was poised with the next shell.

"Hold!" shouted the lieutenant. He raised his binoculars again, searching for where the first would land. There was no burst of earth. Instead, branches tumbled in on themselves at the top of the canopy. In the briefest lull in the firing, Wolf thought he could hear shouting and screams of pain.

The lieutenant's radio crackled.

"Yes sir, yes sir, right away sir."

He turned to the unit.

"Stop firing immediately."

He sent the ammunition holders out to the other units with instructions for them to cease firing also.

"Men have been hurt in the woods," said the lieutenant. "It may have been your mortar."

Your mortar, rather, thought Wolf, but he was shaking. However much he detested the jibes of the Polish soldiers, he knew that they, too, were treated like dirt by their superiors. He had no wish to harm them.

He looked back towards the woods. Already, army-green ambulances, a large red cross on the side set in a white circle, were racing across the rough ground. A light drizzle had begun to fall and the smoke from the different weapons mingled with the mist, so that the wood could barely be seen. The smell of cordite lingered in the air and a robin began to sing its sad song in the bracken behind them.

Wolf could hear the sound of an engine and, tumbling across the scrub, a jeep approached. General Maczek, his uniform now more dishevelled, stepped out. The lieutenant went over and saluted him. He called over the corporal and the three of them stood in discussion for some minutes, then studied the map.

The general pointed to a different part of the wood and came over to Wolf.

"I understand that you fired the mortar, soldier."

"Yes sir, but against my will. I tried to explain to the officer that there might be men in the woods. You said in your address this morning that it had all been planned so that no one would get hurt, but I could see there were reds in there. I felt that perhaps something had gone wrong."

"Or you were being told to target the wrong place," said the General. "Thankfully, no one has been killed. There are some injuries and some people will have to go to hospital. Unfortunately, these things can happen in live exercises. It is a far lighter outcome than real battle."

"Yes sir. I am very glad no one has been killed sir."

"Don't let it be on your conscience, soldier."

He spoke to his adjutant, instructing him to radio the commanders in the field. The exercise would be suspended.

"Now, tell me about these mortars. I understand this is a new, longer-range version."

Wolf showed the weapon to the general.

"And how do you aim?"

For the next twenty minutes, Wolf demonstrated the laying of the mortar, the aiming mechanism, the elevation and directional adjustments.

"Very interesting."

The general looked at Wolf's uniform.

"You have all this knowledge and you are only a rifleman. We'll have to see about that."

"I am Jewish, sir, as are my colleagues here." Wolf took a deep breath. "There is a lot of prejudice in the Polish army, antagonism against us, though we have the same goal as you – to send Mr Hitler back where he came from. You might have noticed – there are no Jewish officers here."

"I see," said General Maczek. "I see. I will speak to your C.O."

47 VOLKSDEUTSCHE

29 October 1943

WOLF'S conversation with the general gave him hope that something might change — perhaps he would appoint some Jewish officers — but that hope was dashed in a minute when his detachment arrived back at Archerfield that afternoon.

Raise the flag! The ranks tightly closed
The SA marches with calm, steady step.
Comrades shot by the Red Front and reactionaries
March in spirit within our ranks

Clear the streets for the brown battalions
Clear the streets for the storm division
Millions are looking upon the swastika, full of hope
The day of freedom and of bread dawns

For the last time, the call to arms is sounded
For the fight, we all stand prepared!
Already Hitler's banners fly over all streets.
The time of bondage will last but a little while now!

Wolf could not believe his ears. He had not heard the song since 1939 but he recognized it immediately. It was the Horst-Wessel-Lied, the anthem of the Nazi party. All sorts of thoughts ran through his mind. Why on earth was this song being sung here? Who was singing it?

It soon became clear. A group of men who had served in the German army and then been captured by the allies – Poles who had lived in Germany, Germans who had lived in Poland, half-Germans, half-Poles, Poles conscripted into the German army soon after the invasion, the so-called Volksdeutsche – had been posted to Gullane. Not just to Gullane but to Archerfield.

"Don't worry," they said loudly, as Wolf and his fellow men entered the building, "Hitler is sorting the Jewish problem out for us."

******

17 November 1943

Every day now, when the mortar unit passed them, the Volksdeutsche would break out into the opening lines of the song:

Raise the flag, the ranks tightly closed
The SA marches with calm steady step…

They'd laugh at the Jewish soldiers' attempts to ignore them.

"Have you got a tight hold of that gun, Hermann?"

"I'm strangling a Jew."

The jibes were unremitting.

"What's wrong with you?" asked Wolf of one of their ringleaders. "We all want to just get back to Poland and live in peace again, don't we?"

"Oh, do we?" the man taunted. He turned to his mates.

"Do we want to live in peace in Poland with the Jew boys again?"

"No way!" came the cry.

He turned back to Wolf.

"Listen mate, we don't want you," he sneered. "We don't want you here, we don't want you in the army, we don't want you in Poland. So I'd watch your back if I were you. Because if you don't get a bullet from the front when we actually get to start fighting, you'll get one from behind."

Wolf was stunned. The others had heard it too. He noticed copies of Der Sturmer lying around on chairs as he left.

"We have to report this," said Zvi. "It's getting completely out of hand."

"But who to? The C.O. will just laugh in our faces."

At that moment, Wolf saw a familiar figure riding up to the building on a motor-cycle.

"Sieradski!" he waved.

"Ah, Wolf, Zvi – it is good to see you. I thought I might find you here. I hear you have become famous in the mortar world, Wolf."

"Huh, that fiasco," said Wolf. "And what have you been up to?"

"They sent me on this driving course in a place called Falkirk, learning to drive lorries and motor-cycles."

He patted his olive-green, mud-spattered machine.

"That is what I'm doing now. I was sent to deliver a package of documents to the C.O. here."

"Ah. Yes, I've heard of the Falkirk driving school. To tell you the truth, I am more than glad to see you. We have a bunch of Volksdeutsche in this place – I don't know what they are doing here. They spend their time singing Nazi songs and taunting us. One of them just told me that, if I didn't get shot in battle from the front, I'd certainly get a bullet from behind."

"It is disgusting," said Sieradski, "but I know it's true. A friend told me that, in his unit, one of them had got a hold of a German newspaper reporting the slaughter of

Jews in the Warsaw uprising. They were in the mess hall, about 200 soldiers in there, and they were all laughing and applauding, gathered around the reader. They were Poles speaking German, insolent, no respect for their own country. And none of them were privates. They were all lance corporals, corporals or even sergeants. Apparently there is some system in the German army where, if you are captured and become a prisoner of war, you gain one rank. It makes you sick."

"We have to do something, Chaim."

48 TALK OF RATS

3 April 1944

CHAIM Sieradski had just finished his breakfast when he was called to the telephone.

"Someone called Janek wants to speak to you. He sounded pretty intense. Have you stolen his girlfriend?"

The bank of black phones in the hallway stood in little booths, but these provided no privacy.

"Hello, Janek? This is Chaim. How nice to hear from you."

"Chaim, I know that you cannot speak on the phone and I have not got much time before I will be overheard, so just say 'yes' and 'no'. Something has come up – very serious and very urgent. I need to speak to you in person. Can we meet outside the cinema in Galashiels tonight at 8 pm?"

"Of course. Yes, we can have a coffee and talk about old times. I will see you then."

Chaim put the phone back in its cradle. He was worried. Janek's tone was urgent.

Janek Scherer was in his mid-thirties. He had been a lawyer in Warsaw before the war and also had an office in Nowy Sacs where he had been born. With particular knowledge of corporate law and fluent English, he had been allowed to join the Polish army, even though Jewish, and had been put to work in the Legal Affairs office at the Polish 1st Armoured Division HQ, a country house not far from the Waverly Hydro in Melrose. Though his rank remained as private, Janek dealt with highly confidential documents and the staff in the HQ building had come to trust him.

******

They shook hands and embraced outside the Playhouse.

"I get the impression you don't want to watch a film. Shall we go over to the café?" said Chaim as cheerfully as he could.

"No," said Janek. "Let's walk over to the park here, where we cannot be overheard."

They sat down on a bench well back from the path that followed the line of the Tweed. It was already nearly dark, but the air held a tinge of spring in the buds that were forming on the birches and sycamores and oaks that stood between them and the river.

"As you know," said Janek, "I work in the Legal Affairs section of HQ. My desk is in a little cubicle that is off the main office. A lot goes on there and there is a lot of communication with other regiments.

"You may know, too, that at the end of last year, Churchill, Roosevelt and Stalin (that bastard who nearly killed us) had a meeting. The word is that they came to an agreement that Britain – and that would include the Polish forces — and the U.S. would invade mainland Europe. That would take the pressure off the eastern front and Russia."

"I follow," said Chaim.

"There was a big meeting at HQ two days ago. The main staff officers and generals were there. General

Kukiel, Colonel Sosabowski, the parachute brigade man. I don't know all their names, maybe Maczek. Even their adjutants weren't allowed in. The place was filled with smoke from all their cigars.

"They all went quiet and then I think it was Kukiel that addressed them. He told them that a plan was in hand to invade the European mainland – he didn't give any details. 'Soon,' he said, 'we will be able to fight our way back into Poland.' Another voice broke in. 'What will we do with the rats, though?' 'Have no fear,' came the answer. 'We have that all worked out. They will be in the first wave. You can be sure that none of them will reach the borders of Poland.'

"I kept very quiet, my head down buried in papers, pen in hand, and pretended not to notice when one of the men looked round the corner of my cubicle."

"My God," said Chaim.

"Yes. Effectively premeditated murder."

He paused.

"So what I have done is this. I have spoken to someone in London who carries a lot of influence. I cannot tell you who he is, but the upshot is that there is an address in London that I will give you. Any Jewish soldier in the Polish army who wants to go there, under the guise of attending celebrations and prayers for Passover which starts next week on the 7th, should do so.

"What you probably do not know, also, is that back in February over two hundred Polish-Jewish soldiers absented themselves from other units for reasons of anti-semitism. The big men at the top in the Polish and British governments allowed them to transfer to the British army. It was after that that those Orders of the Day came out later in the month – you probably saw them – that any acts of anti-semitism would be the subject of strict disciplinary procedure. Did it make any difference? No, not that I saw. In fact, some of them, mainly those Volksdeutsche, would just mutter behind our backs: 'OK, we can't get you here in Britain, but once you're back on European soil, look out. There's a bullet waiting for you.'

"I suggest that you speak to all the Jews in your unit individually and explain the situation. As you can see, there is not much time. People are going to have to make their own minds up – I suspect some people will not join us, fearful of the change, however bad their experience is here. We should be treated no differently to those other two hundred, but who knows what might happen? Are you understanding me Chaim?"

"I am … I think. We go there and desert."

"I prefer the word 'leave' or 'absent ourselves', but yes, and then offer ourselves to the British army. We are trained soldiers but our fellow Polish soldiers would rather we did not exist. It is a problem not of our own making."

Chaim brushed both his hands through his hair. He was only 22. His life, and the lives of other Jewish men, weighed heavily on his mind.

"I will speak to people … of course. I will start right away. When should they get there? How should they get there? Some of them, if I can get word to them, are in Gullane."

"They can go straight away," said Janek. "Leon is already there."

"The ex-Bund leader?"

"Yes."

"That's good to hear."

"They will have to take the train. From here, they will need to go to Edinburgh and then catch a train South. From Gullane, I will have to find out. I will let you know in the morning. The address in London is 91 Gower Street. It is near the centre, an old Jewish hotel.

"When we get to London, I want you to help me organise things and to be our spokesman. No doubt there will be a lot of to'ing and fro'ing between the authorities, but we have to do this."

"I agree completely Janek. I hope I can fulfil your trust in me."

49 A DESPATCH RIDER

27 March 1944

WOLF heard the popping of a motor-cycle engine before he saw it. The rider pulled off his helmet — he was surprised to see that it was Matheus Wachtel, a man he had met with Chaim Sieradski.

Wachtel walked to the office, carrying a folder of documents. The Volksdeutsche had already started humming their Nazi song.

"Not another bloody Jew," one of them shouted as he emerged again.

Wolf went over to him.

"Matheus, hello. What brings you here?"

With a slight turn of the head, he indicated that they should go outside.

"You actually, Wolf. The office documents were just my cover. Thank heavens I didn't have to go in search of you."

"Why? What's up?"

"I have an urgent message for you from Chaim. He says the Poles, senior officers, are plotting against us – they have a plan to get rid of us when the invasion that they keep talking about happens. This is our way out – to leave the Polish army and these morons…" he nodded towards the Volksdeutsche, "and join the British army. But we have to move fast. You need to get to London. I don't know too much more — but take this train tonight from here. You'll have to change trains in Edinburgh. Go to this address in London."

He handed him a small sheet of paper with the details written on it. There was a note at the bottom and Wolf recognized the handwriting.

'Good luck, see you in Gower Street, Chaim.'

"Don't worry. If anyone asks – tell them you are joining the official Polish-Jewish Forces celebration of Passover in London. Chaim said please let the other Jewish soldiers in your unit know. It's up to them – their decision if they want to come, but, again, you have to act quickly."

Wolf was stunned.

"Yes, yes Matheus, I will speak to the others now. I can't believe this."

Wachtel clapped him on the back as he mounted the motor-cycle. He leant into Wolf's ear.

"See you in London," he whispered.

******

Wolf found Zvi first and he did not hesitate. Others agreed to come after some discussion, but a man called Katz was hesitant.

"We could be shot as deserters."

"It's up to you," said Zvi. "But do you want to go on living in this hell with those Volksdeutsche people as your bedmates?"

"I'd have to leave Moira."

"Well, you can always come back to her – if she still wants you. I'm going to be leaving Fiona, but I'll write to her and tell her what's happening. She'll understand – she's seen the Volksdeutsche in town."

"I think it's a gamble worth taking," said Wolf.

He cleaned his rifle. He cleaned all around his bed and his cupboard. He left everything behind, and, in only his Polish Army uniform, walked towards the station.

******

More Jewish soldiers joined their train in Edinburgh and by the time they reached Kings Cross, there were over thirty of them.

Number 91 Gower St stood out from the rest of the buildings in this nondescript terraced row in that the front wall had been raised to convert the dormer windows of the attic into a fourth storey. The brickwork was blackened by the smoke of the Blitz and four years of war. Chimney stacks ran from back to front of the building, the pots standing to attention like guards on parade. In front were rusted wrought-iron railings, broken at one end by a gate to the basement. Two wide stone steps led up to an ivory-coloured portico. The front door was black, its brass fittings unpolished and tarnished. Over the door, a sign proclaimed the name 'King Solomon Hotel.' For some reason, the building reminded Wolf of the Aquitania.

Inside, men greeted friends they had not seen for months or others that they thought had perished. The atmosphere was buoyant, almost boyish, as if they had been freed from unjust imprisonment. Men who had known each other before the war, men who had escaped from Poland together or had survived a Siberian camp together, men who had experienced the long journey out of Russia together or been fellow-soldiers in the Polish army, men who had never met each other before but had such a deep pool of shared experience that it made no difference — all greeted each other with warmth.

Behind what once might have been the hotel's reception stood Wachtel. He asked them to form a line and to provide their name and Army Record number before going inside.

Wolf found Chaim in a large room on the first floor. A wide sofa, its tan material torn and its stuffing spilling out, was the only piece of furniture. Some men sat on the floor, leaning against the wall.

"Wolf, you made it! I am so glad. Matheus told me he had found you. Make yourself at home!"

He waved his arm expansively around the house.

"Let me tell you how we are playing this. We are writing a list of everyone who makes it here – we'll give people a bit more time and then we'll give the list to the British Military Police and tell them we want to join the British army. Then we'll see what happens."

Wolf climbed to the next floor and explored it with Zvi. One of the men had found some coal and a fire was burning in the front room. Old, faded black-out curtains hung limply over two of the windows, the other was bare like the light bulbs. Noise seeped into the room from the street outside.

Wolf was exhausted. He found an unoccupied stretch of floor and slept.

50 GOWER STREET

31 March 1944

IT WAS early on the second morning that Wolf heard a loud hammering on the door. He went downstairs to investigate, but already he could see Chaim standing there with Leon and Janek.

Behind them, on the street, he could see three men in British army uniforms with the red 'MP' arm patch of the Military Police.

"We have received notification that there are eighty-five men here who have absconded from their Polish Army units in Scotland."

"That is correct," said Janek, who appeared to speak English fluently. "We sent you that information. All the men here, myself included, have suffered extreme anti-semitic discrimination at the hands of Polish soldiers to the extent that it became impossible for us to stay in our units in Scotland. We have left those units but we are keen to fight our common enemy – Hitler. We have come here to join the British army and fight with them."

It was obviously a prepared statement.

"Who is in command here?"

"There is no one in command. We are all privates. The Polish army will not promote anyone Jewish."

The military policeman looked nonplussed.

"You understand that you can be arrested for desertion? Thirty of another group of you are awaiting trial by court martial up in Scotland."

Leon, Janek and Chaim looked at each other. They spoke together in Yiddish. Wolf caught the words, "That's what happened to them then…well, they've got no chance against us."

"You have two options. You can return to your units and there will be no charges of desertion; or we will have to arrest you."

"How are three men going to arrest eighty-five?" said Janek, again in Yiddish.

"Carry on," said Chaim. "No one here…" he looked around at those watching proceedings from the stairs and the room behind, "has any intention of going back to their units."

A small crowd had formed behind the Military Police. A woman pushed past them and handed Chaim a basket of fruit.

"Leave them alone," someone cried out from the pavement.

The MP's conferred together.

"We will have to speak further to the Polish authorities. In the meantime, you should consider yourselves under house arrest," they said. "If you leave this building, you are liable to be arrested by ourselves or the London Police force."

******

1 April 1944

The man sitting on the threadbare sofa in what the soldiers called, loosely, the living-room, wore a charcoal suit and a tie that was navy blue with a red motif. His black homburg rested on the floor beside him, revealing a mop of dark hair sleeked back from his forehead. There was an aroma, not unpleasant, of tobacco and whisky about him, but in his eye was a mischievous twinkle. He spoke in the clipped tones that Wolf had come to understand from the radio and from Churchill's speeches as the tones of the British educated classes. His language was harder to understand than that of the British private soldiers he had come across in England or Scotland, but there was something about the man — though he could not put his finger on why, it was simply gut instinct — that made him warm to him. He was a man that he could trust. He must, Wolf realised, be the Mr Driberg that he had heard Chaim and Leon speak about.

The Englishman looked completely at ease amongst the sea of khaki uniforms, many of them now open at the neck, buttons loose, their creases gone. Men squatted cross-legged on the floor or perched on the sofa's arms all around him. He was listening intently to Leon, nodding from time to time.

"Of course, now that Ziegelboim's gone, we have Emanuel Scherer on the National Council here in London. Perhaps you know him?"

"I've met him," said Driberg. "But I think, in terms of your present problem, that I, as a member of the British Parliament, am best placed to help you. As you know, I was able to intercede on behalf of the two hundred of your colleagues who left the Polish army last month and are now happily ensconced in different units of the British army."

Leon nodded.

"I am pleased to say that I have received letters from some of them saying how happy they are at being treated as human beings again, not as pariah or scum, and that their commanding officers have promised them transfer to combat units appropriate to their particular skills once their initial training period is completed."

"That is all we want," said Chaim in Yiddish.

Driberg arched his eyebrows towards him and Janek translated. For over half an hour, Driberg listened as soldier after soldier described the abuse they had suffered in the Polish army.

"To me," he said eventually, "you all tell the same story; your situation is no different to your colleagues last month, but you can never tell what Eden (the Foreign Secretary, that is) might say. He might be frightened that there would be a wholesale desertion of all Jews from the Polish army in Britain."

"Well, there can only be about six hundred in total," said Janek. "That cannot make that much difference."

"No, I agree," said Driberg. "But, as I say, I cannot guarantee anything except that I will fight the cause on your behalf as strongly as I can. It is complicated by the thirty men the Military Police seem to have picked up in Scotland – I suppose they would have been joining you here?"

Chaim nodded.

"They have now been imprisoned and I have been told they are heading for court martial for desertion. It is totally unjust and I will be fighting their case as much as yours. I understand that the Military Police visited you here yesterday – don't worry too much about that for the moment, I am working on it. The earliest that I can do anything is next Wednesday at Question Time in Parliament. Then I will put a question to the Foreign Secretary on the subject."

He picked up his hat from the floor and stood up.

"Gentlemen, it has been a pleasure to meet you. I will do my very best for you."

As he reached the door, he turned.

"Do you have enough food? I don't suppose the Polish or the British army, for that matter, are sending you any supplies."

"We have very little, sir," said Leon, "but you have to understand – most of these men went through the camps in Siberia. It is nothing compared to that."

"I'll see what I can do."

51 TOM DRIBERG IN PARLIAMENT

The Times - 6 April 1944 (reference Question Time 5.4.44)

JEWS IN THE POLISH FORCES - No More Transfers to British Units

Mr DRIBERG (Maldon, Ind.):

Asked the Secretary of State for Foreign Affairs if he was aware that, despite the efforts of the Polish Government, there were persistent and widespread manifestations of anti-semitism in the Polish forces in this country and that a number of Jewish soldiers and sailors were now undergoing or awaiting court-martial for absenting themselves from the Polish forces in the hope of securing their transfer to the British forces; and if, in the interests of the unity of the allied war effort, he would reopen negotiations with the Polish authorities and endeavour to facilitate such transfers, taking as a precedent the recent similar negotiations satisfactorily conducted by his Department and the War Office.

Mr EDEN (Anthony Eden – Foreign Secretary):

The negotiations referred to by Mr Driberg, as a result of which, in agreement with the Polish Government, the transfer to the British Army was arranged of a number of Jewish deserters from the Polish forces in this country, constituted an entirely exceptional departure from the normal principle that transfers from one allied army to another cannot be facilitated in war time. His Majesty's Government, however, took the opportunity to represent to the Polish Government the desirability of making a thorough investigation of the men's grievances and of remedying any that might be found to exist. They understand that a full enquiry has, in fact, been made and that the Polish authorities have taken all steps in their power to ensure that their declared policy of suppressing all manifestations of anti-semitism is brought to the notice of all ranks in the Polish forces and that appropriate action is taken to carry it into effect.

In the circumstances, and having regard to the overriding importance at the present time of maintaining at the highest level morale and military discipline in the forces which are preparing to take part under British command in forthcoming operations, His Majesty's Government and the Polish Government are in entire agreement that it would not be in the best interests of the allied war effort to enable further members of the Polish armed forces to secure their transfer to the British forces.

******

Hansard - 6 April 1944: (Debate on the Adjournment ref. Question Time 5 April 1944)
POLISH FORCES, GREAT BRITAIN (ANTI-SEMITISM)

Mr DRIBERG (Maldon, Ind.):

It is with considerable reluctance that I raise to-day, and raised yesterday at Question Time, the problem of anti-semitism in the Polish Forces in this country, and the possibility of the transfer from those Forces to the British Armed Forces of such Jewish soldiers and sailors as wish to transfer. I should not have raised it at all—I would much rather it could have been dealt with as it had been up to quite recently, by private representation and negotiation—if a climax had not been reached, and if the matter had not been precipitated by the event which took place last week, when military police raided a hostel in London at which a group of these Polish deserters were staying in the hope that they would be able to follow the other two groups of deserters who had already been accepted into the British Army.

... I certainly endorse what the Right Hon. Gentleman (Anthony Eden – Foreign Secretary) said about the good intentions of the Polish Government in this matter; I am not making any attack on them at all; but I am rather afraid that their well-intentioned efforts to stamp out anti-semitism in their own forces have not been successful, and that the conversations which the Right Hon. Gentleman says he will now re-open, if they are to be limited merely to the general question of anti-semitism and are not to deal with the transfer of further troops, will be ineffective—because I do not believe that you can stamp out anti-semitism by instructions, by Orders of the Day, or by anything else of that formal kind. I repeat that I know that the Polish Government's intentions in this respect are admirable: there is nothing whatever to be said against them for the very vigorous way in which they have tried to deal with the matter; but anti-semitism, being essentially an emotional thing, cannot be dealt with in that way. It can be cured only by the process—a rather slow process, probably—of education. Perhaps the more blatant or brutal manifestations of it would be checked—I have no doubt about that—but I am afraid that the underlying feeling and its less obvious manifestations will remain.

Of the existence of this sentiment to a pretty wide degree in the Polish Forces, there is no doubt. I know of it from my own experience. I have during this war met quite a large number of Polish officers, in officers' messes and so on, and extremely gallant, charming, and decent young men they are. But, unfortunately, if one gets on to these awkward subjects—which one naturally tries to avoid if one is talking to them—one finds that they have certain fixed prejudices, one of which is this deep prejudice against the Jews. I have seen it in almost all the Polish officers I have met and talked to. If there were not this widespread prejudice, it would hardly have been necessary for the Polish Government to appoint, as it did, a commission of inquiry into this matter, which, I understand, made certain recommendations with a view to helping to check these manifestations. Above all, I am convinced of the existence of these anti-semitic manifestations by meeting and talking to large numbers of these deserters who have come to London in the last few weeks. I have personally seen both the former groups and the group who were arrested last week, and their story is absolutely convincing. I have talked to them personally. They are a tough, highly-trained combatant type of soldier, most of them, not the non-combatant clerical type or the sensitive intellectual type, although those types are also present in the group. Their stories are quite horrifying and absolutely convincing. I am certain, on internal evidence, of their authenticity.

All along they have emphasised strongly, in their conversations with me, that they were not in any sense trying to run away from the war, or from their duty as fighting men. On the contrary, they want to do it where they believe they can do it more effectively, in the British Army...

...What sort of discipline or morale can there be in the units in which these unfortunate Jews are undergoing these experiences? I have a whole drawerful of personal testimonies to the kind of thing they are experiencing, written out laboriously in Polish or, pathetically, in broken English. What kind of discipline or morale can there be in such a unit among the Jews, or, for that matter, among the Jew-baiters? They certainly cannot have a very good discipline if they disobey the orders which the Polish military commanders have, quite rightly, put out against this anti-semitism.

I am afraid that these orders of the day (of 23 February) have not only not had the desired effect, but they may even have aggravated the situation, because I have talked with Jews who left their units some time after the Orders of the Day against anti-semitism were put out, and they said that these Orders of the Day had made very little difference, except perhaps that it was not done so noisily. Man after man said: Now they say, these bullying sergeants or N.C.O.'s, 'We cannot do anything in this country, because Churchill, as we all know, is in the pay of the Jews; but you wait until we get you on the Continent of Europe: the moment we get you there, in the second front, then every Pole has two bullets—the first for a Jew and the second for a German.' I have been told that more of that sort of thing has been said to them by N.C.O.'s and others since the Polish Orders of the Day condemning anti-semitism have appeared.

52 MILITARY VISITORS

10 April 1944

THEY HAD made an effort to enjoy the Passover Seder. Zvi had got hold of a few bottles of wine and a large box of matzos – Wolf did not like to ask from where. Removal of chametz, the leavened food, had not been a problem – anything that could be eaten had been eaten; but it seemed that the local Jewish population, either for lack of information or fear of repercussions from the authorities, were unwilling to provide food for the soldiers apart from Mrs Friedman, a loud and cheerful woman who had a stall in the fruit market. The men were therefore hungry and the washing of hands and recital of the blessings had soon become desultory.

Tempers were fraying when there was a knock at the door on the Monday morning. It was a courier. He delivered an envelope addressed to Private Leon Kozak.

"A Colonel is coming to see us at midday," announced Leon.

He passed the letter to Chaim.

"Gentlemen," he said as the men gathered round anxiously, "we are to be *honoured* by a visit from Colonel Wolkowski of the First Armoured Corps of the Polish

Army. He says he wants to talk to us in an atmosphere of friendship and reconciliation. Huh! I suggest that we let him in and listen to him, but, unless anyone wants to go back to their units, not to answer him."

It was not long before they heard a car draw up outside. Colonel Wolkowski was accompanied by an adjutant and his driver.

"I'll take it from here," he said dismissively, waving them away at the door. He was tall, with an angular nose. His uniform was immaculate, the white eagle gleaming on his cap badge.

Leon led him up to the first floor living-room. He stood facing the men, his hands behind his back. No one saluted him.

"Soldiers, I have come here in a spirit of friendship to try to sort out this sorry mess. I have seen many of the accounts of the abuse and racist treatment you have received at the hands of some of the N.C.O.'s and soldiers of the Polish army and I am truly sorry about that. We have already instituted new and very strict disciplinary procedures relating to anti-semitism. We recognize that things have not been as they should be, but, even since you have been absent, things have changed for your fellow Jewish soldiers.

"You have been trained in your units in Scotland under the umbrella of the British command for the great operation that lies ahead – it is no secret that, sooner or later, we will be back on European soil and thence to our homeland. It is my fervent wish that you will be able to play your part in that great endeavour and therefore I ask you to return to your units. There will be no reprisal or punishment – your absence will be noted only as Passover leave."

There was silence in the room. The top of a red London bus passed across the large windows and a taxi hooted.

"May I know who is in charge?" the colonel asked.

"There is no officer or even N.C.O. amongst us, sir," said Leon. "Many of us have university degrees and professional qualifications, but none of us has ever been offered a promotion. Do you not think that that is rather strange?"

Momentarily, the colonel furrowed his brow.

"This is very odd. I admit that this episode will convince my colleagues that their policy is wrong and counter-productive."

At this point, several men stood and walked out of the room.

"Colonel," said Chaim, "all of us here love Poland. We are itching to go into battle against the Nazi murderers. But we cannot do that when your fellow officers are saying things like 'We'll get rid of the rats before we even reach the Polish border.'"

"That's absurd. If anyone said such a thing they should be disciplined. Why don't you give me a chance to change things?"

"With due respect, I don't think you can sir," said Chaim. "It is endemic. I do not think you can imagine how impossible life can be in the Polish army when you have been born Jewish. You may be blonde, blue-eyed and speak perfect Polish, but you are derided day and night. Why not try it for a week, sir? Change out of that smart uniform into a private's and go into any unit where you will not be recognized and mention casually that you are Jewish. At the end of the week, you would realise what we are talking about and you'd be here with us."

The colonel sighed.

"I am sorry that I do not appear to have been able to persuade you. My offer will stand until midnight tomorrow. Thereafter, I am afraid I will not have any control over what might be decided."

＊＊＊＊＊＊

11 April 1944

Wolf waited in the queue for the toilet. He stood on the threadbare brown carpet, looking out from the landing window. A blackbird sang loudly from the tree on the other side of the street. Upstairs he could hear a man shouting.

"We'll be shot! Deserters they'll call us. We've had enough trouble. We've been persecuted for two thousand years. How do we know things will be any different in the British army?"

A calmer voice said, "No one is stopping you, mate. You heard the colonel. You can go back to your unit, if you want to. If you want all that shit again."

"The only place where we will really be safe will be Palestine. I wish I'd left with the others when we passed through there after Siberia," came a third voice.

Wolf heard the creak of the stairs behind him. Chaim had come to join the queue.

"I don't know how you do it," said Wolf. "You always seem so calm and under control."

"That might be how it looks on the outside, Wolf," said Chaim, "but on the inside I'm churning. We've all been through so much. I know what we are doing is right, but I have no idea what is going to happen next. I wish I did. Leon, Janek and I just try and make decisions, deal with people, as best we can as things develop."

✳✳✳✳✳✳

12 April 1944

There was a loud banging on the door.

"Police! Open up."

Leon opened the door. Six London police were outside, one of them carrying a door ram.

"How can I help…?"

But the police poured in and past him.

"You are under arrest. Everyone in the house is under arrest for desertion. Officers are outside and at the back in case you try to escape."

Wolf's heart sank. Chaim came forward.

"May I speak to the officer in charge please," he said courteously, in a tone that demanded attention.

The nearest policeman pointed to the sergeant.

"Sir," said Chaim, "I think there is some mistake. We are Jewish and we are Polish soldiers who have left the Polish army because of virulent anti-semitism to join the British army. All we want to do is fight Hitler and end this bloody war. Is that not what you want?"

The sergeant looked nonplussed.

"Yes, mate, but orders is orders. I can't be arguing politics."

"So you want to round up eighty-five Jewish soldiers who are on your side – what do you think Hitler is doing on the other side of the English channel? What are you proposing to do with us anyway?"

"It's not my…"

A taxi braked hard outside. Tom Driberg, his coat flying in his wake, raced through the open door.

"Officer?" he addressed the sergeant. "Are you in charge here?"

The policeman nodded.

"My name is Thomas Driberg. I am the MP for Maldon in Essex. I am dealing with this matter with the Foreign Office and the War Office. You may have seen reports of my questions to the Foreign Secretary, Mr Anthony Eden, on the subject. Things have recently changed. By all means check if you wish to. I can give you or your superiors the name of the person to speak to."

The sergeant seemed unsure, floundering with the words War Office and Anthony Eden, out of his depth. Driberg took control.

"How many officers have you got here?

"Five, sir."

"Right, call them off. They're not much use against eighty-five men anyway. Any questions, tell them I told you to. I am sure all will be explained to you in due course."

Driberg waited quietly as the police left.

"That would have made things very complicated," he said to Leon and Chaim as they closed the door.

"Now, listen, I do not have much time, but I wanted you to know – we are working something out. Between the Foreign Office, the War Office, the Polish army, the British army and Mikolajczyk — your government in exile. It may not help the group who were caught up in Scotland, but it will help you. A Captain Murray will contact you. You can trust him. Work everything out with him."

Driberg shook their hands firmly.

"By the way," he said. "Newspapers all over the country are reporting your story, and support is growing everywhere against the plight of the group in Scotland. Good luck."

******

Friday 14 April 1944

Captain Murray was a short, rotund figure in a navy blue suit. He had chestnut hair and a neat moustache and a face that seemed both cheerful and business-like.

"I wonder if I could speak to Janek Scherer or Chaim Sieradski or Leon Kozak."

Wolf fetched the three men. Murray pulled out his ID and showed it to them.

"Glad to meet you," he said heartily. "I hope someone will have given you my name, told you I'd be along. I work for the War Office, so no uniform today. Better to keep things low key. You three are the spokesmen for the group here, I believe."

They nodded.

"Right, I understand you chaps want to join the British Army. Seems like the top brass have worked something out, you'll be glad to hear."

Wolf was on the other side of the room — he was not quite certain that he had heard correctly.

"What we're going to do is get you to Scotland, and there you'll be released from the Polish army and enlisted in the British. You'll be posted to the Pioneer Corps first, based in Buxton in Derbyshire – it's a beautiful part of the world, I can tell you – and then from there, sooner or later, you'll be sent to other units according to your skills and training. How does that sound?"

A huge smile lit Sieradski 's face. He seemed unable to speak for a few moments.

"That sounds perfect, sir," he said eventually.

Leon, however, looked uncertain.

"Scotland, you say?"

"Yes, to RAF Leuchars. Don't worry, it's nowhere near where you were based."

Leon nodded his head thoughtfully.

"What I need to do first is to go through this," said Murray, pulling from a briefcase beneath his arm some sheets of paper. "This is the list that you gave to the Military Police, I believe?"

"Yes."

"And do you believe it is still accurate? Has anyone left the group or been missed out?"

Sieradski and Leon conferred. They looked across at Wolf. He shook his head.

"No one that we know of," said Chaim.

"Right, well I need to check that all these details are completely accurate. Are you able to fetch all the men down for me?"

"Of course."

As Wolf began to climb the stairs, he passed Sieradski, Scherer and Leon in the hallway.

"How do we know it's not a trick? " Leon whispered. "Even if he says it's not Galashiels or Melrose, it's still Scotland. They could be taking us there to be court martialled for desertion, or else returning us to our units."

"I know," said Scherer. "We just need to get things really straight with him until we are sure we understand what is going on."

******

It was not until after the weekend that three buses pulled up outside 91 Gower Street at 5 a.m. Wolf filed out in the line of men, looking about him warily. A British soldier travelled in each bus and at King's Cross directed them to two carriages that had been reserved for military use on the Edinburgh express. Captain Murray was already there, this time in uniform.

There were sandwiches and coffee on the train and Wolf slept for much of the journey. He was excited, but an apprehension sat behind the excitement. Ever since he had heard Leon use the word 'trick', he could not help but wonder. The thought of the Siberian camp, the journey out of Russia, the anti-semitism in the Polish army – all of them filled him with horror. He did not want to go back to any of them, and yet here he was travelling back to Scotland, to an unknown destination, up the very same railway line that he had travelled down just three weeks previously.

His apprehension was magnified in Edinburgh when they changed trains. The new train was going to Dundee and on to Aberdeen. On the bench was a copy of that day's Scotsman. Zvi was leafing through it distractedly.

"Whoah!" he said suddenly. He pointed to a small article in the bottom corner of a page:

The Scotsman 18 April 1944
COURT MARTIAL OF POLISH JEWS

The Jewish soldiers who left the Polish army because of anti-semitic mistreatment and attempted to reach London to request a transfer to the British armed forces will be placed on trial tomorrow before a Polish court martial, it was announced today.

The number of Jews to be tried is not disclosed, but it is assumed that the accused are the group arrested at a railway station by Military Police late last month and estimated by members of parliament to be 'around thirty'.

The court martial trial will take place in an undisclosed Scottish town.

The Representation of Polish Jews in England today stated that it will soon publish a summary of the anti-semitic incidents in the Polish army. It emphasised that a detailed report of those incidents has been submitted to the Polish authorities. The contents of this report will not be made public during the course of the court martial proceedings, since the leaders of the Representation of Polish Jews are bound to secrecy.

Wolf walked up the carriage until he found Chaim and pointed to the article.

"I'm worried," he said. "A lot of the guys are."

He looked around to make sure Captain Murray was nowhere close.

"Are you sure this Murray isn't double-crossing us?"

"I know, Wolf. Believe me, I'm worried too. And I don't understand why those guys who never made it to London are being court martialled while we are being told we can transfer. I've questioned him again and again. He understands why we would be suspicious, but I trust him. I just hope I am right."

******

As the train stopped at Cupar, the British soldiers walked through the carriages.

"We're out at the next stop," they said. "Leuchars."

A bitter wind swept through Leuchars station and they were glad to get onto the coaches that stood waiting for them. They had come through open countryside, not mountainous like some areas of Scotland they had seen, and, increasingly, the sea had come into view on the right of the carriage. Now, as they clambered aboard the coaches, the air was filled with the sound of gulls and the salt smell of the sea.

The men looked out of the windows, largely silent — apprehensive and exhilarated at once. 'RAF LEUCHARS, Coastal Command' read the sign at the entrance to the camp. They drew up on the apron, in front of a large hangar. Captain Murray got out of the forward bus. An officer came out to meet him. They saluted and walked inside.

Wolf looked about. To the side, two runways crossed, the longer one following the coastline. Aircraft were lined up outside a second hangar, the RAF blue, white and red roundels glistening on their wings.

Two black staff cars marked with the Polish eagle were parked neatly, their backs to the hangar, alongside other military vehicles. Wolf's heart lurched. He looked around at the other men. No one spoke. Zvi was biting his lower lip, tapping his leg, waiting and watching.

Murray came out. He went into the first bus and then came to Wolf's.

"Everything's rosy in the garden," he said cheerily. "All the people we need are here. Shouldn't take long. Just follow the RAF boys in."

They filed into the hangar. In the centre were two sets of desks. Two Polish officers sat at those on the left. Some of the soldiers in front of Wolf saluted their fellow countrymen, others did not. Wolf did not recognize them; he had nothing against either of them and he chose to salute.

"Name?"

"Wolf Albert – 25403."

Wolf thought back to other desks he had stood before over the years – in Lutsk before the Russian officer, in Siberia, in Pahlevi, in Galashiels. He hoped that this would be the last.

The officer leafed through a pile of Army Record books until he found the right one. He turned to page 16 and, copying from a sheet beside him, wrote:

Released from service in the Polish Army to serve in the British Army based on the order of the Ministry of Defence Reg. No. 977/Og.Org.Uzup. II/44 of 3 March 1944.

He was about to pass it across to the major beside him to stamp when he picked up the book and inspected the page number.

He grunted and with a ruler struck through what he had just written.

"Is there a problem?" asked Wolf, his heart thumping.

"No."

He turned to page 6 and wrote the sentence out again. This time the major stamped the entry and scribbled his own signature beside it.

Without comment, he waved Wolf across to the desk on the opposite side of the hangar. Here, the British officer repeated the procedure, but this time he wrote the word 'enlisted' against the date. *Location:* RAF Leuchars. *Posting:* Pioneer Corps, Buxton.

At the back of the hangar, folding canvas chairs had been set out in rows. Zvi kicked Wolf's shin.

"I think we've done it," he whispered. "I wonder how far we are from Galashiels – I could go and see Fiona."

"Don't be daft. If that lot in the 10th Dragoons saw you, they'd lynch you."

When all the chairs were filled and all the men processed, Captain Murray stepped to the front.

"Congratulations, gentlemen. I am proud to welcome you into the British Army."

53 POSTSCRIPT

The Scotsman – 24 April 1944
POLISH DESERTERS - Jewish Soldiers Sentenced
ALLEGED ILL-TREATMENT

After a series of trials by courts-martial lasting five days, some thirty Jewish soldiers of the Polish 1st Army, charged with desertion, have been sentenced to terms of imprisonment of from one to three years. The trials were held in a Scottish town. The men had alleged that they had been ill-treated by non-Jewish soldiers and had therefore attempted to travel to London with the intention of leaving the Polish army and joining the British Army. During their trials, each man was asked whether he would return to the Polish army. All refused. It was because of this refusal that the sentences were relatively heavy.

BRITISH JEWS PROTEST

Professor S. Brodetsky, president of the Board of Deputies of British Jews, stated at a meeting of the Board in London, yesterday, that the result of the courts-martial was against the fundamental principles for which the war was being waged.

"I have seen the statements made by these soldiers," he said, "and they are consistent in their allegations of anti-semitism in the Polish forces."

The Board passed a resolution expressing deep concern at the conditions in the Polish Army. It asked the Government, in consultation with the Polish Government, to find a way to enable those Jewish soldiers in the Polish Army who desired to do so to join the British Army, and hoped that the courts-martial findings might be reviewed.

DELEGATION AT DOWNING STREET

Delegates representing 3000 Jewish clothing workers in London went to 10 Downing Street on Saturday to protest against the treatment of Jews in the Polish Army in Britain.

Belfast Newsletter - 13 May 1944
JEWS IN POLISH ARMY - Jailed Deserters to be set free

THE Polish President yesterday signed an amnesty decree freeing all Jewish and other soldiers in the Polish Army who were recently sentenced by courts-martial for desertion. The decree, which is warmly welcomed by the British Government, covers several military transgressions in order to allow soldiers who had committed certain offences to take an active part in the war's decisive final phase. A statement issued last night by the Polish Ministry of Information declared that the Polish Government and Commander-in-Chief would not tolerate "behaviour lacking comradeship, or racial and religious discrimination" in their forces, but insisted that all Polish citizens must submit to the honourable duty of military service in the Polish armed forces. Among the various anti-Jewish incidents mentioned during the court-martial, only one soldier was found to belong to this category, it was added. 11 of the 21 sentences recently imposed for desertion were suspended. In 10 other cases sentence had not been confirmed.

The Times - 18 May 1944
AMNESTY FOR POLISH DESERTERS - Mr Eden's Statement

Mr Eden, in his reply to a question by Mr Driberg in the House of Commons yesterday concerning the amnesty granted by the Polish Government to Jewish and other deserters from the Polish forces said: "I am informed by the Polish Government that the amnesty, in its application to Polish-Jewish and other deserters, involves complete annulment of the sentences inflicted on them by court-martial. The amnesty applies in respect of all offences committed before May 3rd whether or not sentences had been inflicted prior to that date. I understand that the men have been sent to the central Polish depot, and will be posted to units according to their qualifications and military requirements.

His Majesty's Government warmly welcomes the action of the Polish Government in granting this amnesty. I strongly hope that this will mark the close of this unfortunate episode and that the men affected will now go forward to play their part in the great operations which are impending.

I am satisfied that the Polish authorities, for their part, are doing all in their power to stamp out any trace of racial or religious discrimination in the Polish forces."

In answer to a further question from Mr Driberg, Mr Eden said: "I have made it quite clear that, in all the circumstances, we are not prepared to accept these men in the British Army."

EPILOGUE

WOLF ALBERT

Wolf Albert was posted to the Armoured Division of the Pioneer Corps of the British Army and spent three and a half years there. He experienced no discrimination though he was the only foreigner in his company. He served in France soon after D-Day, then Brussels and Bielefeld in Germany and was demobbed in 1947.

He visited Palestine again but decided to return to London where he had a successful business career. He married and had a son named Daniel, under whose aegis this book is written. With Daniel, Wolf went back to Bledow in Poland in 1989. There he found Hela again. Wolf records that they had a very emotional conversation, but he does not reveal the content of it nor did he speak to Daniel of it.

Wolf Albert

(The account of Wolf's father's death in the book is fictional in that it was witnessed by Hela, but it is a true account given by a different woman about a different man).

Wolf never did hear from his parents or siblings again. Their names are recorded amongst the murdered of Bledow in the Mogielnica Yahrzeit book. It is believed that some or all of them perished in the Majdanek extermination camp.

Wolf died in September 2004.

He concluded the Imperial War Museum interviews by saying:

It's difficult to understand how the anti-semitism was so embedded in people. A hatred so deep, but without knowledge. I find many things, from my previous experiences, very difficult to believe. How am I still here? And why can people not just be people – just people. I may be OK today, I've got all I need, but who knows – it may be me that needs help tomorrow.

Wolf with Hela, 1989

Definitely, we have to show people, for the future, what other people have done to each other and for them to judge. We have to give every opportunity, every answer possible – whoever asks for an answer. We cannot let it sleep. Ever.

Charles Stevens, formerly
Chaim Sieradski

CHAIM SIERADSKI

Well-educated and with strong language skills, Chaim Sieradski was recruited into British Military Intelligence soon after the group's initial posting with the Pioneer Corps in Buxton. He was asked to change his name for strategic purposes. He chose the name Charles Stevens as he was reading a book at the time in which a character was called Charles Stevens and the initials were the same.

After the war, he built up a very successful tailoring business in London. He was also widely recognized as a spiritual healer.

His wife, Rita, who he met in 1946, lives in Borehamwood. They had three children.

Charles Stevens died in 2018 at the age of 96.

TONY LINDSELL

ACKNOWLEDGEMENTS

Daniel Albert – for allowing me to write this story and for providing access to the Imperial War Museum tapes.
Rita Stevens – see Secondary Sources: 'CHAMULEK – A Journey into Manhood' by Charles Stevens (formerly Chaim Sieradski), her husband.
Martin Been – for invaluable advice and information on Jewish culture, religion and language as well as medical and historical content.
Mark Campbell and **Tom Evershed** – for ploughing through the text word by word and offering invaluable observations and input on how the story, and my writing and prose, could be improved.
Paul Budd and Mary Durndell – for pointing me in the direction of the British Newspaper Archive which led me to Charles Stevens / Chaim Sieradski.

TONY LINDSELL

SOURCES

PRIMARY SOURCES:

1) **Interviews with Wolf Albert – Imperial War Museum London** (on eleven reels of tape).
   The transcripts provide the core story upon which this book is based.

2) **Polish Army Record Book – Wolf Albert**

SECONDARY SOURCES:

3) **'CHAMULEK – A Journey into Manhood' by Charles Stevens**

   This is the autobiography of Chaim Sieradski (later Charles Stevens) which his wife, Rita Stevens, kindly allowed the author to read. This book has been hugely helpful in providing further detailed background to what these men experienced in their camps in Siberia, on their journeys to and from there, and later in the Polish army. The lives of Wolf Albert and Chaim Sieradski did actually converge in Scotland and then London in early 1944 and the Stevens account does much to explain the events leading up to their departure from the Polish army and enlistment in the British.

   Stevens writes with great colour and some of his anecdotes (such as the stories of Shwili, Sado, Nina and Chremino) and characters (such as Kmiec, from whom Tomczyk is partially drawn) have also been used, in part or in full, in WOLF, with the kind permission of Rita Stevens.

4) **'My Story' by Berta Klipstein**

5) **'To Our Children: Memoirs of Displacement' by Wlodzimierz Szer**

6) **'A Polish Girl's Journey Across Three Continents' by Monica Whitlock (BBC World Service)**

7) **'Regina Franks. Her Early Life'**
   With particular reference to Chapter 19, the death of Wolf's father

8) **'Joseph Stalin's Deadly Railway to Nowhere' by Lucy Ash (BBC Magazine)**

9) **WEBSITES:**
   https://sztetl.org.pl – Virtual Shtetl / POLIN Museum
   https://swoopingeagle.com – with particular reference to the evacuation by boat from Krasnovodsk to Pahlevi.

10) **British Newspaper Archive**

11) **OTHER SOURCES**: Anonymous accounts, the Wiener Library, Wikipedia.

I would like to thank all of the secondary sources above for the part they have played in the research for this book – from a tiny titbit of colour in a description to a chapter's worth of information, anecdote or account.

ABOUT THE AUTHOR

After graduating from St Andrews with an M.A. in Modern History and Moral Philosophy, Tony Lindsell joined the Hertfordshire Gazette. He went on to write for, and ultimately edit, an alternative newspaper in London before becoming managing editor of Samsom Publications, a business newsletter publisher in the days before the internet.

He later moved out of journalism and publishing and followed an eclectic career that included selling custom interiors and interior components for upmarket business jets and forming a company specializing in the sale of equine hoofcare products. He continues to write the occasional feature article and has written for such magazines as The Lady, Trainer, Horse and Hound and Warwickshire Life.

He has also published Days in the Life, a collection of short stories and poems and Balmanie, a novel.

He lives in Warwickshire and can be contacted on email: lindsell@clara.net.

Printed in Great Britain
by Amazon

71935787R00199